Barnhill

A Novel

By the same author:

Poetry
Slate, Sea and Sky: A Journey from Glasgow to the Isle of Luing

Non-fiction
Grounding a World: Essays on the Work of Kenneth White,
co-editor with Gavin Bowd and Charles Forsdick

Barnhill

A Novel

NORMAN BISSELL

Luath Press Limited

EDINBURGH

www.luath.co.uk

First published 2019

ISBN: 978-1-912147-87-8

The paper used in this book is recyclable. It is made
from low chlorine pulps produced in a low energy,
low emission manner from renewable forests.

Printed and bound by Clays Ltd., Bungay

Typeset in 11 point Sabon and 10.5 point Avenir
by Main Point Books, Edinburgh

For Birgit, Gordon, Susan and Callum

Nineteen Eighty-Four

the demons that drove him
the anguish he suffered
his struggle to finish it
his voice is with us still

Norman Bissell

A Note to the Reader

This novel is based on actual events in the life of George Orwell whose real name was Eric Arthur Blair. The opening scene in Chapter 1 and other scenes in the same typeface are the imagined thoughts of George Orwell. All the main characters are real people. Others are fictional. The Timeline of George Orwell's Last Years provides the actual sequence of events. Further clarification is set out in Writing *Barnhill* at the end of the book.

Chapter 1

IT MUST BE about three o'clock. In the morning. I can't sleep for all these thoughts of my Hebridean island. And Eileen's snoring. She says women don't snore, but how can she know? People believe what they want to believe, not what's true. And that's the way the world's going these days. We're winning the war now and all the little fascists will crawl back into their holes when we do. Until the next time. But we've adopted some of their methods so we can win it. Like tapping phones and letter opening and lying on the radio. I'm glad I'm out of it. Making programmes for the British Bullshit Corporation that no one in Asia listens to. And you can't get through the door unless a little man from MI5 upstairs checks you out. God knows how I got in. But who checks out the spies?

Eileen used to work at the Ministry of Information. So we know how it works. Only the good news gets out, only how we're winning on this front and that one. Propaganda – just like that little shit Goebbels perfected. 'But poor old Goebbels has no balls at all.' Whoever came up with that ditty gave him a piece of his own medicine all right. You can't beat a bit of English humour to keep up morale and bring down the enemy. That's what I like about my *Tribune* column, I can write about ordinary things and say whatever I like. It feels more useful somehow, even though it's not really what I want to be doing. But how can you write a proper book in the middle of a war? I've had this idea swilling around in my head for too long. I must write it down in my notebook when I get up. A trilogy, that's what's needed. And I already have a title for it. *The Quick and the Dead*. Not bad. The first book could be about the down-fall of a hard-up middle class family during the first war told through the eyes of a child. If only I could remember how people spoke back then. Another could be a little squib that shows how the Russian Revolution became the monstrous regime of Stalin, but told as a kind of fairy story. Light, easy reading that even a child could understand. That would be good. Then I'll write a horror story. The proles love a gripping tale of gruesome goings-on (I quite like that). Only this will be set in London in the future when the dictators are in power and they'll do anything and everything to hold on to it. I'll bring in the one party state, Newspeak, the Two Minutes Hate and the party slogans (War is peace. Ignorance is strength. Freedom is slavery). In Part 1 I'll build up the system of organized lying on which society is founded, how this is done by falsifying records, the nightmare realisation that objective truth has disappeared and the loneliness of the writer, his feeling of being the last man. He will have a love affair but in Part 2 it will end in their arrests and torture. The greatest failure will be the loss of memory and the inability to tell truth from lies. I'll call it The Last Man in Europe, an intriguing title. Surely when people read this they'll realise what could happen if they don't do something to stop it?

I think some of my best ideas come when I'm lying in bed. They say Stalin stays up half the night plotting the deaths of his enemies when they're fast asleep. It gives him a certain cruel satisfaction. And here's me lying back plotting his downfall in my books. I could put his face on the posters that are everywhere in my nightmare future. Uncle Joe is watching you. No, Big Brother is Watching You. That's it. Eileen's stopped snoring at last. It's all quiet now the bombs and the anti-aircraft guns have stopped. Maybe I'll get some sleep after all. And dream of my island life. That would be nice. I wonder what time it... is... and...

May 1944, Mortimer Crescent, London

He was used to walking in the dark by now. He rather liked the secrecy of it. And the unexpected way others loomed out of the darkness on their way home during the blackout. They probably wondered about him, a gangling figure in an old corduroy jacket and thick flannels. Recognising the familiar daffodil stumps in the garden, he sneaked into a ground floor flat that had once been part of a grand house. He carefully closed the front door behind him and crept into the bathroom off the hall. He locked the door, hung up his jacket and went to the sink where he dropped his drawers and carefully washed his privates with carbolic soap. Next, his bony hands, face and neck. He smoothed his pencil-thin moustache and thought about Sally. Yet, as he dried himself with a scraggy towel, he started to have doubts. This was the third time this week he'd come home late. What would Eileen say?

He pulled up his pants and flannels, straightened his tie and ruffled his black, tousled hair, cut short at the back and sides. He put his jacket back on and checked himself in the mirror. At six foot three, George Orwell looked every inch the scruffy intellectual. His lined face made him seem much older than his forty years.

Now that he was home, he left Orwell behind and became Eric Blair again. He took a deep breath and made his way into the living room. A plate of bangers and mash lay on the oak table by the oriel window. A woman sat in a large wicker armchair by the coal fire, drawing nervously on a cigarette. Eileen Blair was the same age as him but looked almost as worn out as her fawn cardigan and grey skirt. She was tall, slim, still attractive, with something of the dark-haired Irish about her. He didn't get to sit down.

'Working late again?' More of an accusation than a question. In an educated Geordie accent.

'Sorry, I had to.' Shamefaced, a schoolboy caught coming in late.

'No, you didn't. You could have worked at home.'

He knew she was right. 'I needed to finish something.' His voice was weak and hadn't quite thrown off traces of his years as an Eton King's Scholar.

'Well you've just about finished us. You come in here stinking of carbolic. You think I don't know what's going on?' She started shaking as she went to the table. 'Your dinner's ruined.' She pushed away his plate in disgust.

'Nothing's going on. You always think the worst of me.' He tried to take her arm but she brushed him away.

'That's right, Eric, blame me... I can't take much more of this...' He would always be Eric to her. Others might call him by the pen name he adopted when his first book came out, but not Eileen.

'Look, we've talked before about this. We made an agreement. It doesn't mean anything.'

'It does to me... I know we did, but things are different now. If you want us to have a son this has got to stop.'

'Don't bring him into it. There's nothing *to* stop. It's only sex. We're much more than that.'

She exploded. 'Nothing! You and your bloody cock! After all we've been through.'

His mind flashed back to their narrow escape from death at the hands of the Stalinists in Barcelona, how she nursed him in Marrakesh, their shared privations during the war. She grabbed the dinner plate and threw it at him. He fended it off with his arm and the plate smashed on the floor. Mash splattered down his front.

'But...'

'No buts. It's her or me! It's up to you!' She stormed out, slamming the door behind her. George sank into the armchair, staring into space, shaken by her outburst. What to do now?

This was their worst ever row, he would have to do something. But what? Then he remembered he was hungry. He scraped some mash from his jacket and put it in his mouth. Mmm, not bad. He reached for the sausage on the floor.

Of course, Eileen's right. This is happening too often. It's one thing to agree on having an open relationship, which we had done. Lots of people are trying out alternatives to bourgeois marriage. It's quite another for me to 'work late' as much and not expect her to object. I would have objected if it was her doing it. And yet I can't help feeling aroused by the thought of sex with Sally. I find it hard to give up. And yet I have to stop if Eileen and I are to have a future together. We've grown apart since Laurence died and she's been really down about life. We've been through so much as a couple and now we're going to adopt a baby son. I want that more than anything. And he will bring us together again. Yes, that's it. I'll have to tell Sally it's over. And, whatever she says, I'll have to stick to it. That's the way it'll have to be.

* * *

Sally McEwen entered George's threadbare *Tribune* office and stood meekly in front of a rosewood desk piled high with books and papers. She wore a smart suit and was heavily made up. George, jacket on, folded white handkerchief in top pocket, drew on a roll-up as he carried on clacking away at his typewriter. She coughed. He ignored her.

'Excuse me, George.'

Reluctantly he stopped typing and stared up at her. 'Yes? What is it?'

'Nye wants to know when your column will be ready.'

'Tell him he'll have it this afternoon.' Annoyed, he looked back down at his typewriter and started typing again. He liked

Bevan as an editor and as a committed socialist like himself; they got on well, but he was a hard taskmaster.

She hesitated, then decided to confront him. 'Can we speak?'

She's still here, he thought. Why doesn't she leave me in peace? He stopped typing and glared at her.

'George, please… what's happening to us?'

'Sally, I've a lot on my mind. So much to do. '

'I'm not asking for much. You know I…'

'Look, I'm sorry… but it's over.' Ever since that row with Eileen he'd tried to break it gently to Sally that their affair had to stop but now he had to make it clear once and for all.

She gulped, waited for some words of comfort, but none came. He flinched, and looked away. Holding back tears, she hurried from the room. He took a weary draw on his cigarette and went back to work. The phone rang. He kept on typing. It kept on ringing. Exasperated, he lifted the receiver. David Astor. He placed the cigarette on the edge of the desk.

'Yes? Oh, busy as ever… Uh huh… When's it for? I've got so much on at the moment… Next week? Perhaps that would be possible. Eileen? Yes, she's fine, in spite of being bombed out.'

The cigarette burned down, adding another black circle to the surface of his desk.

'No, it hasn't turned up yet. Yes, my only copy… I intend to have another look. Anyway, let's meet soon. Yes… Goodbye for now.'

He hung up and sighed heavily, glancing at *The Daily Telegraph* front page on his desk. 'Allied Advance in France', said the headline. It was dated 30 June 1944. He could picture all those smug Tory gents sitting in their clubs swallowing its lies and twisted opinions over breakfast and spewing them out over the course of the day. But he believed in the principle of 'know thine enemy'. That's why he made himself read it. He ran his hands through his hair, leaving it even more dishevelled. The war was almost over and he'd still not seen any real action. Being in the Home Guard didn't count – other than the time a mortar shell went off by mistake. At least being a literary editor was more useful than the last few years he'd spent at the BBC making radio programmes about Western culture for the Indian sub-continent that hardly anyone heard. Muggeridge, Koestler, even that mental philosophy professor, Freddie Ayer, had got involved in propaganda work as well.

Now he could write his weekly *As I Please* column about anything that took his fancy. It was satisfying to give what for to those middle class pub socialists. The 'antis' he liked to call them. And there was no-one looking over his shoulder about what he wrote – except Nye Bevan, and he actually looked forward to their debates on what he proposed to cover in his column. He got sent Left Book Club editions, novels and political tomes of all kinds. Books by Harold Laski, Winston Churchill, James Burnham and more lay piled up around him on the floor as well as on his desk. His desk drawer was full of poems and articles from young hopefuls he didn't have the heart to turn down. He could do his author mates some favours in this job, but that's not how he saw it. For him political truth was sacrosanct. To a fault. But he should be *writing* books not doing all this hack work. He forced himself to start typing again. The phone rang again. He ignored it and continued typing. The ringing seemed endless. Angry now, he got up and left the room.

Sally was on reception as he walked past.

'I'll be back in a couple of hours.'

'George, please… can we talk?'

He turned round. 'There's nothing more to talk about, Sally.'

'Can't we at least…?'

'There is no 'we'. I didn't promise you anything. It's finished.'

'You can't just leave it like that.'

'Sorry. I have to go,' he said brusquely.

'Well, go. But you'll never find love this way.' She wiped her eye, mascara streaming down her cheek. Unnerved, he left.

The stairway from his office had seen better days. George rushed down two stairs at a time and almost tripped near the bottom. He stepped out into the Strand and was instantly dazzled by the sunlight. The street throbbed with life. Crowds of people going about their business, war or no war. Despite his troubled mood, he couldn't help but think of the ghosts of Carlyle, Dickens and Burlington Bertie. Many a time, he'd smiled at the idea of himself as a latter day Bertie, rising at ten thirty, living on plates of fresh air and sauntering around like a toff. But today the world seemed a bleaker place.

He hurried into Kingsway, taking in the boarded shop windows, heaps of sandbags and makeshift air raid shelters. War weariness was everywhere, not just in the damaged buildings but on the anxious faces of young soldiers. In Oxford Street he came upon women queuing up outside a baker's and a butcher's. He admired their patience and fortitude as he hurried on. Old English values at their best.

He reached Fitzrovia, familiar territory. How many times had he sampled its watering holes? These days he seemed to be getting more and more drawn into literary circles and the bohemian lifestyle that accompanied them. He must do something about this. He entered Regent's Park and suddenly he was in a different world. Women were pushing prams, couples strolling hand in hand, signs of summer in the very fabric of the place. Funny how life went on in spite of the war. He became aware of the vastness of the sky, the huge, moving clouds.

Rushing on, he came upon empty zoo cages. The animals had been evacuated, along with many of the city's children. He sniffed the fetid remains of animal fodder, held his nose and started coughing. Why didn't they clean this place up? He sometimes thought that the world might be a better place if the humans were behind bars and the animals were allowed to roam freely. They wouldn't be at war for one thing.

At the other end of the park he crossed into a street of bombed buildings, some still smouldering, their inhabitants' lives exposed to the world. Torn wallpaper fluttered in the wind, furniture protruded from half-demolished floors. Amazingly, a canary in a cage had survived in one of the houses. It sang sweetly from a wrecked room on the ground floor as a woman, face blackened and bleeding, was carried on a stretcher into an ambulance. George stopped, stunned by her glazed, grim look. He reached for her outstretched hand but she was whisked away by two stretcher bearers before he could comfort her. On a nearby wall, a poster with Churchill's bull head and clenched fist caught his eye. *They asked for Total War. Let us make sure they get it!* It amused George no end that a phrase about the war that he had once written had been taken up by Goebbels and Churchill in turn. Perhaps he should invent some more phrases?

Gasping and wheezing now, George entered the shell of a partially destroyed house in Mortimer Crescent. The roof, ceiling and some of the walls had fallen in, but it was still familiar. Was this all that was left of his home? He stood blinking amongst the rubble, noticing family heirlooms amongst the debris, recognised his wheelbarrow. Would it still be there or had it been burnt to a cinder like much of the place? The thought spurred him on. He started to hunt amongst the debris and uncovered book after book. Left Book Club political potboilers, *Bleak House* by Dickens, his old favourite *Gulliver's Travels*. He dusted them down with his handkerchief and put them in the wheelbarrow. He came across a bundle of seaside postcards. He picked one out and chuckled at the sight of a fat, red-faced man with a hankie on his head sitting on a beach deckchair grinning at a scantily clad, big bosomed girl and two rounded sand castles. 'That's a nice pair!' the caption read. He blew the dust off and carefully placed them in the barrow on top of the books. It made him cough and spit up some phlegm.

He uncovered a large heap of left wing pamphlets, including some by the Duke of Bedford and Leon Trotsky. He wiped and added some of them to the growing pile in the barrow. Becoming more and more desperate, he cleared away broken shelves and a cupboard. Nothing. He was about to try somewhere else when deep under a shelf he came across a pile of crumpled paper. Frantically he flattened it out. His eyes lit up. The front page said *Animal Farm* by George Orwell. His face beamed, overjoyed at finding his lost manuscript at last.

A hand tapped him on the shoulder. He swivelled round defensively, then relaxed, laughing in recognition. It was Eileen in a grey trench coat and headscarf.

'Ah, you've found it! The girls at the Ministry *will* be pleased.' Excited, she gave him a big hug.

'They're not the only ones.' He felt a huge sense of relief as he gently disengaged from her.

She surveyed the ruins of their home. 'It wasn't a bad billet, you know… But this could make all the difference to us.'

'I know… if I can find a publisher… At least now I've got something to send out.' He gripped the manuscript tightly, the safe return of an old friend. He tried not to let political doubts spoil the moment. He knew it was the best thing he'd ever written and was determined to get it published one way or another.

'Just think of all the things we could do with the money. Perhaps we could buy some nice things for Ricky?'

'I suppose so. I'll send it off to Eliot as soon as possible… Sorry, I've got to get back to the office. Can you manage this lot?' The wheelbarrow was full to the gunwales, far too heavy for her slight figure.

'I should be able to. Have you had any lunch?' He shook his head. 'I thought not. I brought you these.' She took out some egg sandwiches in a greaseproof wrapper from her bag and handed them to him.

'Thanks, I'll eat them on the way back. Are you sure you'll be all right with this?'

'Don't worry. It's not that far to Inez's flat.'

George felt grateful. She always supported him in spite of everything. An air raid siren went off. Passers-by looked up anxiously at the sky and scurried off. He quickly pecked her on the cheek.

'Will you be working late again tonight?'

When would she stop reminding him? 'No. I told you, that's over. I'll see you later.'

'Oh, good,' she looked relieved. 'I'll make something nice for us… so don't be late.'

'I won't.' Chastened, he dashed off, manuscript and sandwiches in hand. Eileen watched his lanky figure striding out then struggled to wheel away the barrow.

September 1944, Canonbury Square, London

'I'd like to propose a toast to my namesake, young Richard here. May he be happy and healthy all his life.' The plummy voice of the balding and stubble-bearded Sir Richard Rees echoed round the living room as he raised his wine glass to the assembled company. George and Eileen had invited some close friends and relations for a celebration in the top flat they had rented in a Georgian terrace in Canonbury Square, Islington.

'To young Richard.' George, his younger sister Avril, known in the family as Av, his friend Paul Potts and Eileen all joined Sir Richard in clinking glasses.

'Well, he looks darn healthy to me,' said Paul, George's younger, but also balding, bohemian pal whose North American twang betrayed his Canadian upbringing. How come so many of his left wing chums were going bald? George wondered, just one of the many strange thoughts that kept popping into his head.

They all looked round from the table to where the baby lay contentedly in his wooden cot. Adopted when only three weeks old, with his chubby cheeks and tufts of dark hair, he looked big for four months. The table groaned under the weight of the many prerequisites of high tea at the Blairs. A plate of kippers, toast, piles of crumpets, jars of jam, marmalade and, of course, a pot of Gentleman's Relish. In spite of their habit of giving away some of their rations to those in greater need, the Blairs believed in putting on a good spread. They'd put away some of their rations for this special occasion. Adding to the general feeling of good cheer, a huge fire blazed in the grate in the otherwise dark and rather spartan, low-ceilinged room. George looked round the table with a feeling of quiet satisfaction. It reminded him of high tea at Southwold after his father had returned from India and how he would sit at the head of the table with him, along with his two sisters and his mother. Happy days long gone, but this was as near as he could get to them.

'He's a sturdy looking lad, alright,' added Sir Richard.

'Thank you, Richard. I certainly hope Ricky will be healthy.' George had named the boy after both his late father and his well-heeled best friend. 'After this beastly war's over, I'd like us to bring him up as far away as possible from the city.'

Five years younger than George, Av had a tiny mouth and big round eyes a bit like a Dutch doll's. She glanced at Eileen to check if this was news to her, but she was giving nothing away. 'Yes, it would be nice to get away from all the smog and the doodlebugs one day,' was all she said in response.

'Will you go back to Wallington?' asked Richard.

'Perhaps. Keep it under your hats for now, but David Astor has suggested I go and visit Jura where his family has some land,' George replied.

'I've never heard of Jura, whereabouts is it?' asked Av.

'It's an island off the west coast of Scotland, Av. It might be a good, quiet place for Ricky to grow up and also for me to write my next book.'

'What's it about?' asked Paul.

'You should know me well enough by now not to ask,' George replied.

'Well, this Jura sounds rather remote, what about Ricky's schooling?' Av seemed slightly disapproving.

Eileen looked uncomfortable. 'Of course, it's still at the recce stage. Eric's going to take a look quite soon. We haven't decided anything yet.'

'And, of course,' Richard suggested, 'your little Wallington cottage would also be a good place to bring up the boy and still within reach of what passes for civilisation these days. And now that you've found a publisher for *Animal Farm* at last, its sales should help matters along rather nicely.'

'It certainly wasn't easy,' said George. 'I sent it to eight or nine of them and Gollancz and the rest were terrified in case it offended our gallant Soviet allies. André Deutsch loved it but was overruled. Even Eliot at Faber wasn't interested. He seemed to think all the animal revolution needed was more public spirited pigs,' he laughed. 'But then politics was never his strong point.'

Paul spluttered, 'They were the pigs if you ask me. It's a real masterpiece, the best thing you've ever written. You know, things got so bad at one stage that I was going to bring it out from my Whitman Press and flog it round the pubs along with my poems. On the train on my way to the printers I burst out laughing when I read it. It was dynamite. I took a look under the seat in case there was any more hidden there.' Now they all laughed. 'I'm darn sure we coulda sold plenty.'

'I'm glad it never came to that,' Eileen sighed. 'Now that

Fred Warburg's taken it up, I hope it'll sell. I know his office got bombed but the sooner he gets hold of some paper to bring it out the better. The girls at the Ministry couldn't wait to hear all about it when I worked there.'

'It sure will sell,' said Paul. 'I've another toast. Here's to *Animal Farm*!'

More clinking of glasses, 'To *Animal Farm*!'

January 1945, Canonbury Square, London

George looked out at the drizzle from a door at the bottom of the brick stairway at the back of their flat. The lawn and borders were enclosed by a high stone wall with a solid wooden gate the only entrance. A few brown hens were scrabbling about and came dashing dementedly towards the door when they saw George. He threw them some grain which they gobbled up. An old goat was tethered to a metal stake in the middle of what was left of the grass but was chomping snowdrops in the border. The white stripe down the side of her head matched the whiteness of the flower heads. No sign of the rain stopping, and the light was fading fast. He turned up his jacket collar and hurried out, some hay, a stool and a small milk churn in hand.

'Come on, Muriel, try some of this instead.'

He held out the hay but she ignored him, still stretching for the snowdrops. Shivering, he yanked on the rope, pulling her towards him. He tied her close and sat on the stool, put the churn under her and felt for her teats. She resisted and kicked the churn over. Exasperated, he threw the hay on the ground. 'Blast!'

Muriel began nosing around and picking at the hay. Relieved, he took her teat and spoke quietly in her ear. 'That's better, old girl.' The teat squirted milk into the churn. One of the hens started pecking at his huge leather shoes but he gently kicked it away. He soon had enough milk, so he got up and repositioned the stake so that Muriel couldn't reach the snow-drops. Churn in hand and stool under his other arm, he made his way back inside and slowly climbed the stairs up to their flat. He gripped the green metal rail for support and stopped on each landing to catch a shallow breath. The staircase felt as cold as the rail. He opened his half-glass front door, went along the narrow, dark hall and entered the living room. Eileen sat in a loose dressing gown in her high armchair beside the fire, nursing a cup of tea.

He put down the stool and placed the churn on the table. 'She was playing up again but I think I got enough.' He was still short of breath.

'Good. She can be stubborn. A bit like yourself.' She got up and walked over, raising her hands to his shoulders. 'But you're soaked through. It'll be the death of you. Come on, let's get this off.' He let her take his jacket off and, as she did so, he wondered if she'd fancy a bit. 'You could do with a good cup of tea,' was all she offered him.

He grinned. Strong, black tea, almost as good as sex in his eyes – as long as it was from Ceylon or India. She went out to the kitchen and he tiptoed over to the cot in the corner where Ricky was sleeping peacefully. He listened to the child's rhythmic breathing which was punctuated only by the sound of water dripping from a crack in the ceiling into a pail on the floor. Eileen returned and set down a large, metal teapot on the table. Seeing him staring at the leaking ceiling, she said, 'You need to get on to them again.'

'I know, it's fitting it in… But even if I do, I can't see it being at the top of the Marquis's agenda.'

'Well, if you don't ask you don't get.' She poured him a mug of his favourite tea. It had a picture of an elderly Queen Victoria on it. He added some milk from the churn, stirred it, put some in a saucer, blew on it and slurped it down. Ricky turned over and started crying. She hurried across and struggled to lift him out of the cot. He was now eight months old. 'You're getting bigger every day,' she said to him. He was heavy to carry and she stumbled. George rushed over and took the boy from her. He walked up and down, rocking him in his arms. 'There, there... There now, lad.' His soothing voice soon began to quieten the boy. He felt proud to have a son at last. Eileen had initially taken some convincing. Perhaps she'd been worried that she'd be left to cope with him on her own? They'd had to wait all those months for the adoption to go through but, since she'd given up her job at the Ministry to look after him, she seemed much happier. They both felt nothing but love for him. 'There's a good boy. It's just coming,' George was more than happy to do his share of caring for his son.

Eileen took the milk churn out to the kitchen to prepare his bottle. By the time she'd returned with it, Ricky had calmed down and, once she was seated in her armchair, George carefully placed him in her arms. He was soon greedily sooking from the bottle. 'It's fine now,' she said. She looked smaller in the large armchair happily feeding him. The dark portrait of Lady Mary Blair on the wall behind looked imperiously down on her as if checking how well she was doing. George felt a twinge of guilt as he admired the pair of them. He tried to shrug it off and started setting out the table for their evening meal.

'He's got a good appetite. I wonder if his sister will be the same?' he asked. George had been keen to adopt a second child for a while now.

'Who knows? One at a time, Eric. Let's hold off a bit longer to see how we get on.'

He hesitated and stared absently at the worn screen divider covered in colourful magazine cuttings, angel scraps and old Christmas cards in contrast to their dark Victorian furniture.

'I've been offered a job by David as a war correspondent in France. It would pay much better than *Tribune*...' Anxious about her reaction, he ploughed on, 'But I don't like the idea of leaving you alone here with Ricky.'

She looked unsure, 'For *The Observer*?'

'He also wants me to do some articles for the *Manchester Evening News*.'

'Would you be going on your own?'

She had to ask didn't she? Would she never trust him again? 'Of course, just me and my old Remington.'

'You're sure about that?'

'Look, I told you, it's just us now. Can't we put all that behind us?'

'All right, all right. But what about Ricky and me? Perhaps we could stay up at Gwen's?'

'That sounds like a good idea.' He was well aware that Eileen couldn't wait to get out of London and it would do her good to see the widow of her dear brother Laurence who'd died at Dunkirk. Eileen had been heartbroken and depressed, almost completely withdrawn, for ages afterwards, she'd loved him so much. She and Gwen got on well, and Gwen was a doctor too, so she'd be fine up there at Greystone, her big house near Newcastle-upon-Tyne. 'So, what's for tea?' Food was never far from his mind, and, now that he'd broached the subject of him going to France, he wanted to change it as soon as possible in case she had second thoughts.

'Potato floddies. And there's still some Victory Pie left. My old Ministry recipes are really quite good, you know.'

He smiled in anticipation and finished setting the table as Ricky fell asleep in her arms. He took him from her and patted his back to make him burp, then carefully put him back in his cot, tucking him in as he did. 'You'll be walking in no time, won't you, son?' he said. Eileen smiled weakly at the thought.

***

'It's bloody freezing, George,' drawled Paul Potts, rubbing his hands together and blowing into them. He'd let his receding hair grow longer since George last saw him.

George cast his fishing line into a still part of the river near the other bank. 'Of course it is. Come on, give it a try.' He knew this tributary of the upper Thames well. He'd fished here on and off since he was a boy. And there was nothing more satisfying than initiating a friend into the joys of angling. Paul tried to cast his line but it disappeared. He looked behind and around him, puzzled, then saw it was caught in the branches of a willow. George laughed and put down his rod to help set it free. He struggled for a while then pulled down line and branch together, his long frame almost falling over in the process. Grinning, Paul thanked him and tried again but his lure dropped a few yards in front of him. George took Paul's rod from him and showed him how to release the catch on the line. 'Remember to let the catch go as you cast.' He handed it back to Paul.

'I don't know if I'll ever get the hang of this.'

'Sure you will.'

Paul cast his line almost as far as George and turned to him, looking all pleased with himself. As if he'd won an angling trophy.

'There you go,' George encouraged him, reeling in his own line, recasting and landing his line near the same spot as before.

Suddenly Paul's line went taut. He became all agitated, 'I think I've got one!'

'Take your time, let it go a little then reel in some more.' George was as calm as the river.

Paul's rod bent as he kept reeling in, almost bursting with excitement. The fish thrashed around in the water as it neared the bank. George put a landing net under it as Paul swung the rod ashore. The fish jumped about in the net on the grass.

'What do I do now?' Paul beamed.

'Watch.' George carefully took the hook out of its mouth, put two fingers inside, pulled them back quickly and broke its neck, spilling blood on his hand. 'Not a bad sized trout.'

Paul looked horrified as he stared at the red blotches on the mouth of the dead fish and on his friend's hand.

'Short and sweet, best way to go. This calls for a celebration.' George put down the trout on the grass and hunted in his fishing bag. Out came a hip flask. He opened it and took a slug. His face screwed up, he gasped and offered it to Paul. 'Here. This'll warm you up.'

'Well, it's a bit early, but why not? You only live once. Down the hatch!' He gulped it down and doubled up spluttering as it hit the spot.

'Firewater! David brought some back from Islay. Very peaty,' George laughed.

Paul downed another one and gasped again. He passed the flask to George who took another swig. As George saw it, Paul was something of an innocent abroad, not just the sponger the London literati took him for. George liked him. The world could do with more socialist poets, even if that arch-Stalinist MacDiarmid had written the introduction to Paul's first poetry collection. They sat down on a faded groundsheet and gazed at the sluggish river.

'You know I'd like to go up to Islay myself some day.' George thought back to that phone call he'd had with David in his office last summer and the delight he felt when he found his manuscript amongst the rubble of his bombed flat.

'Give it time. It won't be long till the little one's up there catching fish with you. Like father like son.'

'Not so little these days... Like father like son.' George weighed the sound of the phrase and liked the thought that one day he'd be able to teach Ricky to fish. 'You know, being a good angler is much the same as being a good writer.'

'How do you reckon?'

'Well, you need to be quiet, inconspicuous and observe things, so that they forget you're even there.'

'The fish or the people?'

'Both.'

'I get ya. Then you reel 'em in?'

'Now you're getting the idea. We'll make an angler of you yet.' George took another drink.

'How's Eileen these days?'

'All right… but I'm afraid she's a bit run down.'

'What's wrong with her?'

'I don't really know… but we've never been so happy since we got Ricky.' He looked around him as if they were under surveillance and almost whispered, 'It's not always been plain sailing, and we've had our troubles. It's a real marriage, you know.' He knew he could safely share secrets with Paul. A close, penniless pal, he owed George. And not just money.

'I know.' Stretching out, Paul blinked in the early sun, its warmth and the whisky relaxing him.

'She's had a lot to put up with, what with my writing and all.' He knew fine well his writing was the least of it.

A fish splashed in the river. They caught a glimpse of it disappearing into its hidden, liquid world and watched the circled ripples spread, then stillness return to the surface. Another one that got away, George thought, and passed the flask back.

'Yeah, you told me. Maybe you need to think more about her, not just what *you* want all the time? She's been a real good support to you.'

'I know. I'm trying to.'

'Women don't let you forget. It might not be that big a deal to you but it is to her.'

'I realise that now. She certainly doesn't let me forget. But she's had more to deal with than she deserves. We both wanted children,' he looked Paul in the eye, 'and, strictly between us?'

'Sure.'

George checked all around and could see only a solitary cow in a field. Unconcerned, it gazed back at him. 'I'm sterile. And she's had some trouble there too.' He pointed down below.

'Gotcha.'

'That's why we adopted Ricky.'

'I wondered… Well, good for you, George. It sounds like the best thing you ever did, bar none.' He put his finger to his lips. 'And mum's the word.' Paul downed the last drops from the flask with a flourish. Now it was George who stared at the dead fish lying on the grass, its bulging eyes, blood-smeared mouth fixed open, its neck broken. He thought about his own ill health and how quickly life became death.

***

'How're you keeping, luv?' Eileen's best friend, Lettice Cooper, spoke with a slight Lancashire accent. She was a stout, homely sort of woman who had recently started a career as a novelist.

Eileen hesitated. She had very little colour in her cheeks. 'Not bad, I suppose. I've been better.'

'Is Eric looking after you?'

'Well, you know him. Always sorting out the world's problems. Never bothers about our own.'

'They're all the same that way. But you're looking a bit peaky.'

'Well, I suppose so. I'm afraid… I'm listless and light-headed a lot of the time. I think there's something working on me.'

'Have you seen the doctor?' Lettice looked concerned.

Eileen put down the fairy cake she'd been nursing and made sure that the women at the other tables in the spacious Lyons tearoom couldn't hear her. 'No, not yet. But living in

London is a nightmare. I feel smothered by the crowds.' It all came pouring out. 'It's like a mild kind of concentration camp. I feel suicidal every time I walk as far as the bread shop.' She got more and more worked up as she spoke.

Lettice looked alarmed and took Eileen's hand to comfort her. 'Look, you have to tell Eric how you feel.'

'I've tried, but you know what he's like. He says we can't leave London until the war's over. We can't possibly go whilst everyone else is suffering. And then he wants to adopt a sister for Ricky and take us all up to Jura so he can write his next book.' She sounded weary, almost tearful, as she glanced at Ricky still asleep in his metal pushchair beside them.

Lettice seemed even more worried. 'Another child, in *your* state? Are you sure that's wise?'

'It's all right; we haven't done anything about her yet.'

'And it's so remote up there, how would you cope?'

'I really don't know. He's had this dream of living on a Hebridean island for a long time. He's such a romantic at heart. But at least it would get us away from here. And the freedom to play outdoors would be good for Ricky. I've written to the Fletchers, who have a farmhouse for rent on Jura, to find out more. At least there'd be no crowds up there and we'd all be together. I'll get myself checked out after he goes to Paris next week. I don't want to worry him.'

'Well, don't leave it too long. You mustn't neglect your health the way he does.'

George emerged from behind where they sat, spotted them holding hands. Caught in the act, they looked a bit sheepish. 'Sorry I'm late, very busy at the office.'

Lettice watched Eileen to see how she'd react. She didn't.

'I didn't know you'd taken up reading palms, Lettice,' he added, trying to figure out what they'd been talking about.

'Just keeping my hand in,' Lettice gave as good as she got, reminding him that she was a writer too. 'Are you still working late as much these days, Eric?'

A loaded question. She knew about Sally, then. 'No, not really, just finishing off things before I leave for la belle France next week. Is that what you've been on about then?'

'I was just telling Lettice how much I'm looking forward to going up north,' Eileen offered.

'Yes, it'll do you good.' He realised they weren't going to tell him anything. He bent over Ricky who was still fast asleep. 'Now what has one got to do to get a decent cup of tea around here?'

***

'Will you be all right up at Gwen's?' George asked Eileen. He held Ricky in his arms and was dressed in the brown captain's greatcoat of a war correspondent. A steam train idled beside them on the crowded platform at Victoria Station. He'd wanted to fight in the war from the outset but had been rejected on medical grounds. His lungs were a mess. His belief that the Home Guard could become the vanguard of the British revolution had proved to be little more than a pipe dream. David Astor was a man with connections and somehow he'd swung it so that George could go to France and Germany to see for himself the end of a totalitarian regime. He was looking forward to it with a kind of stoical relish.

'Don't worry, I'll be fine. It'll be nice to see them all again, like going home. Let's write nice long letters to each other,' Eileen replied. Young soldiers embraced their wives and sweethearts around them. Eileen looked wistfully at George for signs of affection.

'Yes, let's. You will look after yourself, now won't you?'

'Of course. And you must too. Please be careful... And watch out for the mam'selles,' she added, making light of her concern.

'I will. Don't worry, I'm finished with all that.' He hesitated. 'I want to tell you how…' He paused. The guard's whistle blew and the train lurched forward. Other soldiers kissed their loved ones and jumped aboard. George kissed Ricky quickly and handed him to her. He hugged them both and gave her a long, passionate kiss. She was tearful but tried to put a brave face on it. He put on his best stiff upper lip. He threw his suitcase into the carriage and carried his typewriter aboard. Slamming the door, he leant out the window and waved as the train pulled away. 'Take care,' he shouted.

'You too,' she shouted back. She took Ricky's arm and helped him to wave to his father as the train moved further off into the distance. The other women on the platform turned away to leave. Eileen and her son were left alone staring at the empty track.

Chapter 2

March 1945, Paris

George walked aimlessly along a cobbled quay on the left bank of the Seine near Notre Dame Cathedral. He looked unwell and his long greatcoat badly needed cleaning. He stopped and stared at the dark silent river. A couple of fishermen sat waiting, their lines slack, but somehow even fishing didn't interest him that morning. A long barge slipped past trailing smoke in its wake. That year he'd lived in Paris, penniless, near starving, seemed like a lifetime ago. He'd gone to see for himself how the city's poor lived and died; and his first book had exposed the sordid reality behind the facade of its fashionable restaurants. But, like all his other books, to him, it was a failure. The toffs still dined out whenever they wanted and the proles were still little more than slaves. He was shaken out of these dispiriting thoughts by the sound of heavy artillery fire in the distance. He took a letter from Eileen out of his pocket to read. It was long, and he'd read it many times before, but this time he read only one part of it, where she expressed regret for not telling him before he left for France that she had a growth. She had wanted him to go away without worrying about it. And she hadn't wanted to see the doctor in case she had cancer which could have prevented them from adopting Ricky in the eyes of a judge. As always, she had put his needs and their desire to adopt a son before her own.

George walked on. A ragged veteran sat begging on the quayside, First World War medals drooping from his torn jacket. His head was down, expecting nothing. George put some change in his cap. Surprised, the beggar looked up and nodded his thanks. George walked on, remembering how it felt to have nothing. A military ambulance and a steady trail of soldiers crossed the bridge ahead of him. He stopped at a book stall, rummaged about and picked up a copy of Victor Hugo's *Les Misérables*. It would help him brush up on his French and old Hugo was always worth a read, he reckoned. He took out a few francs and paid the vendor who thanked him and put the book in a paper bag. As he walked down a quiet street, he noticed bullet holes on some of the walls and the occasional bunch of withered flowers on the pavement. Café tables sat empty on either side of the street. Heading for the Hotel Scribe, he remembered how he had almost got a job in its kitchen when he lived in the city all those years ago.

Once inside, the clerk at the reception desk recognised George and reached for his key.

'*Merci*,' muttered George. '*Est ce-que Monsieur Hemingway est ici maintenant?*'

'*Oui, êtes-vous un ami?*'

'*Oui, nous sommes écrivains.*'

'*Donc, il est dans la chambre numéro cent quarante au premier étage.*'

Writers are still respected in France, George thought as he went upstairs. He knocked on the door of room 140 on the first floor and a gruff voice shouted, '*Entrez!*' When he entered, George was surprised to find a gun pointed at him. The grizzled, bearded Hemingway sat on the bed, half-packed suitcases strewn around him.

'I'm Eric Blair. I wonder if I could have a word?'

'So, what the hell duya want?' Hemingway kept the pistol aimed at him.

'Well, I'm a writer and I wanted a chat with you about our war experiences in Spain.'

'Eric Blair? Never heard of you. What have you written?' Still on his guard.

'A few novels and *Homage to Catalonia,* under my pen name George Orwell.'

'George Orwell! Why the hell didn't you say so, man?' He put his pistol down on the bed, smiled and said, 'Sit yourself down, George, I've been wanting to meet you.' He pointed to a comfy looking sofa, got off the bed, reached underneath and brought out a bottle of whisky. 'Scotch, George?'

'Don't mind if I do.' George noticed how much bigger and more luxuriously appointed Hemingway's room was compared to his own.

'On the rocks or neat, George? There's no soda. I expect you Scotch take it neat?'

'Neat, but I'm English not Scottish, in spite of the name Blair.'

Hemingway poured out two large glasses of Scotch, handed one to George and sat down opposite him in a brocade armchair. 'Sorry, George. No offence. Here's to us.' They toasted each other. 'Now tell me, have you had a good war so far?'

George felt like saying that no wars were good, but he knew enough about Hemingway to know this wouldn't go down too well. 'Well, apart from the Home Guard back in London and being bombed out of my flat, this is the closest I've been to the action. Bit of a lung problem I'm afraid.'

'Sorry to hear that. Weren't you wounded on the Aragon front?'

'That's right, I caught a sniper's bullet in the throat. And that was just about the end of that.'

'Nasty business. But at least you saw some action. I was mostly stuck in Madrid as a war correspondent, and it was all politics there.'

'Same in Barcelona when I got back, the Republican militia were rounding up all the Anarchists and so-called Trotskyists on behalf of the Stalinists. My wife and I barely got out alive.'

'I know, I read your book… just about the best piece of writing to come out of it… bar my own, of course,' Hemingway laughed. 'Just joking, George. So what are you doing here in Paris?'

'Well, I'm reporting on the war for *The Observer* and the *Manchester Evening News*, and I'm off to Cologne tomorrow to see what life under a dictatorship looks like.'

'Good luck with that. I imagine a lot of the Nazis will have gone inta hiding just like the damned Vichy collaborators here. Everyone and his grandmama in France is a Resistance hero now.'

'I'll soon find out… But I want to ask you a favour. Do you have a spare gun I could borrow?'

'I thought for a minute there you were gonna ask me to fix you up with a little mam'selle,' he laughed. 'I could probably get you one if you're interested… What's it for?'

'No, no. I just need some insurance in case the Stalinists come after me. They detested my book about Spain, and I've another little squib coming out soon they've probably heard about, which is guaranteed to blow up in their faces.'

'Sure, I get it. You don't want the old Trotsky treatment, an ice pick in the back of the skull. Well, try this Colt I nearly shot you with.' He took the gun off the bed and handed it to George, 'How does that feel?'

George weighed the Colt in his hand, looked down the barrel and pointed it at the window. 'That feels good. Not too heavy.'

Admiring the way George handled the gun, Hemingway said, 'Right, you can keep it till after the war. I can easily get another one… Let's drink to that.'

They emptied their glasses and Hemingway poured them another. 'Now tell me more about yourself, George.'

I admire Hemingway as a writer. I like his writing style – short, sharp sentences. To the point, none of your flowery language. He's a man's man, larger than life. I was hoping to find out more about his experiences fighting in Spain. But, as he said, he didn't do any real fighting although he was there at the Battle of Ebro, the last big battle of the war. Spent most of his time in hotel bars picking up political gossip and reading between the lines of what both sides and the other reporters were telling him. The Communist Party was big in France at the time and was vying for power with the Gaullists. There would be nothing revolutionary or communist about their takeover if they succeeded. It was all about power and creating allies for Stalinist Russia. That came before everything. I'd learnt that much in Spain. Not only that, they'd want to silence any dissenting voices – like mine. My press pass and my NUJ card wouldn't save me. That's why I need a gun. Call me paranoid if you like – lots of people have – but I wasn't taking any chances. Life is cheap in wartime. What would another dead journalist matter?

Next morning, rather the worse for wear, George got into the back of a British Army truck that would take him on a long journey across the border to Cologne. The French countryside looked bruised and battered, but he was struck by the number of local people who lined the streets of the villages and towns to welcome them as they drove through. Even some of the farmworkers stopped working in the fields to give them a wave. But by the time they got to Cologne after many hours travelling, George was feeling distinctly unwell. His throat was burning up and he was coughing non-stop.

'I think we better get you to a hospital, sir,' a corporal said. 'Just to make sure you're all right.'

George hardly noticed the ruined city as they picked their way through street rubble, but he saw that the huge twin-spired Cathedral beside the broad expanse of the Rhine had survived almost intact.

They took him to casualty where a young doctor took one look at him, listened to his chest and admitted him right away. After a couple of hours' wait in a busy corridor, during which he felt dreadful and almost passed out, they found a bed for him in a long ward on the second floor. It was full of young men in bandages wrapped around just about every part of their bodies. He fell asleep not long after he lay down, but when he awoke next morning he could hardly move. A British Army doctor examined him and told him that he had some kind of serious lung disease and they would have to do more tests on him. Meanwhile, he must lie as still as possible in case he did himself more damage. Day after day, George lay there helplessly until it gradually dawned on him that this time his illness was really serious. He'd been diagnosed with tuberculosis before the war but he thought he'd made a full recovery. Until now. He knew that a haemorrhage could kill him, and so for once he did what he was told and just lay there, thinking. He'd have to get word to David that there would be no articles for the time being – and ask him to let Eileen know he was unwell. He wondered how she was doing up in Newcastle. Ricky was becoming a bit of a handful. Would she be able to cope? He'd better make clear what should happen about his written work in case he was a goner this time. The hours passed with him thinking about his life and falling in and out of sleep. He remembered being bedridden as a boy and how, lying there unable to do little more than read, books had fired his imagination. Lying in bed was never time wasted.

Next day the doctor arranged for a stenographer to sit by his bedside while he dictated his 'Notes for My Literary Executor' lying on his back. He made Richard his literary executor to make it easier for Eileen. And he specified that *A Clergyman's Daughter* and *Keep the Aspidistra Flying* should not be reprinted because he felt they were no good, but he wanted Richard to try to compile a selection of his essays and have them published in book form. Once it was all typed up and he'd read it over, he made some corrections, signed and dated it, and had it sent to Eileen, care of Gwen's place near Newcastle-upon-Tyne. Lying there day after day he wondered how a devastated Germany would be rebuilt. It could only happen with American money. This would extend their influence over Western Europe whilst Stalin would no doubt grab the Eastern part. The carve-up had probably been agreed with Roosevelt and Churchill at Yalta. It seemed to confirm that he was right in the political assumptions that he'd made in the outline of his next novel.

As the days went by he got stronger and was able to read some of *Les Misérables* and write some pieces for *The Observer* after all. One morning a hospital orderly brought him a telegram. He opened and read it. His face turned ashen.

* * *

Still in uniform, George stood alone by an open grave in a sprawling Newcastle cemetery. The handful of other mourners had gone on ahead, but he didn't want to leave her just yet. Two gravediggers leaned on their shovels as they waited for him to go. He rubbed his eye then hunkered down and slowly ran his hands through the soil. The rain had stopped but the earth felt cold and unforgiving. He threw, then kicked with his huge boots, some of it on to her coffin in the grave. He looked done in. Why hadn't she told him much sooner that she was going to have an operation? By the time he got her letter it was too late to get back in time. She'd died on the operating table whilst he was lying in a hospital bed in Cologne. He'd discharged himself and got a lift back in a military aircraft. Maybe he shouldn't have gone abroad at all? Selfish, selfish, selfish. And now he was on his own with little Ricky to bring up. What to do now?

As he left the graveside, Av came over and put her arm round him as they walked. He looked back and saw the men hard at it shovelling the damp earth into the grave.

'What'll you do now, Eric?'

'I don't know… Things were looking up after we got Ricky…' He almost broke down.

'She didn't look well. The war took it out…'

George interrupted her, 'I didn't realise she was so ill… I thought it was a routine op… And I wasn't there for her…' He choked with guilt. They stopped beneath some high beech trees. The wind soughed through the early leaves on their twisting branches.

'You weren't to know, no one could know… I'll help you any way I can.' She rubbed his arm but George flinched and pulled back from her.

'Thanks.' But he didn't want her getting involved. He didn't want her running his life.

'How will you bring up Ricky?'

'I don't know. But he'll be alright with Gwen for now.' They started walking again.

'I could help you.'

'Look. I need to work this out myself… But I'm not going to give up Ricky.' A determined gleam suddenly shone in his eyes.

April 1945, Canonbury Square, London

George took from his pocket a small black and white photograph of Eileen holding Ricky in her arms and put it on the mantelpiece in his living room. He sat in Eileen's armchair and rolled a cigarette. He lit it, inhaled fully and, with a deep sigh, blew out a cloud of smoke. Eileen was gone. The heart had gone out of the place. The room was more untidy than before.

Half-full pails of water still stood on the lino floor. He couldn't face the pile of unwashed dishes in the kitchen sink. He was alone and full of regret about how he'd treated Eileen. She'd given up a professional career to support him, his writing and his dream of life in the 'Golden Country'. Wallington was the nearest they'd got to his country idyll. He'd sacrificed his time with her for his writing and he couldn't get it back. She'd stood by him in Spain when they were both in mortal danger and probably saved their lives. And she'd cared for him in Marrakesh and helped him to recover his health. She'd stuck it out in London with him during the war because he'd wanted them to, even though they could easily have gone back to Wallington and been safe from the Blitz. She'd listened in bed each night to the latest pages of *Animal Farm* he'd written that day and made helpful suggestions which had improved it. How she'd loved that little book. Now she would never see it come out. Her experiences working in the Censorship Department of the Ministry of Information had even helped him to work out some of the themes of his next novel. How stupid he'd been to have been unfaithful to her.

He got up and went into their bedroom. He opened the door of the old wardrobe which was still full of her clothes. He took out her favourite white blouse on its coat hanger and sniffed it. He could still smell her. He imagined she was still there with him. He could hear her lovely voice, speaking slowly, choosing her words carefully. But his thoughts were interrupted by knocking at the front door. He quickly shoved the blouse back in the wardrobe and hurried along the hallway. Through the glass he saw who it was and opened the door.

'Come in, Richard.'

'I'm so sorry for your loss, old chap.' He tried to embrace him, but George held out his hand. Richard shook it warmly.

'Come on through.' He led him through to the living room.

'Sit yourself down.' He directed Richard to the sofa and sat in the armchair. He noticed how much Richard had aged since they last met the previous year. His hairline had receded further and he looked almost as gaunt as him. Richard was probably thinking the same thing about him.

'It was a terrible shock. How are you bearing up?'

'Not so good… I only found out about her op a couple of days before it happened and couldn't be with her… Now everything just seems so pointless.' The grief started to well up in him.

'That's understandable. But there was nothing you could do…'

'I wanted to tell her how much I loved her that last time… But I didn't.' George got up and took a letter from the mantelpiece. 'The terrible thing is she wrote me another letter just before she went into theatre. Read the last bit.' He handed it to Richard who studied it. It said that she had been cleaned, bandaged and injected with morphia before her operation. She planned to send her letter off quickly after it was over and described the flowers in the garden she could see outside her nice room. The last thing she wrote was that she could also see the fire and the clock.

'You see how her writing gets fainter? That must have been when she drifted off and they took her in,' George said. 'She never got to finish it.'

'What went wrong?'

'She died from the anaesthetic. Maybe she had a bad reaction to it. She *was* quite frail. But, of course, they say they did nothing wrong… The old boys' network as usual. They'll close ranks and back each other up. There's no point in me… It won't bring her back.'

'How awful. Is there anything I can help you with?'

'No, not really. Ricky's being looked after for now. I think I'll go back to Germany and keep myself busy writing dispatches for David. Too many memories here.' He started to choke again and wiped his eyes with his hand.

'Best thing... You and Eileen went through a rough patch. You're bound to feel it now.'

'I suppose so. But it was just sex, you know. I still loved her. She understood me better than anyone.'

'She loved you too, Eric. That's why she put up with it. But sex isn't nothing. Somehow you have to learn how women feel about these things.'

'I know, I know, but it's not easy.' He couldn't shake the guilt. They sat and looked at each other, not knowing what else to say.

July 1945, Canonbury Square, London

'So, could you live in with us?' George asked a pretty young woman sitting on the opposite side of his living room table. The room looked even messier than before.

'Of course. I'm on my own now my daughter's at boarding school,' Susan Watson replied. She glanced round the sad looking room and spotted the photo of Eileen and Ricky on the mantelpiece.

George put twelve spoons of tea into his large brown teapot and filled it with boiling water. She couldn't help but gape. She got up, followed him to the sideboard and lifted a tray with cups and a jug of milk on it. He noticed she had a limp. She'd told him that she was married to a Cambridge maths don and was going through a divorce, and his friends Rayner Heppenstall and Hetta Empson had recommended her highly.

'Can you cook?' he asked.

'Not that well really. When I was married we had our own cook.'

'What about scones, any good at making them?'

'No, not really.'

'Oh well, never mind, we can always live off fish and chips.'
He gave her a big smile. She seemed grateful yet slightly wary
of him. 'Do you like potatoes?' he asked.

'I suppose so.'

'You know, your hands need never be cold in winter; you
can always put a baked potato in each pocket and put your
hands in.'

She couldn't help laughing.

Next evening Susan met George again at Gwen O'Shaughnessy's other house in Greenwich. Eileen's sister-in-law had
looked after Ricky whilst George was back in Germany. She'd
taken time off work to see to her nephew.

'Susan, this is Gwen,' George introduced them. 'And this is
my son Ricky.'

'How do you do,' Susan shook hands with Gwen. 'Hello,
Ricky,' she tried to shake his hand as well, but Ricky wasn't
too sure about her and was having none of it.

'Good timing, I was just about to bath Ricky,' Gwen said.
'Would you like to help me?' Gwen had been through some
hard times. The loves of her life had died within five years of
each other. Her husband Laurence, a heart surgeon and TB
consultant, whom she and Eileen adored, had died in 1940;
her mother followed a year later, and now her sister-in-law was
gone too. But she was determined to help Eric and his son.

'Certainly,' Susan replied.

They all went through to the large, tiled bathroom and
soon Ricky was sitting in the bath playing happily with a
wooden boat his father had made for him. Susan started to
wash his back with a sponge.

'That's it. Give him a really good scrub,' said George, looking over her shoulder.

She did as she was told, but Ricky put his hand between his
legs and started touching himself. She looked at George, em-

barrassed, unsure what to do.

'You must let him play with his thingummy if he wants to,' he said.

Susan smiled nervously at his directness. 'Yes, of course.'

'Not to worry, Susan, all little boys do it,' Gwen said, 'Eileen and Eric decided to adopt a modern approach to parenthood. I'm sure you'll manage very well.'

'Thank you, I'm sure I will.' Susan seemed reassured by Gwen's kindness.

'Right, just one more thing. Do you know Canuto's?' George asked Susan.

'Well, yes. But I've never eaten there.'

'Well, you will tomorrow. Would one o' clock suit you?'

'Why yes, I suppose so.'

Susan and George had just sat down at a table at Canuto's, a plush restaurant in Baker Street, when George got up. 'Would you excuse me? I have to go somewhere. Could you order us a couple of drinks?'

'Why, of course.'

'A pint of mild for me, please,' he said as he left.

But instead of going to the gents, George hid behind a gilded marble pillar just close enough to observe their table without being seen. Minutes passed and Susan started to look anxiously around. A waiter came over and she ordered their drinks. As soon as he brought them and the menus, George emerged from behind the pillar and sat down beside her again.

'Give us a few minutes, would you?,' he told the waiter, lifting a menu.

'Certainly, sir,' the waiter bowed and left.

'Right, you've got the job,' he told her. 'Now let's see what they've got to eat.' He eagerly started scouring the menu.

Towards the end of their meal she plucked up enough courage to ask him why he'd left at the beginning of the meal.

'Ah, I wondered when you'd ask. Just a little test of mine. You see these waiter chaps are very good judges of character. If they'd ignored you it would've been a bad sign. But you passed with flying colours. I'm sure you'll do splendidly, Susan.'

She stared open-mouthed at his revelation then started giggling. George quite liked how innocently she reacted to his little surprises.

'How much would you like to be paid?'

She asked for a pound a week more than she was earning as a child-minder at an international nursery and was delighted when he agreed to it.

One morning a week or so later, George lay sleeping in bed as Susan crept across his untidy room with Ricky in her arms. She showed him how to tickle his father's long toes. The boy followed her lead. This was great fun.

George wriggled and rubbed his eyes. 'I'm not used to a woman waking me up in the morning anymore,' he smiled and patted the bed, motioning her to sit down beside him. She looked uncomfortable, but did so.

'This could become a nice little ritual, don't you think?'

Susan smiled, relieved that this was all he was after.

After breakfast George went straight to his narrow workroom to write yet another article, this time for the monthly magazine *Horizon*. He was churning out far too many pieces each week and was feeling the strain. Ricky came crawling in and tried to lift some of the books piled up on the floor beneath a wooden bench which held a vice for his father's carpentry. George ignored him as he pounded away on his typewriter, a roll-up dangling from his lips, the air thick with smoke.

Chapter 3

November 1980, Blakes Hotel, London

I'VE FINALLY DECIDED to tell my side of the story about George and me because so many false things have been said about us and I don't have much time left. George agreed in his will that he didn't want any biography written about him and all these years I've tried to make sure his wishes were respected. I even asked Malcolm Muggeridge to write one to put the others off, knowing full well he was unlikely to finish it. That worked for quite a few years and, of course, he never did complete it. But eventually when my little ploy was seen through and it became clear that a biography was going to be written, I thought Bernard Crick would do a good job since it was mainly George's political side he was interested in. However, just as George and I had feared, his personal life was raked over and lots of things were revealed that shouldn't have been. I tried to stop its publication but the contract he had me sign had me over a barrel. So, I've finally decided to set the record straight.

I first met George at *Horizon* about a year after the war began when I called in at Cyril Connolly's rather grand office to enquire about a job as an editorial assistant. This lanky, unkempt looking character was there and Cyril treated him like some long lost brother. Apparently, they were at some ghastly prep school together and both of them won scholarships to Eton – 'jolly boating weather' and all that. The old school tie worked wonders in those days, you know. George initially struck me as a bit of a cold fish, even towards Cyril who clearly had something of a soft spot for him. Cyril later told me that George had given up a police career in Burma to become a writer and had written a few books that hadn't sold that well. One was about how he became a down and out in Paris and London. I didn't read it at the time, but it was full of awful goings on in Paris kitchens and London doss houses. Put you off dining out it would, but pretty typical of George – he would always do things the hard way if he could. Apparently Victor Gollancz paid him an advance to sample life amongst the workers up north and write a book about it and that got him into trouble with the socialists for going on about the smell of tripe and making out how he knew best what socialism was supposed to be about. All the sandal-wearing, vegetarian lefties were quite put out by George's diatribe about them. But that was nothing compared to the rumpus he caused with his book about the war in Spain. Auden, Spender and Hemingway went over there at the time and just about every Tom, Dick and Harry wrote about the heroic struggle of the Spanish people against Franco. But George actually saw action at the front and was almost killed. He even had the nerve to criticise the Communist Party and their Popular Front heroes which hardly anyone dared do back then. Well, of course, that made him even more enemies on the left. He became a bit of a political outcast after that. A position, I think, he rather enjoyed. His novels, on the other hand, were pretty well stillborn as far as the London literati were concerned. Until *Animal Farm*, that is.

That first time we met I could tell George had a bit of an eye for the girls. He gave me a right good once-over and practically undressed me with his intense blue eyes. Small talk just wasn't his thing. Perhaps he was trying to hide his public school accent with his clipped, wheezy voice, or maybe he was just shy. I was still going out with Bill Coldstream at the time, if you can call going out receiving long letters almost every day from army training camps all over England. I used to model for him and Lucian Freud and the other Euston Road painters, and they were all rather lively company, if you know what I mean. So, I wasn't in the market back then. I didn't get the job that time but I must have made an impression on Cyril, because a few years later he phoned me up and offered me an editorial post. He liked having attractive young girls around him in his office and that's how I met Janetta Woolley, who became my best friend. Netta and I got on like a forest fire.

George wrote lots of articles for *Horizon* during the war, mostly about politics in some form or another. He was completely obsessed with politics and thought that the war would lead to revolution in England. Apparently, he was a sergeant or something in the Home Guard and expected them to rise up against capitalism the way the workers had done in Spain. Fat chance. He was well-read, though, and wrote lots of book reviews that popped up all over the place. That's how he made his living.

Well, the next time I saw him was after the war at one of Cyril's soirées that autumn. Quite a gathering it was, everyone who was anyone in London literary circles was there. I spotted George as soon as he and Cyril came into the room. All spruced up he was in the nearest thing he had to a suit. But he looked rather lost until Cyril charged his glass and took him over to see David Astor whose father owned *The Observer* and a lot else besides. They greeted each other like old friends and George seemed to perk up right away. I had the usual crowd of hangers-on around me, almost drooling at the mouth some of them were, but hardly a brain between them. I kept half an eye on George and the others, and, sure enough, when he began to lose interest in their conversation, his eyes wandered round the room, caught mine and hurriedly looked away. Next thing, little Cyril was scurrying towards me with George in tow. The long and the short of it: the circle parted and Cyril leapt in.

'Sonia, I'd like you to meet George Orwell, the brilliantly successful author of *Animal Farm*.'

'How do you do, George. I've been wanting to talk to you.' I replied, shaking his bony hand. I noticed it had some strange little tattoos on the knuckles.

I could see he was uncomfortable being the centre of attention, so I shepherded him away from the others' prying eyes and we collected a couple more glasses of claret from Cyril's cocktail bar. We went into the drawing room whose long windows were open and overlooked the square below where we could hear some young folk having fun. It was a clear, balmy night and they seemed quite carefree compared to serious old George. He looked like a shadow of a man, his unruly dark hair and thin moustache barely visible in the half-light.

'So, tell me, are you pleased about the success of *Animal Farm*?' I asked him.

'I suppose so.'

I realised this wasn't going to be easy but I persisted. 'What gave you the idea of using farm animals to express your politics?'

He hesitated. In my experience, writers don't like to reveal where they get their ideas from. 'Well, I once saw a boy whipping a horse and wondered what would happen if the animals were aware of their own strength and fought back.'

'I see. Cyril said you had a job finding a publisher for it.'

'That's right, none of them wanted to offend good old Uncle Joe.' He tapped his nose as he said it.

'Well, I suppose he *was* our ally at that time.'

'That's no excuse for censorship.'

'Maybe not, but there was a war on. I'm just back from

Paris, it's a *real* literary city, you know. I just love Mallarmé. But they're all devouring Sartre and Merleau-Ponty.'

'I like Paris too, but I can't stand all that art for art's sake.'

'But Mallarmé's poetry's so beautiful!' I wasn't going to let him away with that, but he just ignored me.

'As for Sartre, he's a bag of wind and a bit of a Stalinist to boot.'

'I'm not that into politics,' I told him.

'I could tell,' he said with a touch of irony. 'What *do* you feel passionate about then?'

'Well, I went to a convent school for eleven years. Their whole objective is to utterly control your every thought and feeling, to uncover your secrets and totally isolate you. I hate nuns and spit when one passes me in the street. Does that count?'

He looked quite impressed by my outburst. 'It certainly does. My first school was run by Ursuline nuns and they drummed feelings of guilt into one. But are you saying they act like a kind of thought police?'

'Exactly. Those who've been their victims instantly recognise one another. Cynical despair is their only weapon. They meet in secret and lick each other's wounds.'

He seemed to like that. 'The Jesuits say that if you give them a child until the age of seven, they will give you the man. I'm not sure how true that is but it certainly seems we're a pair of rebels,' he smiled. I noticed his yellowish teeth for the first time and wasn't too sure I wanted him licking my wounds.

Just then Cyril came in with another bottle of claret and topped up our glasses. 'Everything all right?'

'We're having a most interesting discussion,' I told him. George nodded agreement.

'I thought you two would get along rather well.' Cyril gave us a knowing grin and went round the room filling up more glasses and mingling with his guests.

'I see Cyril's as nosey as ever,' George said.

'Oh, he just loves a bit of gossip. The juicier the better. But then don't we all? *And* he likes to keep his beady eye on me.'

'Do you need keeping an eye on then?'

'Oh, I have my moments.' He wasn't the only one who could be secretive.

'Well, how would you like to join me and some literary friends for lunch next week?'

'Whereabouts?'

'At the Elysée in Percy Street.'

I could hardly believe it. 'Why that's right opposite my flat! What time?'

'Next Tuesday at one. Will you come?'

'I'll see… If I'm not too busy reading Mallarmé.'

Well, I wasn't too busy reading Mallarmé the following week and, when I arrived at the Elysée, I found George and some friends already seated at an alcove table at the back. He had his back to the wall, a position that somehow seemed to suit him. I ordered a G and T and went to join them. They all stood up and George did the introductions. 'Sonia, this is Richard Rees, my best friend. We go back a long way.'

I shook hands with him. 'How do you do. Isn't it Sir Richard?'

'How do you do. Yes, but I prefer not to use my title,' he said in a quaint, posh voice.

'And this is Malcolm Muggeridge. He's a leader writer at *The Telegraph*.'

I put out my hand but, instead of taking it, he bowed and slavered all over it. 'Pleased to meet you.'

'I can assure you the pleasure's all mine, my dear.' He had silky blonde hair and was good looking in a patrician kind of way, but I was already starting to get a bad feeling about this bloke.

'Sonia is an assistant editor at *Horizon*,' George said.

'We know, old boy. Her fame precedes her,' Malcolm replied. 'How's old Cyril? Keeping out of mischief, I hope?'

Before I could reply the waiter arrived with the menus and my G and T. Greek food – plain but, from past experience, quite palatable. Richard ordered a bottle of retsina and our noses went straight into the menus.

'Cyril's fine. Jean's divorcing him, and Lys and he want to get married,' I threw him some gossip. 'And, of course, he's trying to write another book.'

'He's certainly got quite an eye for the fillies,' said Malcolm in an exaggeratedly toff voice. 'I wonder if he'll ever write anything as good again as *Enemies of Promise*? But I suppose he must still have the old writing bug. We've all got it.'

'Why do you think that is?' I asked him.

'My dear girl, one writes because one must!'

'Don't be such a pompous ass, Malcolm! There's no *must* about it.' Richard intervened before I could. 'I have to drag myself kicking and struggling to my typewriter. In fact, I'm really more of a painter these days.'

Malcolm looked decidedly miffed. The waiter came back with the wine, poured some for Richard to taste and, having got his nod of approval, filled our glasses and took our orders. George went for the moussaka, as I recall. I wondered why he had said so little. Until, that is, he started.

'You know, writers are egotisitical, they think they know more than other people and would like to be immortal through their work. A lonely childhood often leads them to start writing.' He paused for effect, then went on. 'They love beauty whether it's in the world or in the sound of words. They've a burning need to express the world as it really is and to change how others see it. There's no such thing as non-political art, certainly not in the kind of world we live in. Anyone who claims there is such a thing is expressing a political view.' He talked fast and fervently. Our jaws practically hit the floor.

'But...' Malcolm tried to get in. But George didn't let him.

'Writing a book drains the life out of a writer the way a serious illness does. The only reason one does it is because one can't do otherwise. It's like being possessed by some demon.'

Impressed by his obvious passion, I asked, 'So you've a burning need to put the world to rights before you die?'

'I suppose you could say that,' he replied.

'And what demon drives you to write your books?' I pressed him.

'George and I are both driven by political demons, albeit from rather different ends of the political spectrum.' At last Malcolm got a word in. 'But whether we'll be remembered after we die for anything we've written is difficult to gauge. Look at how the once famous are all but forgotten nowadays. What I don't doubt is we'll read all of this in one of George's columns in a few months,' he told us with a wink.

I don't remember much else of that lunch. The food was passable, the conversation lively, if not exactly memorable. After his outburst George seemed to go back into his shell and let the rest of us hog the discussion. Mostly literary I think it was, but by the end of it I'd put Malcolm down as a cynical lech and Richard as a perfect gent. George, however, remained something of an enigma.

The next time I met George was on the Embankment about a week later. He was pacing up and down impatiently checking his watch. I sneaked up behind him and tapped him on the shoulder. He whirled round as if expecting someone was going to knife him in the back.

'Sorry I'm late.'

'I don't have much time.' He appeared put out.

'Time and tide wait for no man, as my dear mother used to say.'

We started to walk along beside the river. Barges were plying up and down, the life of the city was returning to normal. It was hard to believe we had just come out of a war that, at the time, had seemed to last forever. It was turning cold and golden leaves were quietly falling from the trees that lined the Embankment.

'Aren't you talking to me?' I asked.

'What do you want to talk about?'

'About you.'

'What about me?'

I started to wonder if I should bother. 'Where were you born and brought up?'

'Why do you want to know?'

God, it was like pulling teeth. 'Because I want to get to know you better, of course!'

'I don't tell just anybody about my private life.'

I pulled up and looked him straight in the eye. 'Look, George, I'm not just anybody!' That got through to him.

'Well, I was born in India.'

'So was I! Whereabouts?'

'In Motihari in Bengal.'

'I was born in Ranchi in Bihar. Not that far away, really.'

We walked on and I put my arm in his. He seemed to relax and enjoy having me on his arm. As well he should.

'I was brought up in Henley-on-Thames and sent to a beastly prep school.'

'I was brought up in Calcutta and shipped off to that bloody convent school near London after my father died when I was only six. And I was there until I was seventeen.'

We stopped and sat down on some steps that led down to the river. He took something out of his pocket wrapped in newspaper.

'Would you like a sandwich?'

'What's in it?'

He opened it up. 'Corned beef.'

I took one and bit off a piece. 'Ugh! It's ghastly!' I spat it out.

'Actually I quite like it.' He smiled and carried on wolfing down his.

'Now you're a successful writer you should be dining out at the Ritz.'

He practically choked on his mouthful. 'Money doesn't interest me.'

'The root of all evil?'

'The love of it, perhaps.' He stared at the murky river, contemplating its steady flow. 'Have you ever thought that life is like a river?'

'How do you mean?'

'Well, it springs up and becomes a stream that merges with others. It sparkles for a while and eventually flows into a sea of past lives.'

'So you don't think it matters what we do, we're all doomed?'

'At the time it does. But in the end, no, not really,' he sighed.

I wasn't going to have that. 'That's far too fatalistic for me, George. Right now I want to sparkle and shine. Life is a sea of possibilities and I want to experience them all!' I put my arm in his as if to give him a shake. He really could be a gloomy old bugger. He put his hand on my thigh. It didn't bother me but I took it off.

'Maybe I'm just run down and need a break.'

It seemed to me that he was working himself into an early grave to avoid thinking about the wife he'd lost and his other troubles. Some men are like this. Work, work, work. And they tell themselves they have to. 'Maybe you *are* run down.

Now let's see if we can cheer you up. If you had one wish what would it be?'

'I'd like to be irresistible to women!' He grinned at the thought.

I laughed. 'Well, let's pretend you are. Give me a kiss.'

He hesitated then gave me a big kiss. The works. Tongue and all. He put his hands round my waist and started caressing it. I felt quite relaxed about this but carefully removed them. I'd say I'm fairly liberal-minded, but it was a public place after all.

'Not bad.' I gulped for breath.

He looked distinctly pleased with himself. 'What would your wish be?

'I'd like to be a handmaid to an artistic genius.'

'Well, I'll need to see what I can do. Is that why the artists call you the Euston Road Venus?'

'No, it's because I used to model for them.' We laughed again and I felt at last that we were beginning to enjoy each other's company.

'Are you sure that's all you did?'

'Whatever could you mean?' I teased.

For once he seemed stuck for words. 'Eh... I'm sorry, I'd better get back to the office to finish my column.' Damn, just when we were starting to have some fun. He wrapped the rest of my sandwich in the newspaper and put it in his pocket. We started heading back together.

'Next week then?' I asked.

'I'd like that.'

'Perhaps you could buy me lunch at the Ritz next time?'

'Perhaps I could.' He smiled and I gave him a goodbye hug as we left the river behind.

* * *

George and Paul liked to walk in the tiny gardens of Canonbury Square whenever they could. The shrubbery could be seen from the front windows of his flat, beckoning him out. There were still some leaves on the trees but winter was on its way. Canonbury Road cut the gardens in two but to them it remained a little oasis in the midst of run-down Islington.

'I'm really grateful to you for sorting out that business with her ladyship the anti-Semite,' Paul said.

'It was nothing. But maybe you shouldn't have smashed her little Madonna statue just to make the point that Mary was a Jew.' George enjoyed gently winding him up.

'Well, she kind of deserved it.'

'A lot of politicians deserve to have their statues smashed, but you don't see me going around town with a sledgehammer.' George chuckled to himself at the thought. Maybe that wasn't such a bad idea?

'No, George, you smash them far better with your old Remington.' Paul was always good fun.

They sat down on a bench beside the path in the gathering dusk. Some pigeons came waddling up to them looking to be fed.

'You know, pigeons are the proles of the bird world,' George said, gazing at their bright eyes.

'A lot of people don't like them, they think they're vermin.'

'Well, I like them.' George took a paper bag out of his pocket. He broke off pieces of stale bread from it and began to throw some to the pigeons. They fluttered about and hurriedly pecked them down. More arrived to try to get a share of the feast. We must look after the proles, George thought.

'I sometimes worry that you take the world too seriously. There's much more to life than politics,' said Paul.

'It determines just about everything, as far as I can see.'

'What about love? I've just met a girl and suddenly the world's a much better place.'

'Maybe you're right,' George said wistfully as he threw the last of the bread to the scrambling pigeons and put the empty bag in his pocket.

'How's your love life going?' Paul asked.

'It's still hard coming home... All those ghosts... You know, Eileen really understood me and my work. It's only now I realise how much she helped me.' He paused to think back. She didn't deserve an early grave. They would have been really happy together bringing up Ricky.

'It's been tough all right. But isn't there someone new?'

George snapped back to reality. 'There is indeed. Things are looking up since I met Sonia. She's bold and very well read... A bit of a challenge actually.'

'It wouldn't be you if there wasn't a challenge, would it, George? But it's still early days.' They got up and started walking again. 'Fancy a pint?'

'I could murder one.'

The light was fading fast now.

'Only I'm a bit short.'

George smiled. He'd been here before. 'Don't worry, I've got enough.'

They walked out of the gardens into Canonbury Road and along past a row of war-damaged houses to the Compton Arms. The area was dilapidated. Paint peeled from the sides of terraces and metal stumps were dotted along the low walls where railings had been removed for the war effort. But inside the place was noisy and cheerful, and Paul was soon struggling through a haze of smoke with two pints of beer in hand to a table in a dark corner where George sat rolling a fag. Two young women followed behind him, pints of shandy in their hands. A blonde and a brunette, East End girls dressed up to the nines and already well oiled.

'This is Doreen... and this lovely young lady is...?' Paul asked.

'Jean,' the blonde one said.

'They want to meet a famous author. Girls, meet George Orwell.'

'How do you do.' George looked them up and down without much enthusiasm. What was Paul getting him into now? Doreen plonked herself close to Paul whilst Jean practically fell down beside him. He could feel her thigh pressed against his and smell her cheap perfume.

'An are you famous then, George?' Jean asked.

'Not really. But my recent book's doing quite well,' he replied.

'So wha kin of books do you write then, George?' Doreen asked.

'Novels mostly.' George took a deep gulp of his pint, as did Paul.

'Are there any murders in 'em? I like a good murder,' Doreen asked.

'No, but some animals died in my last book.'

'Oh, wha a shame. I could tell you were the sensitive type the first time I saw you,' said Jean and squeezed up even closer to George. He shifted awkwardly in his seat.

'An I've got a sensitive poet all to meself, see.' Doreen tickled Paul under his jacket as he was drinking his beer. Some of it sprayed out onto the table and the girls had a right old giggle at this. Doreen started stroking the inside of Paul's leg. He got the idea and started kissing her.

'Well, they look all set an no mistake. Now, wha are *we* goin to do, lover boy?' Jean slurred. She came on strong as well, putting her hand between George's legs. He started touching her breasts. She bit him on the neck but he broke away from her.

'I'm sorry I don't think I can do this.'

'It's only a bit of fun, luv... It ain't as if we're movin in together.'

'You see I recently met someone rather special.'

'Wha, you mean I ain't special?' She quickly turned against him.

'No, that's not what I meant. I'm sure you're special too, but…'

Jean staggered to her feet. 'This one thinks I'm not good enough for im! Come on, Doreen, let's get ou of ere an find ourselves some real men. They're just a pair of nancy boys!' She practically pulled Doreen off Paul. The pair of them looked a bit dazed but Doreen grabbed her bag and trooped off after her pal.

'I thought we were all set. What happened?' Paul asked.

'I'm sorry, I just couldn't…' George felt bad for spoiling his mate's chances.

'Ah well, nothing ventured… That's the proles for you… Anyway, the night is young.' Paul downed the rest of his pint and George did the same.

Later that night, much the worse for wear, they climbed the three floors to George's flat. George puffed and wheezed. Halfway up the stairs a lovely, dark-haired young woman passed them on her way down. Paul took a long, sharp intake of breath and whistled after her. 'Who'sh she?' He slurred and stumbled as if to follow her downstairs.

George blocked his way. 'A neighbour. I think she's called Anne. A bit of all right… but she'sh hardly ever about.'

Eventually they reached the top landing. George struggled to find the key in his pockets.

'Shpoiled for choice, old man, shpoiled for choice. Thingsh are definitely looking up around here,' Paul announced.

George opened the door and they fell inside.

* * *

Well, of course, I slept with George not long after we started having lunch together. In fact, I used to come over to his flat to help him look after little Ricky on his housekeeper's day off. Susan, she was called, a bit of a mousy young thing, but wouldn't hurt a fly. She was very good to George and his son, and had a little girl of her own who, poor soul, had been packed off to boarding school. The English and their public schools – but I suppose it gave Susan a bit of freedom to do what she wanted. And I heard there was a new man in her life after the break-up of her marriage. Anyway, I liked helping people out and George could certainly do with some help.

One of the times I went over that November, there was no sign of Ricky. I assumed Susan had either taken him out for the day, even though it was her day off, or he was fast asleep. Perhaps George had bribed her with an extra day's pay so he could try his luck with me. Knowing him, I wouldn't put it past him. Well, we had a nice lunch that he'd prepared. Kippers on toast with his favourite Gentleman's Relish, as I recall. And afterwards, well, one thing led to another and we finished up in bed together. I wouldn't say he was the worst lover I ever had, but he certainly wasn't the best. It was all crash, bang, wallop and before you knew it you were lying there thinking, was that it? And he was snoring beside you. No finesse, and scant consideration for a woman's needs. But then most men were like that in those days.

I know I shouldn't be engaging in pillow talk but I feel I've done my bit by George all these years and, the way I am these days, what does it matter? Not only did George snore – find me a man that doesn't – but he used to cry out in his sleep. He was prone to having nightmares, you see, and that time we slept together I remember he shouted 'they're listening to us' and woke up with a start. He seemed upset and, when I asked him why, he told me he had dreamt about Eileen. They were being followed through the streets by a shadowy figure when a flying bomb

shrieked and exploded ahead of them. There was a huge crater
in the back garden lawn with the remains of his goat's rope lying
beside it and crows flew up from the hole as they went past.
When they got home, 'they' could hear everything they were
saying.

'How come?' I asked him.

'They'd planted some kind of listening device in the phone.'

'Who's they?'

'I don't know. Secret police of some kind.'

'It sounds like a nightmare. Do you often have them?'

'I'm afraid so. The world's becoming a nightmare as far as
I'm concerned. But Eileen isn't usually in them.'

I was intrigued. He didn't usually talk about her. 'How long
were you together?'

'About ten years.'

'No wonder you're upset. Do you still miss her?'

'Of course, every single day.' He paused, then brightened
up. 'But I'm not alone any more. I'm so glad you offered to
watch Ricky on Susan's day off.'

'This wasn't quite what I had in mind!' He could be quite
sweet in his own innocent way and I gave him a big hug. Of
course, he took that as an invitation to go again and I had to tell
him, 'That's plenty for one day.' He'd had all he was going to get.

'But…' He looked frustrated and that's when he asked me,
'Have you had many men?' He just came right out with it, and
even I was a bit taken aback.

'Enough,' I said.

'It doesn't bother me, you know. In fact I quite like the
idea.'

This was becoming somewhat tiresome. He didn't seem to
understand that this kind of talk can be off-putting for women.
'A lot of men do,' I replied, 'but let's talk about us.'

Well, the next thing we were talking over each other. He
was going on about some big house on Jura where Ricky

would have lots of freedom and he could write his book, and I was saying how much I enjoyed my work at *Horizon* since Cyril always seemed to be busy and I was able to do what I wanted. Then I heard him say, 'There's no telephone or electricity at Barnhill,' and that's when I realised we hadn't been listening to one another.

'What? You'd need to be a masochist to live like that,' I said.

'I don't mind. It's good for you to do without. The way most people do.'

'Perhaps for you, not for me.'

That seemed to set him off. He took a deep breath and started coughing uncontrollably. He scrambled out of bed, grabbed his shabby old dressing gown and rushed to the bathroom. I lay in bed wondering what was wrong and why he was taking so long. I could hear him coughing and spitting up. It sounded disgusting. I knew he wasn't in the best of health. How could he be with all that chain smoking? He smoked dark, shag tobacco and the place reeked of it. Eventually he rejoined me in bed and I asked him if he was all right. He said it was nothing much, he'd always had problems with his health. I suggested perhaps he should get himself checked out. I was worried about him, but he didn't reply. It was then I noticed the scar on his throat and asked him what happened.

'A fascist sniper got me in Spain.'

'I wondered about your voice.' I took his hands in mine and asked him about his tattooed knuckles. He told me he had them done in Burma and the little blue circles were a Buddhist design.

'They're supposed to ward off evil spirits.'

'You believe in them do you?'

'Well, you never know.' I hadn't realised he could be so superstitious. He went quiet, lost in thought, and suddenly sat up straight.

'I've something important to ask you.' I didn't like the

sound of this, but he pressed on. 'I'm not that well, but I *am* a successful author. We could have some fun together and you would still have your freedom... I don't know if this is the right time... but... will you marry me?'

Well, you could have knocked me down with an elastic band. I'd only been seeing him for a few weeks. He made for interesting company and I admired his dedication to his writing, and, of course, *Animal Farm*. But only George could have thought that after such a short time together I would be willing to marry him. I was just twenty-seven, I had my whole life ahead of me. I was enjoying my job and wasn't ready to settle down and bring up his son for him. It was completely out of the question.

'It's all a bit sudden, George. I hardly know you,' I stammered. 'Of course I like you a lot...'

'You don't have to decide right now. Take some time to think about it.'

He knew he was in deep water, and now he was paddling back as fast as he could. But I had to be honest with him. 'Just because I slept with you doesn't mean I love you...'

'But...'

'I'm sorry, really I can't...' I got up and started dressing as quickly as possible. He got up, put on his dressing gown and looked even more mournful than usual. Ricky came into the bedroom crying. George scowled as he took him out of the room, shielding the boy's eyes. When I came into the living room they were sitting on the floor playing with wooden toy cars that George had made for him. George deliberately crashed one of the cars into the wall and Ricky started crying again.

'I'm sorry I have to go.'

'So soon?' He looked desperately hurt.

'I'll be in touch.' I pecked him on the cheek and left as fast as I could.

Just when things seemed to be going so well with Sonia I managed to mess it up good and proper. Too hasty when it comes to women, that's always been my problem. Too eager, unable to read the signs of when they're ready to take things further. Sonia's a real beauty, glamorous in a voluptuous sort of way and charged with unstoppable, bold vitality. She has a generous, caring spirit and would have been quite a catch. But I tried to reel her in too soon and lost her. She's extremely passionate about literature and cultural life in general, especially when it comes to France. We had such interesting conversations and have so much in common. She just loves literary gossip and her job at *Horizon*, which was at the centre of the world of English letters during the war, suits her down to the ground. She's a true rebel, but real politics don't interest her. Never mind, you can't have everything.

There's something intriguing about her. She's an experienced lover but you always feel she's holding something back. Like she's going through the motions to some extent. And, unusually for a young woman, she exudes an element of sadness about life which is hard to pin down. I suppose that's something else we have in common, however well she tries to play the part of a happy young thing. I was so lonely after Eileen died and desperate to have a woman in my life again, and a mother for little Ricky, who would be prepared to come to Jura with me. I could see that her attitude to remote island life was going to be a problem, but I thought that if she would marry me she would accept that in the same way Eileen was willing to. I'm also annoyed with myself for letting her see how ill I was that last time. That may have been part of the reason she turned me down. What lovely young woman wants to be tied to an old codger who's on his way out? Anyway, it's done now, and all I can do is try to remain friendly and hope she comes round in time.

Chapter 4

GEORGE HELD RICKY under one arm and his battered leather suitcase under the other as he waited in a long queue at Paddington Station. He looked back and saw a beautiful young woman carrying a dainty case coming along the platform towards him. She looked like a film star in her smart tweed suit.

'Are you George?' she asked. He nodded. Up close she looked even more gorgeous. 'And you must be Ricky.' The boy gave her a big smile.

'And you must be Celia.' George replied. 'Arthur said you were coming. Pleased to meet you.'

They shook hands and waited to board the train together. It seemed to take forever and George wasn't one for casual conversation. But eventually, after what felt like hours, they were allowed to board. They had a compartment to themselves and sat opposite each other. Soon they were leaving the grimy city streets behind and passing through the boxed hedgerows and fields of the Thames Valley. In shaded gullies they could see traces of snow sparkling in the low winter sunlight as the train chugged along. George had brought some toys with him and soon Ricky was playing happily on the seat beside him.

'What age is he?' Celia asked.

'He'll be two in May.'

'My, he's big for his age.'

'Yes, but he's not really speaking or walking yet.'

'Not to worry, he will soon enough. He seems quite happy anyway.'

'Have you been to Wales before?' George asked.

'No, but I'm really looking forward to seeing Mamaine again and meeting Arthur. Have you known him long?'

'Oh, about eight years, I think. I read one or two of his books and we started writing to each other and became friends. He's one of the few intellectuals who's not been taken in by the Soviet propaganda machine.'

'Yes, Mamaine said you had a lot of politics in common.'

'Some politics, but not all,' George was quick to stress.

'Well, what do you think of the Labour Government continuing with rationing?'

'Well, ostensibly it's because of the food shortages in Germany. Things are pretty desperate over there, as you can imagine. But I think it's also a means of social control which, now they've got it, could last for years.'

'Surely not. That wouldn't go down well at the next election.'

'Well, put it this way, if they abolish it, I'll be holding on to my ration cards just in case.' George waited for her to quiz him about his reasons for doing so, but she didn't take the bait. She seemed quite smart. He was impressed. 'I do hope they abolish the House of Lords, though. Their superannuated lordships are an affront to democracy.'

'I suppose so. They certainly have a big enough majority in the Commons.'

George noticed her staring at Ricky as she spoke, 'Would you like to hold him?'

'Oh, yes please.'

He lifted up Ricky and put him on her lap.

'He's quite heavy. But he seems all right with me.'

'Yes, he's not strange with people. I think I'm really rather good with animals and, although I say it myself, I think I've trained him quite well.'

Celia gave him a puzzled look. The train steamed its way through the wintry English countryside into Wales and George was pleased how readily Celia helped him to keep Ricky amused for the rest of the long journey.

The large farmhouse which Arthur Koestler and Mamaine Paget had rented was a short drive from the Vale of Ffestiniog in the foothills of Mount Snowdon and had some old woods nearby. A real Christmas tree sat in the corner of the parlour and Ricky was soon fascinated by the twinkling coloured lights and tinsel with which it was festooned. George had to pull him back several times from tugging at it that first evening. Its pine smell reminded him of his own childhood at Christmas. On Christmas morning they all got up early and enjoyed watching Ricky rip open his presents. It felt like a real Christmas having a child in their midst. The boy was soon crawling around the floor playing with his favourite new toy, a wooden lorry his father had made him. Then the adults exchanged presents. Arthur and George gave each other books and the twin sisters exchanged jewellery. Despite continuing food shortages, they had a full Christmas dinner with all the trimmings to go with the goose that Arthur had shot and which Mamaine had plucked and cooked. George gobbled it down as if it was his last Christmas meal.

After dinner Arthur lit a cigar and George made his usual black shag roll-up. Arthur was suave-looking with dark, well-groomed hair and exuded a certain superficial charm. Dense smoke and political discussion soon filled the room once they had added more wood to the fire and sunk into a pair of high-backed armchairs. Arthur poured them each a large brandy whilst Celia and Mamaine cleared the table and went into the kitchen to wash up. Ricky crawled along as fast as he could behind them.

'So, George, I'm pleased you've come round to my way of thinking about revolutions,' Arthur said in a very thick Hungarian accent. He liked to provoke but George found his inability to pronounce the letter 'w' quite amusing.

'What do you mean?'

'Well, in *Animal Farm* you demonstrate very cleverly that revolutions will always fail and lead to dictatorships.'

'That may be your view, but it's certainly not mine. Revolutions led by a centralist Bolshevik Party will always lead to dictatorship. As we've seen in Russia. But if the masses are vigilant and kick out leaders who get too powerful, revolutions don't have to fail. What I saw in Barcelona in the early days taught me that.'

'Yes, but look what happened there. The Stalinists attacked the anarchists and socialists and destroyed the revolution.'

'That's true, but it doesn't mean all revolutions are bound to fail. It's only when middle class intellectuals get a taste of power that things go wrong. That's the big difference between us. You're a pessimist, a hedonist and a nihilist, whereas I still believe in democratic socialism. Otherwise we might as well top ourselves.'

'Come on now, that's a bit much, George. I may like the finer things in life, like good wine and beautiful women. Who doesn't? But, as well you know, I'm still politically active in my own way. I'm more of a realist whereas I see you as still something of a dreamer.'

George was enjoying the cut and thrust of political debate with Arthur. He'd hoped for just this sort of thing when he accepted his invitation to stay with him over Christmas. He took another sip of brandy, as did his host. 'Yes, we're both active in our own way and, if you're interested, I've clarified my views about revolutions and socialism in a preface to a Ukrainian edition of my book.'

'Good, I look forward to reading it some time. In English, of course. My considerable knowledge of languages doesn't quite stretch to Ukrainian.'

'Still, we're on common ground when it comes to exposing

the dangers of totalitarian dictatorships and the spineless intellectuals of the so-called left who excuse their every atrocity for
the good of the cause. Just look at the way they swallowed all
the ridiculous lies in the Moscow Trials.'

'Well, my book exposed how they managed to get the Old
Bolsheviks to confess to even the most outrageous of charges.'

'That it did, but, you know, Rudolf Hess will soon be on
trial in Nuremberg and he could be cross-examined about
Trotsky's alleged spying for the Nazis.'

'I doubt they'll ever let that happen.'

'Well, I think we should start a round robin letter to the
press calling for just that. It would expose Stalin's lies once
and for all.'

'It would indeed, George. Yes, let's do that.'

George thought for a moment then decided to change the
subject. 'So, how did you find living in Palestine?'

'Well, you know it's a very difficult and dangerous situation. The Arabs don't want us Jews there and yet it's the only
place of refuge for those who've survived the horrors of the
Nazi concentration camps. Every other country has refused
to take us in,' Arthur replied.

'I saw those horrors when I was over there as the war was
ending and wrote about them for *The Observer*. But don't
you think it will create more conflict in the long term?'

'It may do, but Attlee should be recognising Jewish rights
there, not just Palestinian rights.'

'The first thing he should do is to pull out of India and
give it its independence.'

'But the day the British leave, there will be 100,000 dead
in Calcutta and a million elsewhere,' Arthur protested.

'Let them kill each other if they want to. It's their business.
At least they'll have the freedom to do what they want.'

Arthur looked horrified at George's callous attitude and
decided to raise another issue he wanted his views on. They

both took a large gulp of brandy. 'I can see we're not going to get anywhere on this. Perhaps we should focus on what we can agree on, rather than our differences, important though they may be. What about this new League for the Rights of Man we've been talking about?'

'Yes, well, on that we *can* agree. Although I'm happy to support Woodcock's Freedom Defence Committee, we need something that's got much greater relevance worldwide.'

'Good. We'll need a manifesto and some cash to launch a magazine. I'll see if I can tap some money from old Rodney. He's always good for a few quid. And I'll talk to Bertie Russell and see if he'd be willing to get involved. Did you know he's got a place not far from here?'

'No, I didn't. It would be good to have a philosopher or two on board. I wonder if we could get Freddie Ayer involved too? Anyway, when I get back I'll draft a manifesto and send it for you to take a look at. As long as we can stop the Stalinists from taking it over the way they did the National Council for Civil Liberties.'

'We're all a lot wiser now and some of us have got the scars to prove it,' Arthur laughed.

George stroked the scar on his throat and said, 'Well, you know something? When I lie back in my bath I enjoy thinking up all kinds of horrible punishments for those bastards.'

'I can just see you plotting away in that bath,' Arthur laughed again. 'But I know you too well, if you met them in the pub you'd be all civil and polite and would end up offering to buy them a drink.'

This time George laughed and sipped some more of his brandy.

'Now tell me, George, why on earth do you want to go to a godforsaken island in the middle of nowhere?'

George was taken aback at Arthur's sudden change of tack. 'Well, I'm becoming more and more like a sucked orange in London. I seem to do nothing but write articles, and my phone never stops. I badly need a rest. And at least up there I'll have some peace and quiet to get on with my book.'

'Perhaps you could do with a new woman in your life?' Arthur lowered his voice, glancing towards the kitchen, 'What do you think of Celia?'

'Well, she *is* rather gorgeous but I can't see her being interested in a withered old stick like me. Damaged goods and all that.'

As they talked they could hear laughter coming from the kitchen where the twin sisters were enjoying catching up with each other's lives. George thought at one point he could hear the ee-aw sound of a donkey that Mamaine was making.

'Don't be so sure about that, George. Mamaine's a bit of a corker, you know, and I think Celia could be interested in you. She would certainly pep you up all right. She's just coming out of a bad marriage, but let me see what I can do.'

George hadn't thought of Arthur as a matchmaker before, and wasn't optimistic about his chances, but he didn't try to dissuade him.

'Typical men, sorting out the problems of the world,' wheezed Mamaine, slightly breathless, when she and Celia came back in with Ricky in tow, 'while we see to their every need.'

'Now then, my dear, come and sit over here and I'll make it up to you.' Arthur patted the arm of his thickly upholstered chair. 'What about a glass of wine? Red or white?'

'I think we deserve some of your best Bordeaux,' Mamaine said.

Arthur went over to the cocktail cabinet, filled two glasses and took one to Celia who sat near George and the other to Mamaine who had perched herself on the edge of his armchair. Ricky crawled over and Celia helped him up to sit beside her.

'He's a little darling,' Celia smiled, stroking Ricky's hair. He looked up and gave her a big smile in return.

'Merry Christmas,' Arthur said as they all clinked glasses.

'Merry Christmas. Ricky seems to like you,' George said to Celia. He looked really happy.

'Oh yes, we get on rather well. Not quite what my aunt had in mind when she put us through finishing school and we became debs of the year,' Celia laughed.

'I'd say bringing up a boy is a much better ambition than that,' Arthur chimed in. 'Not that we're in any hurry, darling, are we?'

'No, we're not,' Mamaine said firmly. 'But George, now that *Animal Farm* has been so successful, what's your next ambition?'

'Oh, I suppose, the usual one. I'd like to be irresistible to women.' They all laughed. The old ones are the best, George thought.

Next morning, George and Celia walked on their own down a track in crisp sunlight. A few snow patches clung on in the woods where the sun hadn't reached yet. It felt good to get away from the London rat race, George thought.

'You know, I've always loved the outdoors,' George said with real feeling. 'Ever since I was a child I couldn't wait to go out to play and see what I could find.'

'What *did* you find?' Celia asked.

'Oh, lots of things. Birds' eggs, grass snakes, conkers, the usual boys' things.'

'Where was this?'

'Henley-on-Thames. And later at Southwold I'd go for long walks across the marshes looking for birds and flowers. Even in Hayes, where I taught for a little while, I used to enjoy taking some of the lads out on walks to find caterpillars' eggs in order to breed them.'

'Did you and Eileen live in the country?'

George's eyes clouded over. 'Yes, we stayed at The Stores in Wallington. We didn't have much money so we re-opened the shop. And grew lots of vegetables, and kept hens and goats. When I go to Jura in the spring I plan to do the same.'

'So that's how you know so much about farm animals. I wondered about that when I was reading your book.'

'Well, you know, politics is a necessary evil. If I'd been born at a different, less barbarous time, I'd probably have written novels that hardly had a political word in them.'

'Perhaps it's possible to combine an interest in politics with a love of nature?'

'Possibly, but the reality of politics has got so dark these days that it tends to take over everything in one's mind. It becomes difficult to appreciate country life with the threat of atomic war hanging over us.'

They walked on together for another hour, growing closer all the time, until George remembered he'd better get back to feed Ricky. It was such a relief to him to stay in the country again and to enjoy the company of a beautiful young woman and a fellow intellectual so steeped in European politics. It confirmed to him that his decision to move to Jura was the right one. He and Ricky stayed for a few days more before they had to say their goodbyes. It gave him a good excuse to kiss Celia for the first time and it was certainly a memorable kiss – at least for him. Arthur ran them to the station in his car. He wasn't the most careful of drivers as he sped along country lanes with the windscreen wipers swishing back and forth. Toad of Toad Hall came to George's mind, but they managed to get there in one piece. Just. They were early for the train and decided to wait in the car because of the downpour.

'So, George, have you had any more thoughts about Celia?'

'Oh, she's absolutely delightful and she's very good with Ricky. He really likes her.' Ricky looked up and grinned at the sound of his name.

'Why that's wonderful. Will you see her once she gets back?'

'I certainly will. And I might even propose to her, although, likely as not, she'll turn me down.'

'I'd be delighted to have you as my brother-in-law, George. You see Mamaine and I plan to get married in a few months. Think of all the great times the four of us could have together.'

'Well, we'll see,' was all that George would say.

'Just you leave it to me… Look, George, I've been meaning to ask you. Why did you write such a stinking review of my play in *Tribune*?'

'Well, it was a stinking play.'

'I know it wasn't my best, but why didn't you just say it wasn't worthy of a gifted writer, why did you say it was muck? Couldn't you have toned it down a bit for your old friend?'

'Frankly it never really occurred to me. It *was* muck. It's what I believe. I hadn't realised it would bother you.' George wondered if Arthur was trying the old 'you scratch my back' game as regards Celia, but he stuck to his guns. 'You'll just have to write a better play next time.'

Arthur laughed. 'Perhaps I will. Anyway, here's your train. Now, remember to let me know how it goes with Celia.'

'I shall.' George grabbed his case under one arm and Ricky under the other, and boarded the train.

A week later George wrote to Celia telling her how much he enjoyed her company when they were in Wales and asked her to marry him. In his letter he explained that he thought they would make a good couple, but realised he wasn't much of a catch because he was a good bit older than her and his health wasn't that good. Still, if things went badly, it might interest her to be the widow of a successful author. It was the kind of offer that was hardly attractive to a glamorous young woman like Celia, especially since she was still trying to get over her failed marriage to Roger Kirwan.

In her reply Celia said she liked George, she admired how well he looked after little Ricky, and she did want to remain friends with them, so she turned him down as gently as she could.

I did it again. Another beautiful young woman with similar interests to my own that even include politics, and I was far too quick. She and Ricky seemed to get on so well and I think she respects the way I look after him and try to bring him up in a modern way by giving him more freedom than children usually have. She even laughed along with me when Ricky shat down the front of Arthur's good suit. I think she would make a really good mother for him. And I definitely have Arthur's support, he's very keen to have me as his brother-in-law, almost to a fault.

I can imagine Mamaine urging caution on her twin sister, having already experienced the downside of life with a temperamental intellectual like Arthur. Were those donkey noises in the kitchen directed at me because of wise old Benjamin in my book? I believe in being straightforward with a prospective partner, but it was probably a mistake to ask her if she might want to be the widow of a successful author. At least she's made it clear she wants us to remain friends and we've kept in touch. But as the months go by, and the closer my move to Jura gets, the more desperate I'm becoming to find someone who will come with me to share the rest of my life.

February 1946, Canonbury Square, London

George staggered along his hallway in the dark. He was in striped pyjamas and was coughing and moaning. 'Susan!' he shouted in anguish. Susan appeared in her nightdress and put on the light. Blood was pouring from his lips. 'Get me some ice,' he croaked at her.

'Go back to bed at once and I'll get it!'

'Thank you.' He turned back to bed.

She hurried into the kitchen and got ice from the ice chest, put it in a jug, took a cloth and went to his room. She wiped his lips and face, placed a cold compress on his forehead and held his hand. He started to relax. 'Shall I fetch a doctor?'

'No.'

'What about Avril? Shall I let her know?'

'No, don't tell Av. And, whatever you do, don't let Sonia know. I don't want them to see me like this.' He looked like death warmed up. But gradually he calmed down. Susan soothed him with the compress and the haemorrhage eventually stopped. She made him as comfortable as possible and stayed with him until he became drowsy and fell asleep. The clock on the mantelpiece struck three as she went back to bed.

George was still unwell a couple of weeks later. He lay wheezing and dozing, his moustache was thicker and the stubble round his jaw made him look even older and weaker. He opened his eyes and was surprised to see an old man carrying a black bag coming into the room behind Susan.

'Now then, my man, what seems to be the trouble?' the doctor said in a mannered Scottish accent.

'I'm feeling a bit rough.' George pointed to his chest.

The doctor took a stethoscope out of his bag and listened to it. He tapped on it a few times with his fingers. It sounded as hollow as the apocryphal dead man's chest. He did the same on his stomach.

'Anything else wrong?' the doctor asked.

'No.'

'Well, it's probably just a touch of gastritis.' The doctor packed away his stethoscope and quickly got up. 'Just keep giving him lots of fluids and he should be fine,' he told Susan as he left the room. She saw him out and returned looking apprehensive.

'I thought that since I'd got the doctor out for Ricky he might as well see you too,' she told him.

'Well, let me decide in future…' He wasn't happy with her. 'At least we know it's nothing to worry about. You haven't spoken to Sonia have you?'

'Of course not.'

'Well, let's keep it that way.'

Ricky was playing contentedly on the living room floor with his cars as Susan held up George's Home Guard shirts and a beret to the window light. She had dyed them black at George's request and wanted his opinion on the results. He was dishevelled and hadn't shaved in weeks but at least he was up and seemed brighter.

'The shirts have come out fine, but I'm afraid the beret's shrunk,' she told him.

George smiled at the tiny beret, snatched it from her and balanced it on his head. He took down a large Burmese sword from the wall and began to waltz round the room waving it above him like a dervish. Susan and Ricky hooted with laughter and George joined in. On his way round he tried to get Susan to dance with him but she shied away. He picked up Ricky instead and danced with him, much to their amusement. Slightly breathless, he put Ricky down and wandered through to his workroom still wearing his beret. Around his workbench, piles of wood were scattered beside a plane, a chisel and other tools. The shelves he'd put up along the back wall were crammed with books and underneath them his typewriter sat on top of a small desk facing the door. He took some tobacco from his pouch and rolled and lit a cigarette. He inhaled deeply and sat down at the desk. He took off the beret and slowly started typing again. He suddenly felt sad and lonelier than ever in his shambolic little room.

* * *

'Would you like some more Gentleman's Relish?' George made it sound highly suggestive.

'No, thank you,' Anne Popham replied, taking a sip of tea from a china teacup.

Anne was the attractive young woman who had passed George and Paul on the stairs to his flat. She sat at their living room table with George, Susan and Ricky; their plates of toast and kippers were half-eaten. She looked embarrassed.

'I haven't seen you around much,' George said.

'I've been away,' she replied.

'Oh... What have you been doing?'

'Governing Germany.'

'Is it interesting?'

'Trying to create order out of chaos is always interesting.'

Susan started clearing the table. 'Go along now, Susan,' George told her. She didn't look too pleased, but took Ricky out with her.

George went over and sat on the divan in a corner. 'Come and sit over here where you'll be more comfortable.' Reluctantly she sat beside him.

'You know, Anne, I think you're a special young woman. And I feel there's something between us.' Without warning he put his arms around her and tried to kiss her. Confused and alarmed, she pulled herself free. Tact was never his strong point. He'd tried this approach with women before, but, despite the fact that it seldom worked, he kept repeating it. It was almost as if he couldn't stop himself.

'I'm sorry. You're very attractive and I'm so lonely... I'm not at all well... Do you think you could care for me?'

'I don't know.' She looked even more confused.

'How would you like to be the widow of a literary man?'

Just then Susan came in. 'Would you like some more tea?'

'No! Please leave us!' George ordered, embarrassed. Susan hurried out again.

'I do so want someone to share what's left of my life and work.'

'But that's ridiculous. I just met you recently. And my fiancé was killed in action... I loved him.' Emotional, she looked at the framed photos of Eileen and Sonia on the mantelpiece. 'Don't you have someone you really love?'

'I did love Eileen. She was a good old stick. But I'm afraid she died a year ago.'

'I'm sorry. It must have been very hard for you.'

'It was.'

'What about her?' She pointed at Sonia's photo.

'I'd rather not talk about her.' He turned away, trying to avoid showing that he still had feelings for Sonia. 'It's just that I've always had women in my life and it doesn't feel complete with just Ricky and me in it.'

'Well, I'm going back to Germany tomorrow. I'm sorry, but I have to leave now.' She jumped up and made for the door.

'Can I write to you?'

'Goodbye.' She hurried off leaving George to contemplate yet another failed marriage proposal. He wrote to her in subsequent weeks apologising for his behaviour and repeating his marriage offer in blunt, almost pathetic terms. But she again turned him down. His letters only served to reveal how desperate he was to find a wife and mother for Ricky.

May 1946, Islington, London

Whatever happens, there's still the great outdoors, George thought. People can reject you, they can spy on you, trample you into the mud, kick you in the teeth, but they can't stop you enjoying a walk in the park with your son. And spring is the best time to go out, when everything is coming to life again after the winter. Nature is everywhere, even in London, and it's free for everyone to enjoy.

He was pushing Ricky along Canonbury Road in a metal pushchair with a wicker basket on the back. As always, a roll-up dangled from his lips. The wee fellow was nearly two now and looked strong and healthy in his little dungarees, unlike George's withered frame in baggy tweed suit, dyed shirt and tie. A group of lads in their school uniforms came along the pavement towards them. A fair-haired one at the front who looked about twelve carried a football under his arm. They were in high spirits and, seeing them coming, the lad dropped the ball onto the pavement and tried to kick it past them off the low wall. But George stuck out his left foot, stopped it and tapped it back.

'Hey, it's Stanley Matthews,' the boy laughed.

'I wish,' George muttered as he weaved his way through their parting ranks. They laughed some more and headed towards Highbury Fields. Lads like them and Ricky were the hope for the future, George thought. Oh, to be young again. He carried on past a bombed out building where workmen were clearing rubble. He noticed the sweat patches on their vests and the weeds that had already started growing amongst the debris. Spring was indeed everywhere. He entered a park and found himself in the company of women pushing high coach-built prams. Some looked like nannies in their starched uniforms, others were young mums proudly parading their offspring. He remembered how he and Eileen had hoped to get a sprung pram like theirs for Ricky. Another disappointment. But it didn't matter now, he'd grown too big for one. A young woman pushing her pram smiled at Ricky and nodded admiringly at George. It wasn't often you saw a man wheeling his son in a pushchair.

A flock of gulls took off and Ricky pointed excitedly at them. Oh to be as free as those birds, George thought. To be able to fly wherever one wished and not be shackled to a desk or a production line. They came to a pond and George took out some stale bread from a paper bag and threw it to the ducks. They came paddling towards them and competed to gobble it down, much to Ricky's delight. George lifted Ricky out of the pushchair and gave him some bread. He threw it to them, laughing and jumping up and down. But he was unsteady on his feet and almost fell into the water. George caught him just in time. He took him and the pushchair over to a park bench, took some reins out of the basket, secured Ricky to the bench and let him loose. Sitting there contemplating the ducks, his mind went back to his own childhood when he would go exploring to see what he could find along the riverbank. 'The best days of your life', his mother had told him, and he now knew what she meant. He was a country boy at heart and soon he would be realising his dream of living on an island where he could relish the seasons and the wildlife that flourished there. He looked at his watch. Time to head home.

An hour later George carried Ricky into the living room, put him in his cot and took off his jacket. As he did so, there was a knock at the door. Through the glass panel he saw a postman standing in the landing with something in his hand.

'Mr Blair? Telegram.'

With a shudder George opened the door and braced himself for more bad news. 'That's me.' He took the telegram. 'Thanks very much.' He closed the door. He ripped open the telegram and scowled at it. 'Oh, no.' He went back into the living room where Ricky had fallen asleep in his cot. He phoned Sonia at the *Horizon* office.

'I'm going to Jura soon. But I've just heard my sister Marjorie has died,' he told her, 'Can I see you right away?'

'I'm very sorry to hear that, George. But it's just not possible. I've got so much to do finishing off the next issue just now.'

George slammed down the phone.

***

I remember how concerned everyone in the office was when George hung up on me.

'Is everything all right?' Lys Lubbock, Cyril's latest conquest and business manager, stopped typing and asked. Another elegant young woman.

'It's George. His sister's died,' I told her. Netta also stopped and looked concerned. 'He wants me to drop everything and go and meet him. But you know how much I've got to do before I leave for the Riviera tomorrow.'

'These types of men are all the same. They only call you when it suits them,' Netta always backed me up.

'I feel bad. But he doesn't seem to realise I've moved on. Lucian's the same, he keeps turning up when he's after something.'

'And we all know what that is!' Netta could never resist a laugh. 'Men are bastards. We're better off without them.' There was a bitter edge to her voice. Her boyfriend had recently left her, leaving her to raise their daughter alone, which rather cramped her style.

'I don't know about that. They're not all the same, surely?' said Lys. 'Cyril and I are getting on swimmingly.'

'Good for you. All we're saying is give it time... And watch out for number one,' I replied.

***

A huge aspidistra sat by the big oriel window. Av, all in black, stood gobbling a sandwich with one hand whilst balancing a cup of tea in the other. George and the rest of the crowded room also wore black. They all stood drinking tea, munching sandwiches and talking in hushed tones. Most of the mourners had their heads bowed, the air was thick with smoke.

They had all the appearance of dark wraiths in a fog. To George it looked like something out of an Edgar Allan Poe story. A grandfather clock chimed three.

'It barely seems a year since we buried Eileen,' Av whispered to George, 'and now Marjorie's gone too.'

Hardly a day passed that George didn't think of death. He'd been with his father Richard when he died almost six years before and, out of some sense of tradition, he'd put two pennies on his eyelids, then wondered what to do with them after the funeral. Eventually he'd thrown them into the sea. Ida, his mother, had died of cancer three years ago and he'd been with her too; then Eileen had gone and now his elder sister Marjorie. When would it end? But he couldn't share these dark thoughts with Av. 'It's hard to take in. We were never that close,' he muttered, 'Age difference, I suppose, and she had a family to bring up.'

'I know, I didn't see that much of her either. What with the war and everything.'

George's brother-in-law, Humphrey Dakin, a short, dumpy man, overheard Av. 'She would like to have seen more of both of you.' He was curt to the point of hostility. He'd lost an eye in the war, but George was never sure which one. Now both the glass one and the real one seemed to be glaring at him as if blaming him for Marjorie's death.

'Life's so busy these days, Humph,' George replied. 'But that's no excuse.' He was full of regrets.

'Are you off to your island soon, then?' Humph demanded to know. It wasn't a friendly question. Humph's youngest daughter, Lucy, joined them. She was only thirteen and her eyes were puffy and red from crying.

'Yes. To Jura.'

'And what will you live off up there?'

'My last book sold pretty well. And I expect I'll catch fish and grow some veg.'

Lucy brightened a little when she heard this. 'Can we come and stay with you on your island, Uncle Eric?'

'Of course. Once I've licked the place into shape.'

'Oh, good. Blair Island, it sounds exciting,' she said.

'You know, you can't possibly do it all on your own,' Av piped up. 'I could help you.'

'I don't need your help, Av.'

'But we're the last of the Blairs. We have to stick together,' she replied. 'I could come and look after you and Ricky.'

'I've got Susan to do that.'

'She's just not capable,' Av dismissed her. 'I can look after you properly,' she insisted.

George looked her in the eye and said, 'It's not you I want to share my life with.'

* * *

George found the entrance to St Andrew's and Jesmond cemetery with some difficulty. It was hidden in a suburban estate that reminded him of Mortimer Crescent. Long rows of standard issue pre-war houses with pocket-sized front gardens you could do nothing with. In a gap in one row was a wall and a wide gate which opened into the last resting place of thousands of souls. He strode along a central path that stretched towards some beech trees and the main entrance at the far end. He peered at the gravestones. All those names that were no longer spoken or remembered. Half a mile further on he reached some trees and saw that their buds were starting to sprout leaves. He recognised a squat building that lay across a side path to his left. He turned into it and walked along, searching for a gravestone with a rose planted in front of it. Ah, there it was. And the rose had taken. New leaves were growing and it would probably flower this summer. Other headstones had been planted near Eileen's. She was no longer alone. He put down his haversack and took out a trowel and some bedding plants which he dug in along the edges of her grave. Pansies, sweet william, violas that would last all summer – and a leek. Food was always close to Eileen's heart and now she would have a nice vegetable to keep her company. He brushed the dirt from his flannels, put the trowel back in his bag and tried to clean his hands on the grass. He stepped back and looked at what he had done.

Poor Eileen, taken from him and little Ricky in the prime of life. He remembered the gravestones outside the church where they were married. And how he had vaulted over the side-gate to greet her instead of waiting for her at the altar. She must have spoken to the vicar in advance because she didn't promise to obey him. Yet she defended him against his adversaries and told him to ignore them. She believed passionately in his work and knew that one day people would recognise its value. Yet she hadn't lived to see the acclaim with which *Animal Farm* was greeted. Now she was gone. Underneath the earth, rotting away. What was the point of life? It had no meaning. He shivered and turned to leave.

Chapter 5

FOR YEARS I had dreamt about living on a Hebridean island. I think it went back to the time when I met Compton MacKenzie not long after the war started, at a Dickens conference (of all things) which he was chairing and he was very complimentary about my writing. He once owned a whole string of islands in the Outer Hebrides and I suppose some of his enthusiasm for them must have rubbed off on me. Lawrence had quite a laugh at his expense in his satirical tale 'The Man Who Loved Islands'. D.H., that is, not T.E. It annoyed old Compton but I thought it was rather funny. I learnt from MacKenzie that many of the Scottish islands are now uninhabited although they have water and some cultivable land. Many have wild goats on them, which somehow appeals to me.

I first went to Jura in September 1944 after David Astor persuaded Janet McKinnon to let me rent a room in their cottage for a fortnight. I was exhausted with overwork and Eileen was only too happy to let me have a break on my own. I suppose it also gave her a break from me. Well, the McKinnons couldn't have been more friendly and they told me a bit about the island and where to go to see its fauna. I did a lot of walking on my own that time and found that it wasn't as cold up there as I expected – something to do with the Gulf Stream that makes it milder on the west coast. That's when I met the Fletchers for the first time in their big house at Ardlussa and they took me up to the north of the island and showed me round Barnhill. It hadn't been lived in for years and was in quite a state, but they said they'd do it up if I wanted to rent it. It had no electricity, only oil lamps and calor gas heaters. And, of course, there was no telephone, so that was a blessing. They were looking for someone to take it on as a small farm or croft rather than it becoming a deer hunting lodge like some of the other large houses on the island. Well, it seemed to me that my prayers had been answered because, although it was quite remote and transport along the rutted track was a bit of a problem, it would be an ideal place for me to write my next book once I had recovered from taking on too much work as a journalist.

When I got back to London and told Eileen I'd found the perfect place for us to move to after the war she wasn't so sure and wrote to Margaret Fletcher with lots of questions about the practicalities of living there. She took quite a bit of convincing, but eventually she agreed. I think it was the idea of getting away from London and Ricky having the freedom to go out and play in safety that persuaded her. And then she died. I so wanted someone to take her place but it just wasn't possible. However, I was determined to go to Barnhill that summer and to get the house in order before bringing Ricky and Susan up there. If that first year worked out, we could move there for good. Now, apart from my work and Ricky, the thing I care about most is gardening, especially vegetable gardening. And so my plan was to grow vegetable varieties which were suitable for the Hebrides and, with fish and venison to supplement our rations, to become as self-sufficient as possible. I've always liked *Robinson Crusoe* and, whilst Jura was no South Sea paradise island, it was the nearest thing I could find to one in the British Isles.

May 1946, Barnhill, Isle of Jura

Barnhill nestled in the lee of a hill that ran down to the sea a few miles from the north-east corner of Jura. It was a large white-walled farmhouse with a barn and outbuildings built in a U shape behind it. That day in late May when George moved in was warm and sunny and the sea sparkled in the bay. Robin and Margaret Fletcher were only too happy to rent out the house to him since they hoped that he would stay there long term and look after the place. They were a lively couple in their thirties and Robin was an old Etonian, like George. They had got on well with George that first time they'd shown him round the place and had put him up at their big house at Ardlussa after his eight hour journey from Glasgow by train, ferries, bus and car. Next day they brought him and some of his things in their Land Rover to Barnhill some seven miles further on.

Margaret opened the door and took him round the seven almost bare rooms which had been tidied and spruced up with a coat of paint since his last visit. She quickly lit the fire in the large black range in the kitchen whilst George and Robin brought in his cases and some of the lighter furniture left at Ardlussa by the removal firm Pickfords. A small table and chairs, floor mats, a rifle case, a typewriter and two suitcases were carried in. It didn't take long.

'Thank you for bringing up some of my things,' George said.

'Not at all, old chap,' Robin said. 'Always happy to oblige.'

'Look, Eric, if there's anything we can do to help with getting food or anything, you will let me know, won't you, because I'm always ready to help,' Margaret said as they made to leave.

'No, I'm fine, I've got enough to eat for now. I'll manage myself, I'll manage myself,' George replied.

Slightly put out at her helpful offer being turned down, Margaret decided to leave quickly. She got into the Land Rover and off it went bouncing down the rough track it had come. George spotted lots of rabbits running around in the grassy patch in front of the house. He struggled upstairs with his old leather suitcase to a sparsely furnished bedroom which had a window facing across the Sound of Jura to the mainland. He put his typewriter on top of a small desk by the window and was impressed by the view. He wondered how much of it he'd see in the months to come. He took out books, blank paper, notebooks and some clothes from his case then inspected the other bedrooms. All were bare and rather cold in spite of the sunshine outside, but that didn't bother him. He was impressed by the depth of the free-standing bath and could picture himself bringing numerous kettles of hot water upstairs to fill it. He returned to the kitchen and emptied out some provisions from his other case. Finally, he took out his favourite metal teapot and made himself a pot of thick, black tea. He sat down at the table and poured some of the tea into a saucer. It looked like treacle. He blew on it to cool it then slurped it down. He looked out the window. It was still sunny outside, so he took his rifle from its case, loaded it and went out to the back garden. It was hoaching with rabbits as well. He took aim, shot at them and killed one. He picked it up and took it into the kitchen, found his large hunting knife and started to skin it. The entrails were pink and red, and his hands were soon covered in blood. He walked through a scullery off the kitchen that led to the byre where he hung up the skin to dry out. He noticed the stalls where cattle must have been kept in winter and the stone floor and gutters to carry away their mess. He went back into the scullery and washed the carcass in the large double sink then hung it up.

Next morning George walked down to the rocks at the foot of the slope that ran from the house and gazed contentedly at the quietly lapping waters of the Sound of Jura. The sun was up and the grey-blue sea shimmered in the early morning light. To the east lay the low hills of the mainland. Not another house in sight. Its rolling hills were devoid of trees but its spare beauty was even more appealing than he had imagined during that last cold winter in the city. It was a far cry from the wildflower meadows and willow bordered streams and pools he had known in his childhood. But where better to be than on a Hebridean island on a day such as this? This is what he had come for; to be part of all this, to give himself space and time in which to think and write, and to make a new life for himself and his son here. It certainly beat the frantic pace and desolate grime of London. Maybe he could borrow or buy a boat from the Fletchers and do some fishing? He went back up to the garden and found a garden fork, a spade and a sieve in a large shed. Someone must have done some gardening here before. He used the fork to break up the dry, stony soil and started to clear it of weeds. It was back-breaking work and he hadn't done any real manual labour since Wallington years before. He went into the kitchen to find a towel to wipe off his sweat. He stripped to the waist, revealing his white, scraggy body. At this rate it would take him most of the week to prepare the ground for sowing. Perhaps by that time the vegetable seeds he'd ordered would have arrived. On the grass he found a fully gorged tick which had probably dropped off a deer or a cow. He cut it open with his knife and the dark, viscous blood oozed out. He'd better watch out for ticks in the future. He didn't want to get any on his body, he knew the damage they could do.

Most nights during that first week he lit a paraffin lamp in the kitchen and noted in his diary what he had seen and done. Some pretty, yellow primroses were still out and there were lots of bluebells on the slopes. He noticed that thick patches of pink thrift and stonecrop grew on the rocks right down to the water. On boggy ground, yellow flag irises were starting to appear and he could see that rushes were spreading in parts of the garden. He'd need to get a mattock to dig them out. He noted down the birds he saw – hooded crows, oystercatchers, buzzards, rock doves, wood pigeons – and found that a pied wagtail had taken over a swallow's nest in the byre.

One morning, he collected some wooden boards from the large byre. With these, and some driftwood he'd picked up from the shore, he hammered away trying to make a trestle for sawing logs. But he battered his thumb with the hammer. 'Damn!' Using the trestle as a base, he made a sledge for transporting things, but it fell apart as soon as he dragged it away, and he had to remake it. Once the garden was dug over, he sowed lettuces, radishes, spring onions and cress in separate rows. He took more pot shots at the rabbits but they scurried off, stopped and stood still to stare at this strange, giant figure, cheekily daring him to try to hit them.

Later that week, spade in hand, George slowly dragged his sledge up a hill. The Fletchers had told him where to find peat which he'd need for the fire later in the year. At the top, he dug up some, breathing heavily and sweating in the hot sun. He took off his shirt, his thin body was browner than before. He piled the peat up in blocks to dry and was surprised how quickly he could cut it. In not much more than an hour he'd piled up about a hundred blocks. A raven flew overhead. He felt content. He'd come here in order to lose himself in this re-mote place that he'd fallen in love with that first time; to do the kinds of things that he fondly remembered enjoying as a boy, exploring and getting to know the territory and going fishing. But now he also wanted to see if he could live off the land and become as self-sufficient as possible, taking it all much further than he had at Wallington. Here he had peat for the fire and all the fruits of the sea at his disposal to top up the meagre rations that he was allowed by law. It was a dream he'd had for a long time and his extensive knowledge of nature's ways should help him to realise it. But he also needed a complete break from any serious writing. That's why he'd given up his *Tribune* job and wouldn't be writing any more articles in a hurry. He knew what his next book would be, and had written a little of it. He'd drafted its structure years back, and here, in what he liked to think of as 'this ungetatable place', he could make a proper go of it at last. But first he needed to clear his head, to rid his mind of all the things that had held him back. He felt suddenly tired. Perhaps he'd overdone it? He headed back and went up to his bedroom and slept for several hours.

A few days later George walked along the track across the hills to the north of Barnhill in bright sunshine. He was carrying an empty milk churn that he'd brought with him from London. He stopped when he saw three wild goats up on a hill staring back at him. They were mostly black with a smattering of white patches. They and the churn reminded him of feeding Muriel at Canonbury Square and, of course, of Eileen. He tried to shrug off his dark thoughts. It was another beautiful Hebridean morning. After walking more than a mile he approached another white-walled farmhouse on a green hillside high above the sea. Kinuachdrachd croft was the home of brother and sister Donald and Katie Darroch. The Fletchers had told him the Darrochs would be happy to supply him with milk and eggs, and so it had proved. George rapped on the door. Katie opened it and gave him a big smile. A plain woman in her thirties, wearing dungarees, her sleeves rolled up, ready for action.

'Hello, Mr Blair, come away in.' The sing-song sound of her West Highland lilt was music to his ears. He'd been scathing about most things Scottish before coming to Jura, mainly based on his unhappy experience of whisky-soaked Scots in the Indian police he'd served with out in Burma, but Katie and Donald were making him reassess his prejudices. He followed her into the kitchen.

'Sit yourself down, I'll just get you a cup of tea.' She shouted, 'Donald, Mr Blair's here for his milk and eggs!'

George sat down at the kitchen table and felt quite at home. Katie put twelve spoonfuls of tea in a pot and poured in hot water from a big kettle on the stove. 'Now, would you like a scone with it?'

'You know I can't resist your scones, Katie,' George beamed.

Donald came into the kitchen carrying another metal churn in one hand and a small egg box in the other. From the way he was weighed down to one side, the churn must have been full of milk. He was sturdy looking and wore mucky old overalls. He put the full churn on the floor near George, sat the eggs on the table and took the empty churn off. 'How're things with you then?' he asked George.

'Oh, I'm settling in quite well, but my vegetable garden could do with some rain,' George replied.

'Couldn't we all. That's about six weeks now without any. Very rare here. Best not to wish, though, we might get too much of what we want,' said Donald.

Katie poured George a cup of tea and gave him a scone on a small plate, a dish of butter and a pot of home-made jam. 'There you are now.'

'Thank you, Katie.' George ladled lots of butter and jam onto his scone, put some milk in the tea, poured it into his saucer and started slurping from it. Katie and Donald still seemed mildly amused by his daily ritual.

'So, what's it like here in the winter?' George asked between slurps.

'Well, it's fine if you like your own company and have plenty to do,' Donald replied.

'I'd have plenty to do all right. Can you make a living out of it, though?' George took a big bite out of his scone and poured some more tea into his saucer.

'Not much of one really. The land's not that good, but we get by. There used to be a lot more crofters on the island, but the lairds, like your friend Mr Astor, seem to prefer the deer.' Donald watched for George's reaction.

'One can't escape the dead hand of the rich even here,'

George suggested, feeling a little uncomfortable at the mention of his friend.

'Especially not here!' Donald agreed. 'But it's a good life all the same. Where else could you feel as free as you do here?'

'That's very true. And freedom is very rare and so important these days.' George wolfed down the rest of his scone and smiled at the contented pair.

'That it is, that it is,' Donald agreed.

'Now, did you enjoy that?' Katie asked.

'I certainly did.' But he was still thinking how the dead hand of the rich extended even to this island paradise.

He was soon heading back to Barnhill, the full milk churn and box of eggs in hand. As he came over the ridge that led down to the house, he caught sight of a woman with a suitcase walking down the slope towards it. Thrilled at the thought that Sonia had taken up his invitation to visit him, he hurried on, milk churn swinging wildly from his arm. He opened the door to the kitchen. He could hardly contain his excitement. A familiar figure stood by the front window. She turned round, startled by the creak of the door.

'Oh, it's you, Av. I didn't know you were coming.' He couldn't hide his disappointment and annoyance.

'I thought it would be a nice surprise,' she grumbled.

'It certainly is a surprise. I was quite enjoying having the place to myself. Would you like some tea?' He couldn't refuse her the kind of courteous hospitality they were brought up on.

'I'd love some. Fancy some scones?'

'I've just had one. But don't let me stop you.'

She took out a bag of flour from her case and started looking in the cupboards for utensils. Later that night George sat alone in his bare room, lit only by a paraffin lamp, and wrote a letter.

* * *

I didn't see George for a long time after that phone call when he told me his sister had died. He was going to that desolate island of his and I had other plans. And, of course, the office was always busy, what with Cyril off gallivanting with his latest floozy, leaving Netta and I to get on with bringing out issue after issue of *Horizon* every month. If truth be told, I enjoyed it. I could choose whose work would go in and whose wouldn't, and I liked the power it gave me over lots of men. Not just the poor, benighted army of unpublished souls, but some of our finest writers. I suppose they resented me for it, but I didn't care. There were some dreadful types who were forever sniffing around to see what they could get from me. So, as far as I was concerned, they deserved all they got – or didn't get as the case may be. And if I did fancy the occasional one or two and give them a bit of what they wanted, well, that was nothing to do with my editorial role. I was still in charge. They needed me more than I needed them – and they knew it.

Of course, Cyril would pop in from time to time, usually to pick up the latest gossip. One afternoon when Netta and I were busy trying to get on with doing his job for him, I remember him asking me, 'How's old Eric getting on these days?'

'I don't know. I haven't seen him in months,' I told him.

'I *am* surprised. I thought you two were rather well matched.'

'We got on well enough, but he really just wants someone to look after him. And he'd like a mother for his son.'

'And that was never going to be you, was it?' Netta, who knew me better than anyone, suggested. 'Anyway, he's a bit of a dry old sort.'

'Yes, he's always been something of a rough diamond,' Cyril offered. 'Perhaps you could use a man with a bit more polish?' He puffed out his chest and practically leered at me. I ignored his suggestion. He could be charming enough and

I greatly admired his extensive knowledge and love of literature, but I just couldn't imagine myself going out with a man whose head looked like a teapot without a spout. I'd led him on a little to get the job, but that's as far as it was ever going to go.

'Well, Eric always knows what he wants. And right now that seems to be you,' he said.

'Maybe so, but it's out of the question. I'm not ready to settle down yet. I've got places to go, people to meet. It was just never going to happen.' I was very determined back then, when I had the best years of my life still ahead of me.

'Perhaps Paris holds greater attractions?' I noticed Cyril give Netta a knowing look, almost a smirk, as he spoke. Who had he been talking to?

'Well, there's nowhere quite like it.' I countered, trying to pretend I didn't know what he meant. Whoever had been blabbing about my affairs over there – and I'd lay a bet that it was Lys – I was giving nothing away to that little smart arse.

A couple of weeks later I was lying in my bathing costume on hot golden sand with the sound of lapping waves for company. Nice was always delightful, whatever the season. Warm, but not too warm, and not too busy. A bronzed young man who looked the part in stylish swimming trunks approached. He was carrying a deckchair. '*Un transat pour mademoiselle?*'

'*Non, merci.*' I turned over and picked up my book. It was *Phénoménologie de la Perception* by Maurice Merleau-Ponty, an up and coming philosopher who had taken Paris by storm in the aftermath of the war. It was quite a tough read but I wanted to see what all the fuss was about. I hadn't been reading long when I became aware of a shadow spreading over me and the book. I turned round and saw a man standing over me, but couldn't make out his face against the bright sunlight. I liked the look of his body though. '*Bonjour, ça va?*' I asked. Later that afternoon we swam in the warm sea together and enjoyed splashing each other, the way children do. The sun beat down as we walked arm in arm along an avenue lined with palm trees. I felt full of the joys of life. That night we sat outside a restaurant sipping pernod before we ordered our meal. We clinked glasses, 'À la tienne!'

When I got back home to London I was on great form. I had lots to tell Netta and, of course, she was dying to hear what had happened. I told her all about the handsome, intelligent Frenchman I'd met and how he'd made me feel. She was almost as excited as I was, so we made plans to go out on the town to celebrate. She came round to my flat carrying a brand new, little black number to wear and we started getting ready together. I poured each of us a large gin and tonic to get us in the mood and put on my pink camiknickers and suspenders whilst Netta laid out her best silk undies. Then I remembered the letter I'd got that morning from George and thought it would be fun to read it to her. I took a large gulp from my glass and said, 'You must hear this.'

Netta, who was making a face as she applied her lipstick in front of the large mirror of my dressing table, turned round. I picked up George's letter and read, 'Dearest Sonia, I'm sorry about what happened. I feel now I was rude in hanging up on you, but I did so want to see you. I'm settling in well at Barnhill and have been sowing lots of veg. It hasn't rained for weeks and some of the plants are dying.'

'Quite the farmer,' Netta interrupted, taking a drink from her glass. She leaned her head to one side to brush her hair.

'I haven't started on the novel yet but I know it's going to be my darkest book yet,' I continued. 'That's gloomy old George for you.' I took another sip from my glass. 'It takes half a day by train and boat to get here from Glasgow. We're about seven miles from Ardlussa, the nearest village, and it's another seventeen miles from there to the shop in Craighouse.'

'That's your hermit George, you've had a narrow escape,

you know.' Netta started to giggle, took another drink and changed into her silk undies.

'I can live better off the land here, but I'm missing you terribly,' I read. 'At heart he's quite a romantic. But can you imagine me up there?'

'Not really. Somehow I can't see you shovelling pig shit in the back of beyond!'

We both laughed and knocked back some more drinks. We slipped into our cocktail dresses before I resumed.

'Avril has arrived and is trying to take over my life,' I continued.

'George, the proud cockerel. He doesn't want a mother hen clucking around him!' Netta hooted.

'A size twelve boots cockerel!' I retorted.

'So it's true what they say about size?' she asked. We broke up in fits of laughter. More drink was consumed.

'He's got a strong sex drive. I suppose that's part of it,' I said.

'A big part of it,' Netta added. We laughed again.

Eventually I calmed down and picked up the letter again to read out the last part, but saw the words: 'Take care of yourself and be happy. With much love, George.' My mood changed abruptly. Here was I laughing at poor old George stuck on a remote island with his book to write and he was sending me such warm wishes and missing me. I felt almost a sense of pity for him. Thankfully Netta saved the day. 'Come on, let's get going,' she said, 'those bright lights won't last forever.' We grabbed our handbags and silk wraps and headed off for the bright lights.

* * *

The drought on Jura continued throughout June and the spring that supplied Barnhill with water almost dried up. But

George kept working away. He put up shelves in his bedroom for some of his books and found more jobs to do outside. He built an incinerator out of large stones that he collected on his sledge and, as he did so, came across an adder sunning itself on a rock. He killed it with his knife, cut it in half and, picking up the wrong end by mistake, was almost bitten by it. Funny how they seemed to live on for quite a while after they died, he thought, must be their nerves or something. He repaired an old creel, baited it with rotten fish heads and tied a rope to it. He attached it to a jagged rock and threw it into the sea just down from the house. Next morning he was delighted to find two fair-sized lobsters in it. He filled a large pot with water, boiled it on the kitchen stove and, once it was bubbling, carefully dropped in the two navy blue lobsters. Fascinated, he watched them struggling desperately for dear life and quickly turn salmon pink. Their legs twitched and their claws scratched and scraped on the sides of the metal pot before they died. That night he and Av sat down to a feast.

'This is the life, Av, the sea's bounty should keep us going very nicely here.'

'I know, but we must get that boat from the Fletchers,' Av said. 'Then we'll really be able to fish.'

'All in good time. I'll see to it. But, you know, you couldn't get lobsters as fresh as this in London, no matter how much you were prepared to pay.'

'True. I'm sure we'll get by very well here.'

Despite George's assurances, Av had to keep on at him about the boat until he finally went down to Ardlussa and brought back an old 12 foot rowing boat with an outboard engine, a jerry can of petrol, some two stroke oil and a pair of oars and rowlocks, just in case. On the way back, he had to keep bailing it out, but eventually he got there. Once he'd caulked the hull it was fine, and the pair of them went out most nights at dusk to fish, the best time for a good catch.

Soon they were dining off saithe and rock cod, as well as the occasional lobster and crab. They were never happier together than on their fishing expeditions.

They got their weekly groceries from the island's only shop at Craighouse which were sometimes brought in a van to Ardlussa for George to collect. Other times he would drive the twenty-four miles to the shop in his old Rudge Whitworth 499CC motorbike to bring them back. He would pick up an occasional newspaper there and his mail was delivered twice a week. He was sent magazines like the *New Yorker* that he'd contributed to, but his main contact with the outside world was by means of a crackly old battery wireless. He had come to Barnhill to get away from it all for now – until he was ready to start on his book.

Early one luminous July morning, George set off on his motorbike to catch a ferry at Craighouse and travel on from there to Glasgow then London to collect Susan, Ricky and her eight-year-old daughter Katie, and bring them to Barnhill. He was looking forward to seeing them again, despite the long journey. But he had only gone a couple of miles when his motorbike had a puncture, not for the first time. He dismounted and tried to fix it but couldn't. Frustrated, he gave up and started walking the remaining five miles of rough track to Ardlussa. Robin Fletcher offered to give him a lift in his car to Craighouse which George reluctantly accepted, but by the time they got there the ferry to the mainland had gone. So Robin took him further on to Feolin where he took the little ferry over to Port Askaig on Islay instead. He had hoped to catch a plane to Glasgow but it was fully booked, so he took a bus to Port Ellen where another ferry would leave for the mainland in the morning. It was getting dark now and he had nowhere to stay. Perhaps someone in that pub would know a place? He went in and found it was packed with farmers having a great old time. He struggled through the crowd with his case and ordered a pint of beer. When the stout bartender brought it he asked him, 'Excuse me, do you know of any accommodation that might be available here tonight in Port Ellen?'

'Och, you'll have a hard job finding anywhere here tonight, so you will,' said the barman in a lilting west coast brogue. 'The boys who're here for the cattle show the morn have taken all the beds.' He winked at some of them who were holding up the bar. 'Mind you they say that Geordie Robertson might still have a bed or two. That's if you're not too fussy.'

The others started to snigger. 'That's true,' said one, his ruddy complexion beaming.

'I'm not fussy. Where is his place?' asked George in all innocence.

'Why, it's just along the road on the way to the pier, you can't miss it,' said the barman. 'It's got a big sign outside that says Police Station.' A roar of laughter went up from those nearest him. 'And be sure and tell Geordie that Lachie MacKenzie sent you.'

George smiled at the way Lachie had caught him out. The ruddy-faced man turned to him and said, 'Sure, but that was a good one and no mistake, was it not? But you took it well. I'm Angus, by the way. I've got a farm up at Keills.'

'It certainly was. I'm Eric, I'm staying at Barnhill.'

'Oh, you must be that writer fellow then.'

George wondered how on earth he knew, but twigged that the islands' grapevines must have done their work. There wasn't much that happened locally that wasn't commented on. They blethered away about farming for a while until George finished his pint. 'I better go before all the beds at Geordie Robertson's place are taken,' he joked.

'Aye, you better. Some of the boys are just getting going,' Angus said, pointing to some hefty farm lads downing pints as if there was a beer drought. 'The cells could soon be filling up.'

George stepped out into the pouring rain and soon found the police station at the end of the road not far from the pier, just as Lachie had said. It looked just like a detached stone house except for the blue door and the sign outside. George had once made a point of getting himself arrested when he was younger so that he could sample the delights of being in jail, but he'd never been in a Scottish police cell. This would be interesting. He went up to the well-worn, wooden counter at the end of the rather dilapidated entrance hall where a burly policeman gave him a suspicious look.

'I can't find a place to stay for the night and Lachie MacKenzie said you might be able to help,' George said.

'Did he now? Well, I suppose I get a lot of custom one way or another from Lachie,' the policeman replied, looking him up and down. 'But I'm sure we can fit in a gentleman like yourself. You look soaked to the skin but I'm afraid you'll have to share a cell and sleep on the floor.'

'Oh, that's quite all right by me.' George had shared and slept in worse places.

'I'll need to take a few particulars first. Name?'

'Eric Blair.'

'Address?'

'Barnhill on Jura.'

The policeman stopped writing and asked, 'And how are you getting on up there, Mr Blair?'

'Not bad, actually. It's taking a while to get things into shape, but I'm getting there.'

'That's good, that's good. Well, give my regards to Robin and Margaret will you?'

'I shall.'

Once he'd finished his paperwork, the policeman led George along a narrow corridor that led to the back of the building where the cells were. They passed one small cell where an old man in a frayed coat looked like he was sleeping off the booze and came to another larger one which lay open. George was surprised to find a young couple with a baby settling in for the night. The baby was wrapped in a shawl and lay asleep in her pram. The policeman told them, 'Here's another lost soul for you to share your room with tonight, Roddy. This is Mr Blair.'

George shook hands with the young, ginger-haired man saying, 'How do you do, I'm Eric Blair,' as if he was meeting someone at a dinner party. 'How on earth did you land up here?'

'I'm Roddy Macinnes and this is my wife Fiona. It's a long story.'

George shook hands with Fiona who looked no more than twenty. 'And who is this little one?' His eyes lit up at the sight of the tiny head sticking out of the shawl.

'That's Catriona,' Fiona said. 'She's a good wee babbie.'

'So I see,' George smiled at the sleeping child, thinking of the baby girl he might have had who would have been a friend for Ricky. If only...

'We were supposed to get the ferry today, and we caught the bus in good time, but I didn't realise you had to be there half an hour before it left, and they wouldn't let us on,' Roddy said.

'That's a bit much. Especially when you had your baby with you,' George sympathised.

'Maritime regulations I suppose,' said Roddy.

'Och, he's always late for everything, no matter what I say,' said Fiona. 'And, of course, we had nowhere to stay, what with all the fermers in toon for the cattle show in the morn. So we landed up here.'

'I had the same problem. Still it's better than sleeping under a hedge.' George was the kind of man who almost took delight in adversity. As if he was serving a penance for ever being born.

The couple looked more closely at this tall, rather shabby gentleman with his white handkerchief dangling from the top pocket of his brown tweed jacket. It was true. He looked as if he could have slept under a hedge in his time.

'Well, I suppose we better get some sleep,' Fiona grimaced at Roddy. 'We've got an early start if we're going to catch the first ferry.'

'Indeed we have,' George replied.

'I'm sorry we're a bed short in here,' Roddy added, looking round the cramped cell as if another bed might miraculously appear at any moment.

'Not at all, I've slept in many a worse billet. I'll be fine,' George replied, thinking back to the lice and rat infested trenches on the Huesca front. A bit of hardship and discomfort meant nothing to him. He turned away to let them get into their bunk beds, took the coarse, brown blankets the policeman had given him and started laying them out on the stone floor. Fiona snuggled into the bottom bunk and Roddy climbed up into the top one. George exchanged his wet clothes for his striped pyjamas and stretched his long frame out with one blanket underneath him and the other on top. The blankets weren't long enough and his thin toes peeked out from the holes in his socks. He lay thinking of all those months he'd spent in Spain and how close he had been to death. He stroked the scar on his throat where the sniper's bullet had gone right through.

That night he had troubled dreams. In a bare prison cell a vicious looking man in a black uniform and jackboots punched and taunted a frail, younger man who begged him to stop. 'There's no point in lying. We know everything about you. Do not resist the inevitable.' In the middle of the night the couple and their baby were wakened by George's moans and screams and the baby started to cry. George woke up and apologised, 'I'm very sorry. I must have had a bad dream.' Fiona settled the baby by breastfeeding her and soon they all went back to sleep again. Except George. He lay back on the blanket and could feel the coldness of the stone floor rising through it. He couldn't get that torture scene out of his mind no matter what he did. He realised he'd have to start writing his novel at some point that summer if he was to exorcise these nightmares he kept having. He was unable to get back to sleep the rest of the night.

* * *

George felt full of the joy of being alive as he put his foot down to speed his motorbike along the track. Katie clung for dear life to his back and a large rucksack was roped to the pillion behind her. He'd got hold of an old sidecar in Craighouse and in it the crouched figure of Susan gripped Ricky tightly on her lap. The girl squealed as they bumped over a hill. As they approached another rise George shouted, 'Hold on, here comes another one!'

They bounced up, the bike skidded on landing and came to a crashing stop. George tried to start it several times but it wouldn't go. Katie got off the bike. She looked quite like her mother. Ricky and Susan squeezed themselves out of the side-car and Susan hurried to her daughter's side. 'Are you all right, Katie?'

'Yes, that was fun.' Katie was excited.

Relieved, George said, 'I'm afraid this thing won't go. We'll just have to walk the rest of the way.' He put the ruck-sack on his back and lifted Ricky on to his shoulders. The boy whooped with delight at being up so high and able to see the hills and the sea around him. They all trooped off to-wards Barnhill with Susan limping along trying to keep up. George strode out and didn't seem to notice the problem she was having. When they reached the farmhouse and entered the kitchen, Susan was surprised to see Av there. She looked at George but he turned away to drop Ricky down. He felt bad about not telling her, but it was done now. Suddenly he felt tired.

'Careful, George,' Susan said, concerned in case Ricky fell.

'What happened to you?' Av asked.

'The bike broke down again and we had to walk the rest of the way,' George replied.

'Well, you make some tea while I show them to their rooms,' she ordered and took them upstairs. Ricky and Katie raced ahead excitedly whilst Susan struggled up the stairs carrying her heavy rucksack. They went into a plainly decorated, sparsely furnished large room. Ricky crawled over to look out the window and Katie followed him.

'This room is yours and Katie's,' Av said.

'Oh, it looks fine,' said Susan, putting a brave face on it. She started to unpack.

'By the way, his name's Eric, not George.'

'But he asked me to call him George.'

'Well here you must call him Eric. You see, I fight for what I want.'

'I don't believe in fighting.' Susan realised for the first time the situation she'd unwittingly stepped into.

Av took Ricky's hand, 'Come along now, Ricky, and I'll show you your little room.'

Next morning Susan entered George's bedroom with Ricky to waken him in their usual way but was surprised to find Av already there. George was sitting up in bed slurping tea from a saucer.

'Eric always gets up at seven. He's done so since he was a boy,' Av informed them.

Ricky and Susan looked disappointed and left them to it. They'd planned to tickle his toes as they always did. George was puzzled by their reaction but got up and dressed to go downstairs for breakfast. Soon after, Av was clattering bowls of steaming porridge on to the big table in the kitchen.

George looked glumly at the unappetising mess in front of him and sprinkled some sugar on it. He was bleary-eyed and feeling a bit rough. Susan and Ricky poured some milk on theirs and started picking at it. They were joined by Katie who had slept in.

'Could you pass the sugar please?' Susan asked George. He pushed it over to her and she spooned some over her and Ricky's porridge. 'My friend David will be arriving in a couple of weeks.'

'Who?' George asked.

'My friend David Holbrook, remember?'

'Oh, yes. Sorry, I'm still half asleep.'

Just then a young pig came in, snuffling along the floor. Ricky laughed, jumped off his seat and tried to catch it. Great fun. It ran around the room with Ricky crawling after it until Av took a broom to it and chased it outside. Ricky, Katie and Susan rushed outside after it with George and Av following to see what would happen. The pig ran off and, as the children and Susan followed, some white geese that George had bought tried to peck their bums. Susan shooed them away and Ricky grinned as he and Katie kept chasing the pig. Susan hobbled after them but couldn't keep up.

'You see, I told you he's too quick for her,' Av said to George as they went back inside.

* * *

Cyril's flat was awash with well-heeled literary types that summer night we launched yet another issue of *Horizon*. David Astor and Malcolm Muggeridge were in attendance and a goodly sprinkling of authors whose work featured in the new issue. Of course, Netta and I had to be there and Lys stuck close to Cyril to make sure his wayward eyes and well-worn chat up lines didn't lead to anything else. Naturally there was no shortage of fine wines and even some bubbly. Cyril always liked to put on a good show. He regarded it almost as part of his vocation of demonstrating the value and importance of the arts and culture for Britain during and after the War. I took some glasses of champers over to David and Malcolm. 'Champagne, gentlemen?'

'Thank you,' said David in his soft, cultured voice. Always the gentleman.

'Oh, rather, my dear,' said Malcolm.

'Thank you for coming along.'

'Not at all. I've supported *Horizon* from the very beginning,' replied David. 'I wouldn't miss it for the world.'

'I'm really only here to sample whatever rare vintage Cyril has to offer us from his cellar,' the cynic in Malcolm joked. But it wasn't far from the truth.

David quickly changed the subject. 'Have you heard from George lately?'

'No, not recently. I got a letter from him not long after he went to his island,' I told him.

Cyril tapped his glass with a spoon to get the attention of the crowd. He stood on top of a stool and stretched his thick neck so they could see his podgy little figure. 'Thank you for coming along and for supporting *Horizon* these last six years. During that time I think we've demonstrated to everyone that we have a modern culture that was worth fighting for. And I'm delighted that some of the new writers and artists we've introduced to the world are here with us tonight. Not forgetting the not so new ones, of course.'

Some of the crowd chuckled and acknowledged his welcome, whilst Malcolm and I kept gulping down the champagne and David nursed his.

'I'd particularly like to thank Sonia whose editorial flair has been invaluable to me, and Peter whose unstinting support and advice have made it all possible,' Cyril continued. He raised his glass to us and a few in the audience politely clapped. I smiled and nodded my gratitude. Peter Watson, my wonderful friend who bankrolled *Horizon,* seemed unmoved, but shyly acknowledged Cyril's praise.

'But, enough from me,' Cyril added. 'Tonight we have some rather fine wines for you to try. Enjoy!' General applause, everyone went back to drinking. A queue quickly formed at the large table where Lys was charging glasses. No one went near the forlorn looking piles of magazines on the other tables.

'Short and sweet, Cyril old boy,' Malcolm commented. 'I must try some of his wines. Did either of you see George's splendid article in *Gangrel* about why he writes?'

'*Gangrel*, now there's a strange name. But yes, I did; you were right about that monologue of his,' I replied. 'It's a very honest, well-written piece.'

'Well, you know, he's not honest about everything,' said Malcolm. 'He conceals the old Etonian in him so he can lay claim to being the political conscience of the Left.'

'Why shouldn't he?' I said. 'No one knows more about politics than George… If only he wouldn't drive himself so hard.'

'He never thinks twice about his health, I'm afraid,' David agreed. 'I do worry about him up there. He's so far from a doctor.'

'Well, most men won't go near a doctor anyway,' Malcolm pointed out. 'You know, he wouldn't be the first artist to destroy himself for the sake of his work. Perhaps one must just accept that no one can save old George from himself.' This intrigued me.

'Well, I suppose he's a bit of a Don Quixote on a motorbike,' David smiled wryly. 'He's always tilting at windmills of some sort.'

'A knight of the woeful countenance indeed,' said Malcolm.

'Then Paul Potts must be his Sancho Panza!' I added, to everyone's amusement.

'Yes, I suppose Paul's a bit of a waster, but you can't tell George that. I hear he's gone up to Jura to live off him for a while. But I do hope George will be all right.' David raised his glass. 'I'd like to propose a toast,' he said. 'To Don Quixote up on Jura!'

We put our glasses together and toasted George, 'To Don Quixote!' The drinking and the chatter continued for the rest of the evening, and everyone grew merry as more and more fine wines appeared and disappeared. Needless to say we didn't sell many magazines, but Malcolm's remark about no one being able to save George from himself had got me thinking.

July 1946, Barnhill, Isle of Jura

George sat puffing on a roll-up at the desk by his bedroom window. He took some paper from a drawer and wrote the words 'The Last Man in Europe'. He paused to gaze out at the silvery bay below the house and thought about the opening sentences of his new book. It would begin in April, the cruellest month according to Eliot, and with a clock as his other novels had. His hero Winston Smith would be leaving his home in a high building in which the lift didn't work when he pressed the button. In his mind's eye George could see a door opening at the end of the passage and an aged prole thrusting out a grey, seamed face. He stood for a moment sucking his teeth and watching Winston, a scrawny man in blue overalls who looked like George. Winston saw the prole, but immediately averted his gaze back to the lift. It would do for a first draft, George thought. He could always come back to it later. The important thing was he'd made a start.

That night round the dinner table Paul Potts was rabbiting

on to George while Av, Susan and her boyfriend, David Holbrook, listened. Paul announced that when he met David on the ferry he had found out that he too wrote political novels and much admired George's work.

'Is that so?' George replied, noticeably cold towards David. Under the table, Katie looked at Ricky and pointed to George's toes poking out of the holes in his socks. His old leather slippers lay beside them. Ricky crawled towards them, his big, round eyes full of mischief.

'George – sorry – Eric,' Paul glanced at Av. 'Do you remember those marvellous high teas we used to have in your flat with the table piled high with kippers and toast, and loads of crumpets for afters? Oh, and always the Gentleman's Relish, and a roaring fire in the grate!'

George smiled wistfully at the memory. Underneath the table, Ricky tickled George's toes. His smile broadened involuntarily.

'It's just so amazing to be up here, you know. I've always liked being in the country, but this kinda takes your breath away. It reminds me of parts of Canada. If I can't get a poem outa this I might as well give up,' Paul added.

'Yes, I hope to get some inspiration for my writing here too,' said David.

'I'm sure you will, David. What are you working on at the moment?' asked Susan.

'My novel. But I've only just started it,' David replied.

Av and George seemed distinctly uninterested. 'I'm tired. I'm going to turn in.' George looked like a very sleepy, sad Don Quixote.

Underneath the table, Katie and Ricky started giggling as George struggled to put his slippers back on and his feet disappeared. They emerged suddenly from under the table and Katie shouted 'Boo!' Everyone laughed.

Next afternoon Paul arrived at the back door carrying an

axe and some green branches from a hazel tree. He proudly showed them to George and Av who were standing outside smoking and chatting, and told them, 'This should keep us going for a while.'

George was mildly amused, but Av was angry. 'You fool. That's the only tree for miles around that bears nuts. You've killed it... And it's so green it won't even burn.'

'I'm sorry, I didn't realise,' he looked shamefaced.

'Never mind, Paul,' George consoled him. 'It's perfectly obvious you're no country man. But I hear there's some nice roast beef on the menu tonight.' George put his arm round his younger friend and took him inside.

Av followed them in, pointed to the pile of dishes in the sink and confronted Paul, 'When are you going to start doing your share of the washing up?'

'I will, but I'm working on a poem sequence at the moment. I'll do my fair share once it's finished,' he protested.

'Well, we can't eat poems. So if you want to eat, you better start earning your supper.'

The following morning George sat at the kitchen table drinking tea as Av busied around him looking for paper to light the fire in the stove. She found some sheets which Susan had crunched up into a ball and lit the fire with them.

Paul came into the room looking worried. 'Has anyone seen my manuscript?'

'I wonder if that was the papers I lit the fire with?' Av answered breezily.

'What? Surely... you wouldn't have?' Paul asked angrily.

Av wasn't bothered. 'I don't know, I didn't read what was on them.'

Paul stormed out in a rage, grabbing his coat as he went. George took his coat off the back of the door and followed him. The rain had become a light drizzle as they set off walking towards the north of the island. Going up the hill George found it hard to keep up and had to ask him to stop so he could get his breath back.

'Av deliberately burnt my manuscript,' Paul blustered. 'How would you feel if it was one of yours?'

'I'd be angry too,' George puffed. 'But I can't believe she knew what she was doing. It could have been Susan, you know, and she certainly wouldn't have meant to either.'

'You would stick up for your sister, wouldn't you?'

'Not always. She can be rather a pain at times.' George had recovered and noticed a buzzard circling above them on its way south towards Barnhill. He also spotted David Holbrook who appeared to be following them from a distance. 'Don't look now, but we're being followed.' He made it sound like a conspiracy. 'You know, I made some enquiries about David. He's a card carrying member of the Communist Party.'

'You don't say.'

'Well, I smell a rat. Stalin murdered Trotsky in Mexico by infiltrating an agent into his house who was the boyfriend of one of his supporters. One day as the old man was writing at his desk he crept up behind him and smashed his skull with an ice axe.' George illustrated the action with his arm. That got Paul's attention. 'And you know what? Trotsky was writing a biography of Stalin at the time. Maybe that's why David's here. The Stalinists hate *Animal Farm* with a vengeance and they may have heard I'm writing a new book which could damage them even more.'

'I can't believe you're serious.'

'I'm deadly serious.' He turned away so that David couldn't see him and showed Paul the Luger pistol stuck inside his belt under his shirt. 'I got this from Rodney Phillips after I gave Hemingway back his Colt. You never know when you'll get a bullet in the back of the neck.'

Paul shook his head in disbelief. 'Don't you think you're being a bit paranoid, George?'

'No, I don't. I saw a lot of things that the Stalinists did in Spain that I'd never have believed. And I wouldn't be at all surprised if MI5 have got files on both of us.'

'What, a penniless poet like me? Why would they want to know what I'm up to?'

'Well, they tap the phones and open the mail of anyone who has any connection with the Communist Party and, after all, that Stalinist MacDiarmid did write an introduction to your poetry book.'

'But that was poetry not politics. And anyway, I'm more of an anarchist.'

'You think MI5 make any distinction between anarchists and communists?' Everything's political as far as they're concerned.' George knew he sounded paranoid to a political novice like Paul but, he thought, one day it'll all come out. Some of his best friends like Astor and Muggeridge had been spies during the war. Perhaps even Freddie Ayer, whom he'd met in Paris, wasn't just there in pursuit of language, truth and logic? And who knew whether any of them still had some connection with the secret services?

They started walking back towards the farmhouse and met David on the way.

'Are you following us?' George fingered the Luger under his shirt. Paul looked alarmed.

'No. I'm just getting some fresh air,' David replied.

'Well, watch out for the stags. They can get rather aggressive sometimes, you know.' They walked on, leaving David looking quite puzzled.

In the middle of the night George was wakened by a thud from below his bedroom. He carefully took his Luger from under his pillow and got up. He made sure it was loaded and crept downstairs in his pyjamas, gun pointing ahead of him. The wooden stairs creaked. He stopped still and listened. Had someone broken in? Had he been burgled by some agent? He thought he heard noises in the kitchen and lunged in, brandishing his gun in different directions. Paul stood smiling at him as he stuffed his rucksack full of leftover venison and scones. A large suitcase lay beside him. George felt relieved and tried to conceal his gun.

'What were you goin to do with that?' Paul asked.

'You can't take any chances,' George was looking rather sheepish now. 'It could have been that young spy up to no good... Do you have to leave?'

'Much as I like it here with you, George, I just can't take any more nonsense from Av.'

'I'm sorry. I know she's not the easiest woman to get on with.'

'You never said a truer word.'

'But at least stay until morning, will you?'

'Look, George. I really don't wanna see Av again. It's cleared up outside now and it'll be a nice night for a walk. I'll be fine.' Paul went to hug him but George warmly shook his hand instead. 'You look after yourself now and keep that Luger handy.' He threw the rucksack on his back and lifted the suitcase to leave.

'Goodbye, Paul. If you see Sonia, give her my love.'

Next morning Susan was dressing Ricky in the kitchen. He yelled as she pulled his jersey over his head.

'You should smack him,' Av told her.

'But Eric told me that's his job,' Susan replied. 'He said he and Eileen were against that kind of thing.'

'Well, in any case, life here is quite unsuitable for you. You're not really able to look after Ricky properly. He's too quick for you now and you can't get around fast enough.'

Ricky scooted off to join Katie outside and they began playing tig. David came into the kitchen and followed Susan outside. It was bright and fresh as they walked down to the bay together. She told him what Av had said.

'You know, that's completely out of order. She's no right

to speak to you like that. And George hardly talks to me. It looks like Paul's gone. I wonder if they're trying to get rid of us next,' David said.

'It would be a great shame if we had to leave. I do like it here and Katie is such good company for Ricky.'

In the kitchen that afternoon, Susan sat darning a sock whilst Av was busy knitting. She watched the difficulty that Susan was having. 'Call yourself a nurse, you can't even darn a sock.'

'But I never said I was a nurse. I'm Ricky's nanny. It's just that my co-ordination's a bit odd. That's why I sometimes make mistakes.'

They continued working in silence for a while and then Susan left the room. She went upstairs and knocked on George's door. 'Come in,' he called. She went in, saw he was typing at his desk by the window and waited for him to stop.

'What's wrong?' he asked, turning round.

'Well, I'm just not getting on with Av. She said I should smack Ricky although you told me not to. She also told me I shouldn't be here because I can't get around fast enough for him. I really can't go on like this.'

'I'll smack Ricky if needs be. I'm sure she doesn't mean it. You must realise I can't very well ask my sister to leave. Could you try your best to get on with her?'

'All right, I'll try. I like it here and Katie gets on so well with Ricky.'

'Yes, she does. And he does need another child to play with. I've been rather worried about how slow he's been to start speaking. But he's come on a lot since Katie's been here.'

'I think so too. And they both love the freedom they have to play here.'

'Right, well, let's see how it goes. It won't be long till we're back in London, and then I don't imagine Av will want to come back here next year.'

* * *

One evening a couple of weeks later, Susan and David sat drinking tea in the kitchen as George and Av droned on about when he should go and try to rescue the motorbike which he'd again had to abandon miles down the track. They ignored the young couple and a feeling of gloom seemed to settle over the room. The boat was leaking once more and George wasn't sure whether to try to fix it himself or whether to ask Fletcher to find someone to repair it for him.

George turned to Susan and David, 'Oh, I meant to say that Fletcher and his shooting party will be dropping by to-morrow afternoon. Av will make some scones and perhaps you could serve us some tea in the sitting room, Susan?'

'Of course,' Susan replied.

'Good, and I'd be grateful if you and David could enter-tain his beaters in here.'

'Naturally,' said David, trying not to show his amusement at the idea.

Next day in the sitting room, George and Av, Fletcher and one of his shooting pals were waited on by Susan whilst their beaters sat in the kitchen with David. The talk in the front room about the shooting season was somewhat restrained, almost genteel, whilst hearty laughter could be heard coming from the kitchen. Afterwards when their guests had gone and George and Av had gone out for a walk, Susan and David fin-ished clearing up and washed the dishes. Katie and Ricky were playing outside.

'George might be a socialist but he still practises the same old class divisions he was brought up on and claims to have rejected at Eton,' David said.

'I don't know, I suppose he was just fitting in with what Mr Fletcher expects. He is our landlord after all,' Susan replied.

'Maybe so, but if he was a real socialist, he'd be challenging that kind of thing,' David wasn't letting go. 'I wonder what his new book is about. I'd like to have a look at it.'

'I don't think he'd like that.'

'Come on, it'll be fun and it won't do any harm. I'll take a look and see if the coast's clear.' David went outside and, beyond where the children were playing, he could see George and Av turning along the track heading south. He came back in, 'They'll not be back for a while. And Katie and Ricky seem quite happy.' He took Susan's arm and led her upstairs to George's room. The door wasn't locked so he hurried inside and Susan followed him hesitantly. He went over to George's desk which had some papers on top of it. 'Now let's see what we have here,' he flicked through the opening pages then started reading quickly from the beginning. Susan hung back listening anxiously at the open door.

David looked up at her, 'He's just started on it but it's pretty grim stuff, almost as dismal as George himself. There are lots of good things happening in the world now the war's over, yet he seems to be painting a picture of a miserable future in which there seems to be little hope at all.'

'I really think we should go back down. I need to see that Ricky's all right,' Susan said, her anxiety growing.

'Well, I've seen enough. He really is a gloomy old bird.'

Outside in front of the house, Ricky was crawling after Katie, trying to catch her. He was still unsteady on his feet but he could crawl almost as fast as she could run. Susan and David came out and stood looking down at the glistening bay, enjoying the warmth of the late afternoon sun.

'You know this does your heart good,' David said. 'He should be writing about cheerful places like this.' Susan was about to reply when George and Av came back round the corner of the house. As they approached, David whispered, 'Here comes His Lordship of Barnhill.' Susan wasn't sure whether or not George had heard him, but David persisted.

'Did you enjoy your tea with the laird?' he asked. George and Av merely scowled and walked on past them into the house.

A few nights later, George knocked on Susan's bedroom door and entered. Katie was fast asleep and Susan was sitting on her bed. George sat down on the only chair.

'Look Susan, I'll come straight to the point. I'm sorry it's not been working out between you and Av. And I'm afraid that David and I don't really get along.'

'Yes, I'm sorry too that things haven't really improved.'

'I realise that no one's happy about the situation, but I really can't ask Av to leave. We could try to work it out for a few months more until we return to London, or you could leave now and I'll pay you sixty pounds in lieu of notice. I don't want to lose you, but something has to change. What do you think?'

'Well, I don't think we can go on like this. It's not getting any better, no matter how hard I try. But I do worry about Ricky. How would you manage with him if I'm not here?'

'Av would look after him. He'd miss you, of course, and be upset for a while, but children are very resilient, you know.'

'Well, perhaps it would be better if I went now. Could I still come and see Ricky once you're back in London?'

'Of course. Whatever you think best. You'll always be welcome. And I'll be happy to provide you with good references. I'm just sorry it hasn't worked out between you and Av.'

Next morning after breakfast, Susan, David and Katie left. They lugged their cases up the track and round the hill as George stood in the doorway holding Ricky to see them off. The poor boy cried and cried at the loss of his nanny and his only friend. Once they were out of sight George took his son inside. But he wouldn't stop crying no matter what he did to try to quieten him. Eventually he fell asleep in his arms. He took him upstairs to his room and laid him down in his cot, still sleeping. He went into his own room, lit a cigarette and started typing away. But he soon had to stop in a fit of coughing and wheezing. In his mind, Winston was a lonely ghost uttering a truth nobody would ever hear. But so long as he uttered it, in some obscure way, the continuity would not be broken. It was not by making yourself heard but by staying sane that you carried on the human heritage. He imagined Winston going back to a table in a corner that was hidden from a telescreen, dipping his pen, and writing. George wrote:

Winston Smith rolls a cigarette and lights it. He looks out of his window. His room is worn and bare. There are no signs of his personality in it. He goes to a table in a corner hidden from the telescreen which has the face of Big Brother on it. The face looks like Joseph Stalin. He takes out his secret diary and writes to an unknown reader living in a time when freedom and truth are possible and history cannot be rewritten. He reaches out to someone who knows nothing of Big Brother and Newspeak – and wishes them well.

Chapter 6

I REMEMBER OPENING another letter from George late that summer. He told me that Susan and her boyfriend David had left Jura. He said he came to spy on him or worse, but he got rid of him and now he and Avril were getting on well on their own. He gave me detailed instructions of how to get to Barnhill, but I had other plans. You see, that was a very special summer for me. I'd met Maurice Merleau-Ponty in Nice in May and we seemed to get on like the proverbial house on fire. Of course, he had a wife and a young daughter, but that's never stopped a Frenchman. We arranged to meet up in Paris in July and where better than at the Café de Flore?

We sat down at an outside table in glorious sunlight. 'À la tienne!' Our wine glasses clashed and we gulped some down.

'You know, your *Phenomenology of Perception* is amazing,' I said. 'It's caught the public imagination much more than Sartre's *Being and Nothingness*.'

'*Merci*. I quite like Sartre, but, you know, I heard his tome sold well because it weighed exactly a kilo and could be used to weigh things at the market.'

'Miaow,' I joked. 'I quite believe it. I tried reading it once but found it impenetrable.'

'I didn't think the English were that interested in French philosophy.' Maurice seemed amused.

'They're not. But I am.'

'Tell me more about you then.'

'Not much to tell really. I'd like to see a special issue of

Horizon on art in France. It's much more dynamic than English art, don't you think? What with Klee, Miró and Picasso all living here?'

Maurice wasn't so sure. 'I don't know that much about the art world here. But I could offer you an essay for your magazine on the so-called humanism of Orwell and Ayer.'

'There's nothing *so-called* about George.' Perhaps I was a bit over-protective of him. Guilt, I suppose. I downed some more wine.

'Do you know him well?' Maurice seemed intrigued.

'Well enough to know he's not got a phoney bone in his body.'

'He must be very strange indeed not to have a funny bone like everyone else,' Maurice chuckled.

'Of course he does.' Then I realised he was teasing me. His English was better than I thought.

'I'm surprised you admire such an eccentric political writer.'

This time I didn't take the bait. 'I'll suggest your article to Cyril. But I can't promise anything.'

'What more can I ask?'

I looked into his eyes. He was handsome in that extremely stylish French way. He might be a philosopher but he knew how to dress well, not like Freddie Ayer or your typical Oxford don. We clinked again and drank the rest of the wine.

'How would you like to try out a new bar I've discovered? We could meet up with Sartre and the Beaver and dance the night away.'

De Beauvoir and Sartre, now that *would* be interesting. 'Oh, that would be delightful.' I couldn't wait. I so loved the sophistication of life in Paris and here was I enjoying life with one of France's up and coming philosophers and going to meet his even more famous intellectual friends.

A few nights later I found myself in Maurice's arms dancing round the dark basement of a bar in Montparnasse. He'd treated me to a lovely meal at the Deux Magots and now here we were tripping the light fantastic to the sound of Sidney Bechet and sharing the tiny dance floor with just two other couples. He really was a wonderful dancer. Graceful, elegant, charming, everything a woman dreams of.

'Koestler's as clumsy a dancer as he is a philosopher. No finesse,' Maurice whispered in my ear.

'He's no Fred Astaire, that's for sure. And Simone's no Ginger Rogers,' I smiled, nodding in the direction of a suave, middle-aged man and a small, sophisticated woman lumbering round the dance floor. 'Try not to look, but Sartre's not much better... poor Madame Camus.' A rather ugly little man in a crumpled suit was dancing out of time with a tall, attractive young woman. He looked like he was enjoying himself much more than she was.

'Koestler's an oaf and a windbag,' Maurice said.

'I agree. What's more he preys on women.'

'Tell me more.' I'd clearly caught Maurice's interest.

'Perhaps another time.'

'Will you also tell me what lies behind your sense of despair about life?' he asked.

'What despair? I'm having a great time.' I wasn't for telling him too many secrets just yet, in case I scared him off.

The music ended and we all went back to our little table in the corner. The men threw back some more beer and we sipped our wine. There I was, squashed between the cream of the new wave of Parisian writers and thinkers, and I wasn't going to miss this opportunity. Only Francine Camus and I hadn't published any books. Poor Albert wasn't well again, but she'd been allowed a night out whilst he looked after their newly born twin daughters. Tiny Sartre, bespectacled and old-fashioned looking, almost down at heel, didn't look like much of a catch. But his lover Simone was the height of French elegance, if a rather stern looking, glorified hospital matron. Of course,

I'd heard they'd agreed to have an open relationship, and half of Paris seemed to be talking about it.

'Do you believe in free love?' I asked Sartre.

'I believe in free everything!' he replied. Everyone laughed at his *bon mot*.

Simone weighed in, 'Love is a bourgeois trap. It shackles and destroys relationships. Show me a happy monogamous couple.'

'You know, when love comes along reason flies out the window. But free love can be destructive too,' Maurice offered.

'Maybe, but monogamy is unnatural to man. Man has urges that must be satisfied and he will always be unhappy if they're not.' Koestler's heavy Hungarian accent made him hard to follow, but I got the gist of it. Typical male chauvinist.

'We all know about your urges, Arthur. But it's always the woman who's left holding the baby,' I countered. They seemed quite impressed by my candour, especially Francine. Everyone except Koestler, who gave me a dark scowl. We all drank some more. This was getting interesting.

'Absolutely. There can be no freedom whilst women remain oppressed,' Simone said. I knew I'd have her support.

'You're right, Simone. Complete freedom is anarchy. It's unsustainable. Our biological needs must be met, but not at the expense of women,' Maurice argued. I could have kissed him there and then. Simone and Francine must have noticed.

'That sounds more like free sex than free love,' I suggested.

'Precisely,' said Simone, 'and there's nothing wrong with that. Sartre and I have an open relationship and it certainly works for us.'

'Perhaps I'm an anarchist with my heart and a socialist with my head.' Clearly Sartre didn't want this to go any further and closed down the conversation just when it was getting going. Maybe that's why philosophers love abstractions. They enable them to avoid the personal and all the problems that go with it.

'It's all right for you lot sitting here pontificating. Since I had the twins I can't even get Albert to take me out dancing!' Francine exclaimed. We all laughed and took another drink. It was going to be a long night.

* * *

George sat on a couch weighing a glass paperweight in his hand. He admired the beautiful pink coral inside and the way the light hit it. His full milk churn and a box of eggs sat on the floor of the Darrochs' house. He got up and went over to look through the contents of a small bookcase. He selected *Our Scots Noble Families* by Tom Johnston and took it back to the couch, watching the door anxiously. It portrayed the Scottish aristocracy as rogues and robbers and called for redistribution of the land to the people. It was much more radical than he'd expected from a Labour Secretary of State for Scotland in Churchill's wartime coalition. He must have been much younger when he wrote it, George thought, and he could picture him and his flunkeys nowadays desperately trying to buy up all the copies in the second-hand bookshops. An amusing image, George concluded. As he read, he heard the creak of the front door opening. An attractive woman entered. Sally McEwen. She hurried over to him. He put aside the book, stood up and embraced her.

'What did you tell them?' he asked.

'I just said I needed to go a walk to get some fresh air. The children are playing.'

'Good. I've thought about you a lot.' He started stroking her neck.

'I've thought about you. Is it safe here?"

'They're away for the day. No one knows we're here.' He was enjoying the clandestine nature of their assignation. It reminded him of their affair. When she'd accepted his invitation to visit Barnhill he'd hoped this might happen. In fact he'd imagined this moment many times since then. He started to kiss her neck and she bent back onto the couch. He kissed her passionately.

'Don't be too rough,' she pleaded.

'I won't. You know, I still think about you a lot.' He pulled up her skirt.

'Take your time and, remember, it's only a bit of fun. Have you brought a French letter?' she asked.

'We don't need one. I told you before, I'm sterile. And besides they're beastly things.'

'But, but…' It was useless to argue with him, he was such an old-fashioned man when it came to making love. They were soon lost in their lovemaking and enjoyed picking up where they'd left off several years before. There seemed less pressure on them now. But, of course, it brought back his feelings of guilt when he thought of Eileen and how he'd betrayed her. When it was over Sally insisted she had to get back.

She and her daughter only stayed for a couple of weeks and then returned to London. George missed her, or rather he missed their secretive sex life. Still, he had plenty to keep him occupied. Every fortnight after that he travelled by motorbike to the shop at Craighouse to stock up on supplies of all kinds. In the height of summer the rushes in the centre of the track and at the sides grew so high that he took a long scythe with him to mow the worst of them along the way. One morning in a smir of rain and with the mist closing in, he set off on the bike for Craighouse in his oilskins and goggles. He had gone about half-way to Ardlussa when, for the umpteenth time, his motorbike broke down. He tried to get it going but there was nothing to be done, so he decided to walk the rest of the way to see if some of Fletcher's men could come and fix it. This was becoming a terrible nuisance, he must get a more reliable vehicle. He reckoned that if he took his scythe with him at least he could still cut down some of the rushes so he slung it over his shoulder, pulled an old wide-brimmed hat over his ears and set off. But as he neared Ardlussa, he was surprised to see Robin Fletcher looming out of the mist. Fletcher looked as if he'd seen a ghost, 'By jove, Blair, I thought you were the Grim Reaper come to take me away!' George laughed, realising how his tall, skeletal figure carrying a scythe must have scared his friend the laird. They went back to Ardlussa and had a dram or two whilst Fletcher got one of his men to fix the motorbike yet again. As a result, George was able to fetch his supplies later that afternoon, load them into his sidecar and return to Barnhill. On his way back, it amused him to think of himself as the Grim Reaper. He had no shortage of candidates for his services.

I suppose it's time to take stock before I go back to London. I've made a start on my book but I still have a long way to go. I've had an outline of it lying about for years and now it's much clearer to me where it's headed. Like all true rebels I know what I'm against, but what am I for? Well, I suppose it could almost be summed up in the French revolutionary motto 'Liberty, Equality, Fraternity' – with the all-important addition of Truth, however uncomfortable. Liberty means the freedom for every individual to say what he likes, as at Speakers Corner in Hyde Park – and what a variety show that is. It's the freedom to write whatever you like, except that there's no such thing as freedom of the press as long as it's owned by a handful of the rich in this country and by the state in Soviet Russia and Spain. In fact, the biggest restriction on freedom of speech is the prevalence of self-censorship where people won't say what they think but keep within what they know is acceptable to the majority and the powers that be. And when it comes to Equality, of course, 'we're all born equal'. Tell that to the miners who've slaved for the coal owners for generations. But we must strive to create equality and that means abolishing the House of Lords, the public schools and the whole class system by nationalising the means of production and the rest. Only that way can we create a universal brotherhood in which people care for and support each other through thick and thin. Solidarity might be a better word for it than Fraternity. But as we've seen under fascism and in Soviet Russia, none of this can happen without Truth. Because once you suppress the truth you're on a slippery slope towards not just inequality but dictatorship. In a time of deceit and lies like ours, telling the truth is the best policy. There is only one truth. One must dare to be a Daniel, dare to stand alone – whatever the consequences. I tried to put some of this into the manifesto I wrote for Koestler and the League for the Rights of Man earlier this year but he and Bertie Russell appear to have fallen out and the idea seems to have died a death. The only real hope for all this to come to pass is when working class people ignore all the petty distractions that keep them in their place and get up off their backsides and take power in the way I saw them do in Barcelona in the early days of the fight against fascism. It cannot succeed in one country alone, but perhaps a United Socialist States of Europe could show the way to the rest of the world? That makes me a democratic socialist in my book.

To me this just seems like common sense. I can remember a time when human decency was the norm, and people valued ordinary things like high teas, antiques, cricket, saucy postcards, angel scraps and stamp collecting. I will forever love and cherish the Earth and everything that lives on it. I've always loved animals and the English countryside – except for rats and snakes – and now I've experienced Jura for myself I hope to live here for the rest of my life. Of course, I'll miss raking about in junk shops and second-hand bookshops, but the compensations of island living far outweigh such minor pleasures.

Naturally, one must be willing to change one's views in the light of experience. There are no guarantees about any of this, but being alert to the opportunities for deep-going social change, as well as their dangers, is the only way it could work.

My book will show the very antithesis of all this if the world keeps on the way it's going. It will portray the kind of society we're heading towards if we don't act to stop it. I want to alert the world to the dangers facing us by taking to their logical conclusion the totalitarian tendencies which I can see are already well underway in today's world. I only hope that I can finish it, that my efforts won't be in vain and that its readers won't see it as a fantasy of my twisted imagination. I expect I won't get much more of it written in London over the winter but the one compensation in going back to that hellhole is that I should get to see Sonia again when I'm down there.

* * *

When I got back from Paris, another letter from George was waiting for me. He said he was sorry I hadn't made it to Barnhill since the autumn colours were very beautiful and he'd seen what looked like a whale and several otters. The stags had started rutting and there was good fishing since the mackerel were running. I can't imagine why he thought any of this would interest me, but I suppose it must have reminded him of all the things he loved about his childhood. He told me that he and Av were coping well. I felt a bit sorry that he'd lost Susan. After all, she looked after him as much as she did Ricky, and now he was left with his rather frosty sister who wouldn't be nearly as much fun. He said he'd soon be back in London and hoped to see me then.

So, come October, there we were in Highgate Wood gazing into a pool in which little fish flitted about in the dappled morning light that shone through tall, ancient trees. George seemed happy to be with me again. Or perhaps he was just wondering if he should have brought his fishing rod. You could never really tell with him. We walked along a winding path through the early mist. He kicked piles of copper leaves which rustled and swished in the high, empty wood.

'Did you never kick leaves as a child?' he asked.

'I suppose I must have.'

'People have forgotten these simple pleasures, yet all this is right under their noses.' He indicated the woods around us.

'Perhaps they don't find it that interesting.' I half hoped he would realise I was speaking about myself.

'It's all so wonderful, how could they not?'

'But it's rather gloomy, don't you think?'

'Not at all. It's a place of dark secrets.' He just loved anything remotely secretive.

We sat down on a thick log in a little clearing. He put his arm round me.

'How's your book coming along?' I asked.

'I've written about fifty pages so far, but I've still got a long way to go. You're going to be in it.'

Now this was real news. 'Am I? Well, do tell me more.'

'I would, but it'd be bad luck. I've already said too much.'

What a tease. 'Well, you'll have a ready market for it since *Animal Farm* did so well.'

'I suppose so. If I ever finish it. It's already proving a bit of a struggle. And it's a lot darker.'

'How do you mean?'

'Well, I'm trying to warn people what could happen if they don't realise what's going on.'

'You mean in Russia?'

'Not just Russia. It's the way the whole world's going.' He looked uncomfortable talking about it and quickly got off the subject. 'But what about you? How are things at the office?'

'Well, Cyril and Lys aren't long back from their travels in France and already he's planning another trip to America. He seems quite addicted to travelling.'

'That'll mean even more work for you then.'

'I don't mind. I enjoyed editing that last issue about how all you authors earn a living.'

'Oh, that one. I don't need a lot to live on.'

I'm still not sure why he didn't like it. I suppose he just felt that writers should keep the details of their lives private. Part of his need for secrecy. We started walking again. Deep in the wood, a roe deer appeared through the mist. He pointed to it. 'Look, there, a phantom of the forest. We've got lots on Jura... You know, Barnhill really is a magical place. And I'm still desperately lonely. You would like it there.'

We stopped and stared at the solitary deer grazing by the side of the path, its white rump bobbing in stippled sunlight.

'I'm sorry, George. I'm not going to give up my career. And, anyway, you know how much I'd miss London. But, you know, if you stayed on here we could have some fun together.'

'That would mean abandoning my book. I just can't do that. But I need you with me.'

'You know you can get by without me, George. Anyway, you've got Av to look after you now.'

He pulled a face. I gave him a hard look. 'It's up to you.'

'I'll think about it.'

Chapter 7

ON THE LAST day of the year George arrived at Central Station in Glasgow. He had left Ricky in the care of Av and taken the overnight sleeper from Euston. But it was two hours late in arriving and he realised he'd missed his connection. He wished he hadn't cut it so fine because now he'd have to find a place to stay in the city for a couple of nights since there would be no transport available on New Year's Day. He carried his suitcase along the platform and, not for the first time, marvelled at the huge glass roof above the concourse and the window gallery high above where all day long some poor devil had to change heavy notice boards showing the train times and destinations. The station was crowded with middle class families who all seemed intent on hurrying to places unknown before the year was out. Presumably the city's workers were still working a full shift that day. He made his way through the crowd and emerged into bustling Gordon Street where a newspaper vendor was shouting something incomprehensible at passers-by. George knew that the Central Hotel in the station would be out of his league price-wise so he bought an early *Evening Times* from the vendor and asked him if there was a cheap hotel nearby.

'Aw, aye. That's The George you'll be waantin. Nothing fancy but they'll see tae ye awright.'

'And how do I get there?'

The rasping seller had one eye on the paper sales he was missing. 'Evenin Taiaimes, Citizzen, gechyer Taiaimes Citizzen!

Hugmanaay Speshaal!' he stretched the words as he bawled. Then back to George, 'Well, ye go right alang here tae Buchanan Street, then ye turn left an go right up as far as Cathedral Street. It's on the corner. Ye cannae miss it.' He pointed directions as he spoke. 'A gey old place it is, but ye'll be awright there. A Guid New Year tae ye when it comes.'

George wasn't sure he followed all of that, but set off anyway. These Glasgow chaps weren't so bad after all. He went up Buchanan Street past the subway entrance and spotted the old hotel up ahead of him on the corner. Right where the man had said it was. A dirty red sandstone Victorian building with nothing to see at street level except a wooden door to a public bar and a short pair of marble pillars which must be the main entrance. Inside, the high ceilinged hall was dark and dingy and there was no one at the reception desk. He pinged the bell and waited. A bit run down, he thought, but it wouldn't cost him much. The George Hotel. Named after him, of course. Eventually a small man with a grizzled face shuffled out of a back room and took up position behind the desk. 'Whit can a do ye fur?' he asked, giving George the once over.

'I'd like a room for two nights, please.'

'We dinnae check in til wan o'clock an we're pretty fu, it bein Hogmanay an aw, but ah'll see whit ah've goat.' He opened an ancient, leather-bound ledger and ran down the page with his finger. 'Well, yer in luck, big yin, wu'hve still goat a room oan the first flair, jist as weel ye came early. Ye can leave yer case here an come back at wan an ah'll check ye in then.'

George thanked the man, handed him his case through an opening in the counter and turned to leave. Outside the brightness was dazzling after the hotel's dark interior. He decided to wander the streets for a few hours and head down towards the river. But first he had to see what the city's famous George Square looked like. Part way down Buchanan Street beneath the old steeple of St George's Tron Church of Scotland, he was given more directions by a helpful old lady who pointed across and told him George Square was just round the corner. They must have known I was coming, George chuckled to himself. A hotel, a square and now a church all named after him. The square was a good sized civic space surrounded by high Victorian buildings. He walked across it, scattering crowds of pigeons before him. It was peppered with trees and statues and he noticed that the one at the top of an eighty foot doric column was of Sir Walter Scott. The father of the historical novel, but a strange one to find here, he thought. Scott was more associated with Edinburgh and the Waverley novels in his mind. Still, at least they appreciate their writers. A tall, unlit Christmas tree stood almost as tall beside the column and coloured lights that were draped around the Square. He approached the white stone war memorial with its lions on either side and noticed that lots of new names had been freshly carved on it. At the far end of the Square stood another imposing turreted building which he reckoned would be worth taking a look inside. As he entered the hallway he was approached by a plump, straight-backed commissionaire with war decorations on his lapel. 'Can I help you, sir?' the man enquired.

'Just having a look. What is this building?'

'It's the City Chambers, sir, where the Glasgow Corporation councillors meet,' he explained.

'I see. Mind if I take a look around?'

'We'll be closing early today, sir, but you'll have time to take a look at the main hall and the grand staircase. We're not known as the Second City of the Empire for nothing, you know,' he said proudly.

George had his own thoughts about the Empire but peered up at the pink and brown marble on the floors and walls. 'I see what you mean.' He wandered through an archway to the foot of a wide staircase and was amazed at the extravagance of the

City Fathers in this display to the world of the fruits of their commercial success. Success that had been built on the hard labour and brutal conquest of millions of exploited souls throughout the British Empire, as he knew from his years in Burma. The Scots had shared in the spoils of that exploitation. Perhaps Glasgow's Tobacco Lords traded in slaves as well as cotton and tobacco.

He felt a sudden urge to get back out into what passed for fresh air in Glasgow. He thanked the commissionaire on his way out and left. He headed east, past the high archways behind the City Chambers and into Montrose Street. On the opposite side he came across a large group of women of all ages in pinnies and headscarves standing on the pavement. A dark hole had been cut into the tall building for goods to be delivered and taken away. They were chatting and laughing, probably in high spirits because they were on their break and the next day was a holiday. They looked just like the kind of working girls he'd seen going to work in Lancashire mills in the early morning years before. As he approached, one of them, noticing his long frame and huge shoes, gave a wolf whistle and they all laughed.

George smiled and asked her, 'Excuse me. What do you do here?'

'Och, wur in the rag trade. I'm a machinist and Jeanie here works the big press,' a red haired girl, who couldn't have been more than seventeen, replied. The others gathered round this nosey stranger. It wasn't every day a visitor took an interest in them and their work.

'And what do you make?' George asked.

'Shirts, blouses, caps an pyjamas for S&P Harris,' Jeanie, the older woman, said. 'They supply them tae the big stores like Marks an Sparks. They own this hale buildin an hunners o us come in fae aw over Glesga every day tae work here.'

'And do you like it?' George asked.

'Och aye, it's no sae bad – especially oan Hogmanay,'

another older woman laughed and they all giggled. 'Thur a bit mean, the brothers, but oor foreman's awright. Here's Robert noo.' She made way for a good looking man of about thirty who wore a grey smock.

'What's all this then?' Robert joked, looking George up and down.

'I'm a writer and I'm just trying to find out what you all do here,' George replied.

'A writer, eh. For a newspaper?'

'No, not really. Just for my own interest.'

'Well, what do you want to know?' asked Robert, reassured.

'Well, what was it like here during the war?'

'I was in the Navy during the war, but there was no shortage of work here making uniforms and shirts and, of course, caps. Just about every man in Glasgow wears a bunnet,' Robert laughed.

'So I've noticed,' said George. 'And is it well paid?'

'Well, put it this way, nobody here's getting rich – including me – but it's steady work and we earn enough to get by on,' Robert said. The girls agreed.

'Maybe we dinnae do as well as you writers, but we do awright,' Jeanie added.

'An speakin o' work, our break time's up. We better get back in, it's an early finish the day,' Robert said.

'Thanks very much,' said George.

'Don't mention it,' said Robert.

Some of the women went up the stairs whilst others joined Robert in the hoist that took them up to the higher floors. George walked round the corner into Ingram Street and read the plaque beside the main entrance: S&P Harris textile manufacturers. He went down Candleriggs past the Fruitmarket which was already starting to close up for the day. Cabbage and cauliflower leaves and squashed oranges and pears littered the cobbles, but he was able to buy an apple from a fruiterer without showing his ration card. Perhaps this was where the expression 'fallen off the back of a lorry' originated? He turned into Argyle Street and went along as far as Glasgow Cross with its Tolbooth Steeple. Two men were erecting metal barriers for the New Year celebrations. They must be expecting a big crowd that night. He looked up at the blue steeple clock and realised it was time for him to get back to the hotel to check in.

The George Hotel was a warren of a place with dark, wooden panelling on every wall which had once been state of the art, but now looked dingy. He collected his case and his key but got lost in a maze of corridors and finished up in the public bar. As he entered, a handful of men wearing bunnets standing at the bar turned round as one, gave him a quick glance, and turned back to their half pints. He told the barman he'd got lost.

'Don't worry, everybody does. What room are you?' asked the skelf of a barman.

'102,' said George.

'Right, just go back the way you came and take the second corridor on the left, then up the staircase and it's on your right.'

George did as he was told and this time found his way to his room. It had a high ceiling with cornices stained yellow with smoke, an old wooden chair that had once been stylish, a cheap imitation chandelier and a single bed that looked like it would be too short for him. This would do, he thought. He emptied his case and lay out on the bed, wondering what to do that night and the next. Everybody he'd met that day had been friendly and helpful. Maybe Glasgow wasn't that bad a place after all. He hadn't slept much on the so-called sleeper, so he soon dozed off. When he awoke a few hours later it was already getting dark and he felt hungry. On his way out of the hotel he thought he could smell fish and chips and followed his nose to a chip shop round the corner which had already attracted a queue of hungry customers. Three teenage lads were ahead of him in the queue and a stout man in a white smock behind the counter asked them, 'So, whata you want, boys?' in a strong Italian accent.

'A fish supper, a single fish an a black puddin supper,' one of them replied.

'Just a wee minute, boys. We ara waitin ona chips. And what about you, sir?' he asked George.

'I've never tried black pudding before, so I'll have one as well. With chips.'

The lads had a quiet snigger to themselves at his accent but appeared to admire his courage in risking the unknown.

'Two black puddin suppers, a fish supper an a single fish comin up,' the man announced to himself.

Soon George was tucking into his black pudding and chips laced with salt, vinegar and ketchup, which he'd seen the lads spread on theirs. It was certainly different from anything else he'd ever tasted, but he reckoned he could grow to like this Glasgow Italian speciality. By the time he'd got to the Underground entrance in Buchanan Street he'd polished it off and wiped his hands on its newspaper wrapping before throwing it in a bin. He bought a ticket at the kiosk inside and went along a green and white tiled corridor and down some steep steps. The smell was overpowering, somewhere between ozone and damp washing – different from the London Tube. A cold draught blew into his eyes from the tunnel deep below. He shivered. On the narrow platform, he could hear the rumble of an approaching subway but couldn't tell which direction it was coming from until suddenly it whooshed and hissed in beside him and the others crowding there. A lot of people got off and others squeezed on. George wanted to go south to Bridge Street and waited for the next one going the opposite way. A deep rumbling sound got louder and louder until another subway flashed into the station with a screeching of brakes, a loud swishing noise and a sudden jolt. Two long carriages half emptied and he got on, ducking his head to avoid banging it on the low wooden roof. He managed to find a leather seat to sit on. As the subway got up speed, he and the other passengers were thrown from side to side as it rocked and rattled its way along the tunnel. An old guy in dungarees opposite smiled at the look of surprise on George's face at the violence of its motions. St Enoch was the next stop and a crowd of people got off. He looked at the Underground plan above the seat opposite and saw that there was an Inner and an Outer Circle. Bridge Street was the next stop. Only a handful of people got off with him and hurried their way upwards into the street.

Outside he noticed a lamplighter lighting gas mantles on the other side of the street. He took a roll-up out of a tin in his pocket, straightened it out and lit it with his lighter. Ah, that felt better. To his left he was amazed to see not one but two large cinemas right next to each other. The Coliseum with its high red sandstone tower and the art deco New Bedford. Glaswegians must like their films, he thought. An escape from their daily lives. He was in no mood for a film, and they looked closed anyway, so he turned the other way into Norfolk Street. Two pubs on opposite corners of the crossroads had their doors open and were packed with working men just finished for the year. Gorbals Cross was the same, a pub on almost every corner and every one of them busy. He spotted what looked like a Gents with railings round it and went down the scuffed steps of a narrow stairway under the road. The smell of stale piss nearly knocked him over and his eyes stung, so he did what he came for and got out as fast as he could. No sign of the Glasgow hard men portrayed in that awful book *No Mean City*, just little men in their working clothes staggering about the place as happy as larry. In the distance, he caught sight of flames lighting up the smoke-filled night. Probably some ironworks blasting away, he thought. A scene from Dante's Hell.

The tenement walls were blackened with soot and the crumpled faces of passers-by were a testament to their hard lives. Some women were hanging out the windows of the tenements blethering to each other whilst waiting for their men to come home with their pay packets. Others were on their knees at the mouths of closes scrubbing cold stone floors. One old lady looked up at him and said proudly, 'Jist gettin rid o aw the dirt o the auld year, Mister. Aw the best tae ye when it comes.'

'And the same to you,' said George.

On an impulse he decided to see what was round the back of the tenements and went through a close half lit by a spluttering blue gas mantle. He emerged into a dirt backyard enclosed on all sides by blackened tenements. Lots of children of all ages were playing in the dark. Some boys were pushing another seated in an orange box on wheels in and out of a large filthy pool. It splashed over other children who were playing dares to go near it then run away. He could smell the stagnant water from where he stood and was astonished that the children seemed oblivious to the filth around them. They were having great fun... until they saw his tall figure approaching.

'Quick, skedaddle, it's the polis!' one boy shouted and they scattered in all directions. Two older boys came out of a close opposite to see what all the fuss was about. They weren't scared of the polis and one said to George, 'Dae ye waant a hurl in oor bogey, mister? Only it'll cost ye.' George understood enough of this to know that it was time he left and replied only, 'No, thanks. I must be going.' He strode past them through another close into the street. He didn't feel threatened in any way, after all he'd been surrounded by much bigger crowds in Burma years before and the boys could probably do with some change. His abiding thought was that something must be done about these appalling slums for the sake of these Gorbals children who knew only germ-filled puddles to play in. He decided to head back towards the river and came to a wide bridge which looked eerie in the dim gaslight. Mist was gathering over the river. To the east, past a railway bridge, chimneys belched out smoke for as far as he could see. Beyond a weir, the river looked almost rural with trees on each bank, but the stone wall of the bridge he leaned over was black with dust. To the west he could see an elegant footbridge with a crowd of folk sauntering across, singing as they went. The party was starting early. Beyond that, two steam engines passed each other, arriving and leaving.

So this was the famous River Clyde. A fair size, but as black and dank as the walls of the Gorbals slums. Debris of all kinds floated silently past below him and it stank of stale oil. He crossed into Stockwell Street and came to the Scotia Bar. The sound of a fiddle and an accordion wafted out into the street and tempted him inside. The place was thick with smoke and heaving. All the people inside were men. He had to push his way through to get to the bar. The music came from a long, narrow lounge adjoining the bar where a few women were sitting. His head almost touched the ceiling but he liked the look of old varnished wood everywhere and was struck by the feeling of good cheer and expectation that seemed to prevail on that last day of the year. Old guys in raincoats and bunnets stood hunched over the bar nursing their half pints and whisky glasses.

'A pint of mild,' George shouted above the hubbub.

'That'll be a pint o light, you'll be waantin, big yin,' the barman suggested. He'd served plenty of Englishmen in his time.

'Where ur ye fae?' asked an old boy standing next to George.

'London,' George replied.

'A thocht as much. An how dae ye like Glesga?'

'It's quite a place.' George tried not to sound too negative.

'Aye, yer right there,' said the old guy. 'Ah've aye lived here, this'll do me.'

The barman put down his pint on a damp mat, George paid him and turned away to let someone else in and to avoid having to discuss the merits of Glasgow with the proud old local. Before he could leave, the man clinked his glass and said, '*Slàinte Mhor*. Yer good health.'

'Cheers,' George replied, peering through the crowd. At the far end he spotted what looked like a snug with leather seats round three sides of a table. It had one empty place. He weaved his way towards it saying 'Excuse me' and got surprised looks up at him from men in working clothes. Eventually he got to the edge of the snug and ducked his head in, 'Is this seat taken?'

'Naw, yer aw right,' the man nearest to him said.

George sat down and took a quick gulp of his pint. There were five other men gathered tightly round the wooden table that you had to squeeze past to get in or out. Snug indeed, George thought, taking in the black and white pictures of old Glasgow on the walls. They were talking in groups and everyone seemed in good humour. On the back seat he recognised Robert, the young man he'd met outside S&P Harris's, who was talking to an older, white-haired man. In a gap in their conversation Robert looked to see who the new arrival was and nudged his friend, 'Here, Andy, it's that writer I was telling you about.' Some of the conversations faltered when they heard the word 'writer'. The man next to George gave him an admiring look and asked, 'What do you write?'

'Novels mostly... and journalism.'

'Would I have heard of any of them?' the man asked.

'You might have heard of *Animal Farm*.'

'I certainly have. I'm Johnny, by the way,' he shook George's hand eagerly. 'Look lads,' he announced, 'This is George Orwell. He put the boot right intae Joe Stalin in *Animal Farm*.' The others stopped talking and a couple of them also shook George's hand. He felt unexpectedly proud.

'Ah've read some o yer articles in *Tribune*. Ah really liked that wan aboot the toads in spring,' Johnny continued. George looked surprised.

'And what are ye doing in Glasgow on Hogmanay?' Robert asked George. George noticed his speech was clearer than the others'.

'I was on my way to Jura this morning, but I missed the boat, so I'm stuck here for two days.'

'Missed the boat? That's the story o ma life,' Johnny laughed. 'Still there's worse places tae be stuck ower Ne'erday.'

'Jura, eh. Your boat must go doon the watter past Dunoon on your way there?' Robert asked.

'It does,' George replied.

'Me and my pals frae the Toonheid used to go camping in Dunoon, that's where I met my wife,' Robert smiled.

'Look, let me get ye a dram tae go wi yer pint,' Johnny said. George tried to say no, but Johnny wasn't having it. 'Jist you move up wan so ye can talk tae yer freen.'

George got up to let him out. He hardly knew Robert but that was enough to make him a friend. 'How did you meet her?' He asked Robert once he'd sat down and shifted up.

'At a Friday night dance in the Masonic Halls,' Robert replied. 'She's from Glasgow too, from Kelvinhaugh, but she was there on holiday.'

'Any children?' George asked.

Robert looked troubled for a moment, 'Just a boy, he'll be one in January. What about you?'

'I've got a son too. He's almost three. But my wife died a couple of years ago.'

'I'm sorry to hear that,' said Robert. 'That must be really hard.'

'It is. But my boy Ricky's coming on well. He loves it on Jura, it's a great place for him to grow up.'

'Ach, ye canna beat growin up in the country,' old Andy chipped in, 'Ah'm frae Stonehoose, it's a great place fer lads tae grow up as weel.'

'You're right there, Andy. Partick's fine and I've got a plot there tae grow some veg, but I'd love my boy to grow up in Dunoon if I could get a job there. I started pushing a barrow for Harris's after I left school at fourteen, and worked my way up. I got my job back after I came home from the Navy... and it's a good job, though I say it myself.' Robert was starting to get a bit fu.

Johnny sat down beside George again, put down two whiskies and raised his glass, 'Tae George an *Animal Farm*!' The whole snug clinked George's glass, repeated the toast and knocked back their drams.

'They didnae hae ony Islay malts but ah goat ye a Bell's. It's the next best thing. An this here is wan o the Scotia's ain writers, Freddy Anderson. He wants tae meet ye.' He pointed to a thin little man with a sharp red face and a goatee beard who looked like a leprechaun. He offered George his hand to shake.

'Who would have thought it, the great George Orwell sitting here in the Scotia at Hogmanay? Now but you couldn't make that up, sure you couldn't.' Freddy said in a strong Irish accent, his eyes twinkling.

'And what do you write?' George asked.

'Oh, this and that. I've written my fair share o scurrilous verse since I came here from County Monaghan and I've started on a play I'm going to offer the Unity Theatre. Tell me, George, have you ever heard o the great John Maclean?'

'Yes, but I don't know much about him.'

'Well, he was one o Glasgow's revolutionary socialist heroes. He taught Marxist economics to thousands o workers and went to jail for agitatin against the so-called Great War. There was nothin great about it, I'm sure a man such as yourself would agree. They poisoned him in Peterhead jail, and the streets in Pollokshaws were jam-packed at his funeral.'

'It sounds like his life would make a great play,' George suggested.

'That it would, that it would,' Freddy was getting excited.

At the back of the snug Robert was feeling merry and started singing,

Sing me a song o Bonnie Scotland
any old song will do
round an old campfire
a rough and ready choir
will join in the chorus too.
Ye'll tak the high road
an I'll tak the low
it's a song that we all know
tae remind us all of Bonnie Scotland
where the heather
and the bluebells grow.

He stood up and gestured to the others to join in. At the mention of Bonnie Scotland, George decided it was time to go. 'I better be getting back,' he announced.

'Och, the party's just gettin started,' said Robert, disappointed. 'But I suppose I'm in the same boat. I never go to the pub after work. May doesn't like me to. But it's New Year after aw.' He flashed his bottle of whisky sticking out of his jacket pocket and asked George, 'Have ye got your Ne'erday bottle yet?'

'No.'

'Don't worry, there's a licensed grocers up the street,' Johnny checked his watch. 'If ye go noo ye'll maybe still catch thum afore they shut.'

George finished his pint, bade his farewells and told Robert it was a pleasure to meet him.

'I'll maybe see you again sometime on a boat goin' doon the watter. Say hullo to Dunoon for me,' Robert joked.

Out in the street, the cold cut through George like a blade. He started coughing as he set off looking for the off-sales. He liked these Glasgow men, they seemed much friendlier than most Londoners. He looked at his watch. Ten to ten. Another year was slipping away. He got to the grocer's just in time and bought a quarter bottle of Bell's to take back to the hotel with him. The streets were still full of people scurrying about, shopping bags in hand, whilst others waited for tramcars to take them home. Revellers with carry-outs were staggering about looking for wherever the party might be. George Square was now a fairyland, its huge Christmas tree all lit up and a myriad of coloured lights blinking around the Square. When he got back to the hotel, he could hear a sing-song coming from the bar and wondered if he would get any sleep that night.

George opened the window of his shabby little room. He leant out and heard church bells ringing and foghorns sounding along the river to mark the New Year. One boat's horn tooted after another, and air raid sirens wailed as they would have done during the war. There was something strangely moving about this Glasgow ritual that welcomed in the promise of a new start to the year. A roaring in his ears, a shiver up his back, his feelings about life welled up in him. He thought of all the members of his family who were no longer here to greet the New Year. His father, his mother, Marjorie and, above all, Eileen. Never to be seen again, or even remembered? Would anyone even think of them except him? The Scots make such a lot of this dismal time of year, he thought. Or perhaps they just like to wallow in their misery? A bit like himself. But perhaps they were right to mark this time of change, this old tradition that predated Christmas? A drunk man looked up from the street below and shouted, 'A Guid New Year! Ur ye no comin oot tae join the party?'

'Happy New Year. No, not this year,' he replied.

'Well, yer missing yersel,' the man staggered off. George shut the window, wondering what he meant. How could he miss himself? Was this an unanswerable philosophical question? A Glasgow koan? He smiled to himself. Still, it was a truly proletarian city. If there was one place where the revolution would break out, it would be Glasgow. It nearly had after the First World War when Lloyd George's Government sent tanks into the city after police scattered the huge crowd of men with their red flag who were demanding a forty-hour week to create jobs for returning soldiers. He must find out more about John Maclean. The poverty in the city was tangible. He could see it in the worn faces of the shipyard workers and labourers, and in the skin and bone of their wives and children. The very stones of its buildings were black with smoke, but the Glasgow people he'd met seemed irrepressible in spite of everything. He poured himself a dram from his bottle and toasted the New Year and Glasgow's proles. Perhaps he'd finish his book this year? He lay back on the bed thinking about all this, then coughed and spat up phlegm into his handkerchief. A solitary figure. Who knew what the New Year would bring?

New Year's Day meant a late breakfast of ham and eggs and some of that black pudding that George had taken to. Outside he found a deserted city. Everything was closed. Still, he'd managed to get a good night's sleep in spite of his feet dangling out the bottom of the bed and the drunken singing in the street below that went on into the early hours. He decided to go further east and walked along Cathedral Street towards the High Street, the oldest part of Glasgow. He passed Collins the publishers and came to the Cathedral and the Royal Infirmary, standing side by side with equally black walls. Even the Cathedral was closed today so he wandered into the Necropolis. He crossed an arched bridge that resembled a drawbridge over a castle moat and came to what looked like a shrine to the Merchants House of Glasgow which proclaimed that they had built the bridge 'to afford a proper entrance to their new cemetery'. He slowly wound his way uphill past tall stone monuments to the dead on all sides. He stopped at a modest one to William Miller 'The Laureate of the Nursery, author of Wee Willie Winkie, 1810–1862'. Columns, obelisks, arches, mausoleums and carved angels marked the last resting place of merchants, builders, colonels and ministers. This seemed to be where most of the city merchants ended up. All their wealth couldn't save them from the same fate as the poor. He wondered where their graves were? Probably hidden away in other less grandiose graveyards, segregated, as they had been in life.

By the time he reached the huge statue of John Knox on a large pedestal at the top of the hill he was panting for breath. The inscription all around it sang the praises of the man, the Reformation and the martyrs who had died for the Protestant cause. Somehow it seemed fitting that this fierce Calvinist figure kept watch over the copper-green roof of the Cathedral and the inhabitants of the city beyond. To the south, George could see low hills beyond the river and a jumble of tenements, factories and chimneys, some still pouring out a pall of smoke that rose over the landscape. It struck him that the city was situated in a wide valley through which the Clyde ran, where people must have scratched a living for a thousand years. The pretentious engravings on some of the gravestones made him smile. He'd make sure his would be simple when the time came. The thought bothered him and he decided to leave before his high hopes for the New Year had all gone.

Emerging from the cemetery, he caught a strong whiff of hops from a brewery and saw a high prison-like building with a sign that said 'The Great Eastern Hotel'. Some old fellows were sitting between pillars on the steps outside the entrance. They looked down on their luck and he understood at once that this was no hotel, but a model lodging house where the poorest of the poor could buy a cheap bed for the night.

'Excuse me, what's it like?' he gestured inside to one of the men.

'Ach, it's no bad... if ye dinnae mind the fleas.' He looked suspiciously at George. He looked tall enough to be a policeman.

George smiled, remembering the dosshouses he'd slept in after he came back from Burma. 'Are there any more lodging houses around here?'

'Och, aye, thur's wan doon by the river near Glesga Green. If ye dinnae mind huvin tae pray an sing hymns afore they gie ye yer breakfast. The Sally Ann runs it.'

'Thanks,' said George and headed up Duke Street and down between the crumbling High Street tenements in the direction of the river. He came to a huge park, which must be the Green, with another tall monument in the middle, and in the distance a squat glasshouse. The park was empty except for flights of sparrows and starlings flitting around bare trees by the riverbank. He came to an impressive, thick-pillared building carved with the legend 'High Court of Justiciary' and, beside it, a low, stone and red brick one with the word 'Mortuary' above the entrance. There seemed to be no escape from death in this city. Round the corner, sitting on the entrance steps of what must be the Salvation Army hostel, he came upon a haggard group of men and women passing what looked like a bottle of methylated spirits between them.

One of the women gave him a glazed look, held out the bottle and asked, 'Dae ye waanna swatch, son?'

'No thanks,' George replied and walked on. He appreciated her gesture, but didn't want to catch something, or drink meths for that matter. Next to the hostel was a dirt lane that ran along the side of railway arches. The arches' doors were closed but on the waste ground opposite lay rags and litter of all kinds, and a fire around which more down and outs sat huddled. They looked as if they had picked up some of the rags and put them on. As George approached, an old geezer looked up from warming his hands at the fire, sized up the visitor and said, 'Welcome tae Paddy's Market.' George realised he had stumbled across the place where the poorest of Glasgow's poor gathered, probably to exchange rags, and no doubt sleep under the railway arches if they could. It brought back vivid memories of his tramping days all those years ago. He walked up the lane and out into the street and found himself back at the Scotia Bar which was closed. He wandered back along the riverside and up through the deserted streets to his hotel.

There were no trains to Gourock on the second of January but George found out from the hotel that an early morning boat left from the Broomielaw. He boarded the paddle steamer, the *Jeanie Deans*, just after seven o' clock and peered from the upper deck at a handful of passengers crossing the gangway in the dark. The city still seemed half asleep and its street gas-lights hardly penetrated the morning gloom. The steamer left promptly at eight and sailed downriver past the passenger fer-ries that crossed the Clyde like pond skaters, and by the Kingston, Queen's and Yorkhill docks where big cargo boats lay tied up along the quays. Shipyard cranes dwarfed the sta-tionary two-tier vehicular ferry that linked Govan and Partick. Silent shipyard after shipyard with ships at all stages of con-struction. Further downriver a fellow traveller pointed out John Brown's where the famous *Queen Mary* transatlantic liner had been built for the Cunard Line before the war.

George stayed on deck that first part of the journey, curious to see what remained of the river's industrial and shipbuilding past. Quite a lot really, but some of the cranes and the yards looked clapped out. Clydebank had been blitzed during the war and its flattened streets reminded him of London. Very few of the bombed houses had been replaced. The Labour Government was still struggling to overcome serious food shortages and transport problems which meant that building new houses had to wait. As the river opened out, George went down below to the cafeteria where he ordered ham and eggs and a pot of strong tea. Not as strong as he liked, but it would have to do. Afterwards he went down to the engine room and marvelled at the smooth, circling pistons and the steady beat of paddles thumping round and round, water dripping from them.

The first stop was at Gourock at the Tail o' the Bank where a few more passengers came aboard. The river had become a wide firth and, back on deck, George could see snow on the distant hills. The sun came out and, as they approached Dunoon, it felt like he was indeed going 'doon the watter' as Robert and generations of Glaswegians had done before. They crossed a wide bay and tied up at a fine looking pier from which he could see the Argyll Hotel and what looked like a castle on a hill above well-kept gardens opposite the pier. He asked a passenger next to him about the statue of a woman that stood at a corner of the gardens looking out to sea.

'Och, that's Hielan Mary, wan o Rabbie Burns's lassies,' the man replied.

Not often you see a statue of a woman, George thought. She must have been highly regarded. Rothesay was the next stop and, with its ornate Pavilion and gardens, it too looked like a holiday resort where Glasgow people would go in summer. The Kyles of Bute was always George's favourite part of the journey because of its rugged beauty and the narrows through which the steamer had to squeeze. As they approached Tighnabruaich he saw some red deer that had come down from the higher ground to forage for something to eat. When the steamer reached Tarbert at twelve noon, George and the remaining passengers got off and caught a bus that took them to West Tarbert where a smaller boat was to ferry them to Craighouse on Jura. The sun had gone by this time and a wild westerly wind had got up. The ferry crossing was rough and George spent the best part of the next three hours throwing up over the side. The waves were so high it took the boat half an hour to tie up at the pier and the handful of passengers had to scramble across the gangway as it raised and lowered perilously. Fortunately he got a lift all the way to Ardlussa and walked the remaining seven miles of track as the night closed in.

Next morning at Barnhill the sun had reappeared on one of those days early in the year that does your heart good. George took a look round the garden and saw that all his pansies, lupins and cheddar pinks had disappeared. The wire he'd put round the flower bed wasn't pegged down and the rabbits must have got under it. The cabbages, turnips and strawberries he'd planted had almost all gone, although his carrots had survived. The wire round his vegetable patch was still sunk into the ground but the rabbits must have jumped nearly three feet over it to get at the veg. He made a mental note to set some traps before he left. It rained most of the next day and the gale force winds were so fierce he could hardly stand up in them. It was a day for staying indoors, for reading and for drawing plans of where his fruit trees would go.

The following day the wind dropped and, although it was cold and overcast, he managed to plant two morello cherry trees near the house, a dozen apple trees, a dozen each of red and blackcurrant bushes, a dozen gooseberry plants and rhubarb roots, and six rambling and climbing roses. He seldom shied away from hard work. The day after was sunny but cold, and the wind had got up again, yet he managed to plant two dozen raspberry bushes. At night he recorded the details in his diary. It's good to be back, he thought to himself, perhaps he would spend the whole of next winter up here. He checked his fuel supplies and found that he had enough paraffin, calor gas and coal to last a couple of months. The week just flew in and soon it was time to return to London. But he'd managed to plant his fruit trees and felt happier than he had in a long time.

Chapter 8

THAT WINTER WAS the worst in living memory. George's landlord, the Marquis of Northampton, still hadn't got the roof fixed and it now leaked in a dozen different places. The rain was incessant and the cinema newsreels carried aerial pictures of rivers that had burst their banks and had flooded fields and villages all over England. People paddled from house to house in rowing boats. But in the city, the cold was even worse. His flat was like an icebox. One morning when Av got up, the living room was perishing and icicles had formed on the insides of the windows. She beat her arms on her body to try to warm herself and went to light the fire.

'We're out of firewood and coal,' she told George who was still in his dressing gown.

'Don't worry I'll get you some wood,' he replied sleepily and lifted Ricky's wooden boat and rocking horse and took them out of the room. Ricky carried on playing with his lorry and some clothes pegs he'd laid out into roads. In his workroom, George jammed the boat in his vice and started sawing it up. He struggled to do the same with the rocking horse, put all the bits in a large canvas bag and took it back through to Av. 'That should keep us warm today at least,' he almost seemed to take pleasure in their misery. Av took some of the wood from the bag and started to light the fire with it. Ricky was still playing away happily, but when he saw bits of his rocking horse being set alight he started to cry. A long, pained cry that wouldn't stop.

'Daddy, please don't.'

'There now, we need to keep warm,' George tried to quiet-en him but couldn't. The boy's tears and cries kept on and on. George went to the window and looked out. Nothing but smog outside. He could smell it. Canonbury Square didn't exist. He felt cut off from the world.

***

'George, this is Harry Richards, he's been with us a long time. Harry, this is George Orwell,' David Astor introduced one of his compositors to George. *The Observer* case-room reeked of metal and oil.

'Pleased to meet you at last,' Harry wore his Cockney ac-cent with pride.

'Pleased to meet you, Harry.'

'You know, it's a real pleasure to set your stuff. It's always really nice and clear to read. I enjoyed reading your dispatches from Germany.'

'Why, thank you.' George beamed.

'And well, I read your *Tribune* columns too… we know you're on our side and you're not afraid to say so,' he glanced at David. George positively glowed with satisfaction.

'I thought you two would get on. Harry's one of the aristoc-racy of labour around here,' David joked.

'If only I earned half as much as they do!' Harry gave as good as he got. Broad smiles all round.

David and George walked on along polished stone floors into the machine room. The huge printing machines sat silent, almost menacing, waiting for that moment when a switch would be turned and they would spring into life. When the machine minders saw them coming they started looking busy by wiping down the edges of the rollers.

'How's the paper doing?' George asked David.

'This weather's playing havoc with our printing and distri-bution. We've lost two issues to power cuts so far.'

'It's been hellish cold… And I'm not feeling great either,' George started coughing and spat some black phlegm into his white handkerchief.

'What's wrong?' David looked concerned and somewhat disgusted.

'It's my lungs. This cold and smog are killing me,' George panted.

'You really must look after yourself. Let me know if there's anything I can do.'

David led George through a maze of passageways to his plush office upstairs. A big oak desk was piled with papers and two Chesterfield sofas sat facing each other. A cocktail cabinet stood behind the desk and on the floor beyond the sofas sat an-other wooden cabinet with two doors at its front.

'Would you like a whisky? I've got something to show you.' David went over to the cocktail cabinet.

George sat down on one of the sofas. 'Certainly. I always enjoy your Islay malts.'

'It's a twelve-year-old Bowmore. You can't get much more Islay than that.' He poured out two glasses, but before bring-ing them over he went to the other cabinet, opened the doors and pressed a switch. The box began to hum to life. He took the glasses over, gave George one and sat on the sofa opposite.

'*Slàinte*,' they said together.

'Here's to the future,' added David, looking towards the tel-evision screen. A grainy picture of a BBC News announcer dressed in a dinner suit could barely be seen. In a rarefied up-per-crust accent he introduced a newsreel. The narrator's voice over the shadowy images was just as posh: 'Here Soviet troops are parading in Moscow's Red Square before Joseph Stalin and other members of the Politburo. Russia is continuing to build up its armed forces and would like to develop a nuclear capability.' Stalin and his chums looked all-powerful standing stiffly on the podium in their grey uniforms.

'My God, David, what a horrific invention. That infernal machine will give them control over everything we think and do... We'll be watched day and night, once we let them into our homes... People are sleepwalking into a nightmare... We have to wake them up!' George got more and more agitated.

David went over and switched off the television. 'I think you're being far too pessimistic, George. I'm sorry, I didn't mean to upset you.' David looked worried.

George began to calm down. 'At least they can't reach me up on Jura. I can't wait to get back to finish my book... if my health holds up.'

'Well, once it's finished, you could still write the occasional piece for me from up there,' David seemed relieved.

*　*　*

I met up with George a couple more times during that horrendous winter. Early in the New Year he threw a bit of a party the night the BBC Third Programme broadcast his dramatisation of *Animal Farm*. It was quite a gathering. His friends Tosco Fyvel, Inez Holden, Humphrey Slater and another old flame of his, Celia Kirwan, all turned up. Av managed to get Ricky down to sleep before the play came on. The small living room was chock full as we all sat, glasses and ciggies in hand, listening to the old mahogany wireless that sat in the corner. It was a good production, as well it should be, since George himself had written the adaptation, and we all laughed at the grunting noises when the pigs spoke, especially that little creep, Squealer. And, of course, the girls all shed a tear when good old Boxer got taken away to the knacker's yard. At the end, when the pigs became indistinguishable from the humans, we all clapped and George shyly took a bow.

'Wonderful, George,' Tosco said. 'You really caught the essence of your story.'

'I'm glad you think so,' George replied. 'I gave Heppenstall a couple of extra lines to clarify my message, but, of course, he didn't include them.'

'Don't worry,' Celia chimed in, 'everyone got your message. They'll be wringing their hands in Moscow and King Street as we speak.'

Av wasn't sure what she meant and asked, 'King Street?'

'That's where the Communist Party HQ is, where Harry Pollitt plots death to the Trotskyists,' said George. 'As long as it's not sabres they're rattling!' He seemed in a good mood. It had all gone off rather well.

Celia and Inez went through to the kitchen carrying their wine glasses and I followed them to top up mine and indulge in some girls' talk. I'd heard they were cousins who hailed from the landed gentry and were quite close to George, so there was a good chance of some juicy gossip. Celia looked about the same age as me but Inez was a good bit older. As I squeezed into the tiny kitchen where they were topping up their drinks, Inez asked Celia, 'How did you all get on at Arthur's place that Christmas?'

Celia looked unsure what to say when she saw me come in, 'We all had a good time. George is very good with Ricky, and we had some nice long walks and talks together.'

I started pouring myself some more wine.

'Yes, he's much better with children than most men,' Inez said. 'He really cares about the boy, but, of course, he's been very lonely since Eileen died.'

'That's true,' I butted in. 'He doesn't like to show how much it affected him, stiff upper lip and all that. But her death cut very deep.'

'Yes, after she died he called in on me as soon as he got back and was really upset,' said Inez. 'He was almost unrecognisable when I opened the door, standing there in his greatcoat. He looked so ill. I saw him off at the station when he was going up north to arrange her funeral. I think it was only then he realised how much she meant to him.'

I took a gulp of my drink. I'd heard she'd had an affair with George during the war and was still very stuck on him.

'He didn't say that much about her when we were in Wales but I certainly got the feeling he was desperately lonely,' Celia said. 'Arthur was doing his best impression of a matchmaker up there and…' she hesitated. 'Can you keep a secret?' Inez and I nodded vigorously. 'Well, he wrote and proposed to me after we got back.'

Inez looked disappointed, but tried not to show it. 'Why, you must have been over the moon, dear… But still you turned him down?' To be honest, I also felt a bit let down by this news. So, George had his sights on other attractive young women as well as me?

'It was difficult. Although I like him and adore little Ricky, I couldn't really see us together. I was just getting over Roger, and besides, there was too big an age gap between us. Of course, I tried to break it to him as gently as possible, so we could stay friends.' Celia replied.

Inez recovered her composure. She was about the same age as George and she was still pretty looking, but she'd put on a lot of weight and was no match for Celia's looks. She'd written a couple of novels and could probably hold her own with George in discussions of a literary nature, but I really don't think she stood a chance. 'I can understand that,' she said. 'He doesn't keep well these days and you don't want to be a widow at your age.'

'Well, strangely enough, he was very frank about that and even suggested I might like to be a literary widow if things didn't work out for him. It wasn't that romantic a proposal, to be honest,' Celia replied. He's still punting the same line, I thought. Men don't change.

'His loneliness runs very deep, you know, right back to prep school… But we better go back through,' Inez suggested. 'We don't want them thinking we're talking about them, do we now?' We all laughed and took our glasses through. She'd found out what she wanted to know. And I'd got more juicy gossip than I bargained for.

A few weeks later George came over to my flat with a nice bottle of red wine and some bottles of beer in hand and we weren't long in polishing them off. As the night wore on I got more and more tipsy and let him lie out beside me on the sofa. A big mistake. He started stroking my neck and tried to kiss me but I shrugged him off and sat up.

'Have you decided whether to stay on in London?' I asked.

'I've been thinking a lot about it. And I'd love to see more of you, but, between the smog and the cold, London's killing me. Are you sure you won't come to Jura?'

Bloody Jura. 'It's just not my kind of place, George. I didn't really think you'd stay. But you know I can't give up my life here.'

'Maybe we'll find a way one day. Until then we'll both be unhappy.'

'No one's ever completely happy.'

'Yes, but whatever I write, it's always a failure to me. It's never as good as I hoped it would be when I started out. And when it's finished, other people just drag me down with their false praise.'

Drag me down. Why did he have to say that? It brought it all back, the thing that troubled me most in the whole wide world. But I couldn't stop myself. 'I know all about being dragged down by others,' I told him. It all came back as if it was yesterday. I suppose it must have been the drink, but that night I told him my deepest secret.

'Once I almost drowned in a Swiss lake when the boat I was

in capsized in a sudden squall. None of my three friends could swim and one of them panicked and tried to drag me down with him. He grabbed my legs and pulled me under. I tried to fight him off but he wouldn't let go.' I could feel the tears welling up in me. 'The only way I could get free was to hold him down until he loosened his grip. I can still see that look in his eyes as he drifted away… I was the only one who survived.' I burst into floods of tears. George put his arm round me and tried to comfort me. He could sometimes be a decent old sort. Gradually my sobbing subsided and my tears began to dry up.

'How long ago was this?' George asked tenderly.

'It must have been about ten years ago. We were all in our late teens. That's why I find it difficult ever to be perfectly happy.' I could feel the tears coming again.

He gave me a squeeze, looked me in the eyes and said, 'I think I understand you better now, Sonia. I've killed people too, and I don't just mean fascists. But we must try not to let others drag us down.'

I often wondered what he meant by that and it was only years later that I found out from Cyril that he'd put some kind of curse on another boy at Eton and the boy died when very young. George could be really superstitious at times. Well, we sat like that for long enough until I became very sleepy. But thank goodness I knew better than to let him stay over, however caring he'd been. I went over to the sideboard and took out a bottle of brandy I'd bought for him. I handed it to him and said, 'This'll help to keep you warm on Jura.'

Chapter 9

SOMEHOW GEORGE, AV and Ricky managed to get through that hellish winter in London. He couldn't wait to get back to Jura, and so, at the first sign of spring, they were back on the long road to Barnhill. It took him quite some time to get over the extreme cold of the city that had seeped into his bones and sapped his strength. Jura wasn't as cold as London had been, but it hardly stopped raining that first week back. Yet again he threw himself into hard, manual labour; digging his garden, tearing down corrugated iron sheets from the side of the house and building a large wooden henhouse. But, as before, he overdid it, and within a week he had to take to his bed to recover. Even then, he went back to his novel and wrote well into the night, lying in late and, after breakfast and doing a few chores downstairs, retiring to his room to write some more.

Late one morning Av came into his bedroom as he lay snuffling and wheezing in bed. Ricky trailed in behind her and sat on his father's bed.

'Another long lie then?' Av sounded disapproving.

'I was up late writing.'

'Well, I've had a letter from Humph to say that Hen, Jane and Lucy are going to come in August.'

George brightened up, 'That's good news.' Ricky bounced up and down on the bed and George smiled and ruffled his hair but made no effort to get up. Av left them to it. Ricky found some blank paper and a pencil on his father's desk and started scribbling whilst George lay daydreaming, a smile on his lips.

A drift of bluebells shivered in the wind. Winston Smith walked towards them through an old silver birch wood somewhere in southern England. Julia, a beautiful young woman who wore a scarlet sash tight over her blue overalls and looked like Sonia, walked beside him. They stopped and he picked a bunch of the bluebells. They walked deeper into the wood but he kept looking around and above him until they came to a clearing and sat down.

'It's safe to talk now. There are no hidden microphones here,' Julia said.

He gave her the bunch of bluebells. 'For you.'

She smiled. 'Why, thank you.'

'What's your name?'

'Julia.'

'Where do you work?'

'Oh, I'm in the fiction department churning out porn for the proles. As soon as I saw you I knew you were against the Party. I hate all it stands for.'

'Well you certainly fooled me. I thought you were one of their zealots.'

'That's what you were meant to think,' she laughed.

He lay back enjoying the sun that shone through the birches and created shifting patterns on the grass. This is what life was meant to be like. Why couldn't it always be like this?

He looked into her eyes. Slowly she moved her lips towards his and put her tongue in his mouth. He lost himself and his world in her kiss. He pressed her down on the grass amongst the bluebells, caressed her and carefully opened the buttons of her overalls. Suddenly he was certain that they were being watched. He stopped and sat up.

Early that summer a young ex-army officer came to lodge with the Darrochs at Kinuachdrachd. Having given up studying agriculture at the University of Glasgow, Bill Dunn came to Jura to try his hand at farming. He had placed an advert in *The Oban Times* looking for work and the Fletchers took him up on it. He was young, strong, and was so keen to make a go of farming that he worked for nothing except his keep. He'd lost a leg during the war but that didn't stop him getting around as fast as the next man. George had a wry smile to himself about the phrase 'lost a leg'. It was as if Bill had gone out one day and mislaid it. Soon Bill was helping out at Barnhill since George was working on his novel most of that summer. He and Av seemed to get on well.

After writing for much of the day, George liked nothing better than going out fishing in his little rowing boat. He would go down to the bay, start up the outboard and head out as dusk approached. It was early in the season, but the mackerel thrashed and glistened a silvery blue as George reeled them in, several dancing on one line. His old friend Richard, who had come up for the summer, was also catching some.

'You know, Richard, this is the best time to fish. The water's boiling with them.' George picked three off his line and quickly killed them. He was in his element.

'You don't get beauties like these down south.' Richard unhooked his. He was becoming as enthusiastic about fishing as George. Less experienced than him, he copied his method of breaking their necks. They cast their lines again and sat in silence taking in the sheer beauty of the Sound of Jura whilst waiting for the fish to bite. A grey heron stood silently on the rocky shore, lit up by the dying sun.

'What more could you ask than this?' George broke the quietness, gesturing to the sunset over the water and the hills known as the Paps of Jura to the west. Richard stroked his stubbly beard and nodded in agreement as George continued,

'I've been meaning to say, the farm needs looking after and I'm just not well enough to do it. I also need to get on with my book, so Bill Dunn's been helping me out. What do you say we ask him to take it on?'

'Well, he seems keen enough. But do you think he would be able to, what with his one leg and all?'

'Oh, he's mobile enough… and he's certainly keen. But I think I'd need to invest some money in the place to give him a fighting chance.'

'Well, I don't mind helping out. I could put, say, a thousand into it to buy some decent transport and some tools and seeds.'

'Could you? That would be marvellous, Richard. It would take a huge weight off my mind.' He stared at the water swirling around his line. 'You know, it's good to get away from the book for a while.'

'Painting's the same. Even up here, surrounded by all this beauty, it doesn't come easy.'

'Yes, but the book's taking me over. I can't think straight…' George hesitated and took a deep breath. 'Richard, I'm dying… And I don't know how long I've got… I must finish the beastly thing while I still can.'

Richard looked shocked. 'Surely not. What's wrong?'

Looking over his shoulder and back, George told him, 'Strictly off the record, I think it's TB.'

George's line tugged away from him as he reeled it in. He pulled another two mackerel on board, removed the hooks and this time thumped their heads off the wooden sides of the boat as if in protest at his fate.

'That's terribly bad news, Eric. Have you seen a doctor?'

'Only once. In London last year. He was useless. Told me it was gastritis. I'd like to live at least another ten years…' He cast his line again.

Richard didn't know what to say. 'But, surely…'

'Long enough to see Ricky going to a good school. I'd like

him to be a farmer when he grows up, perhaps the only job there will be left after the atom bombs. He's good with his hands,' George continued. He looked at his own calloused hands gripping the rod. 'Sonia wants me to return to London but I don't think I could face living there again.'

'Couldn't she come here?'

'I'm afraid she'd be rather a fish out of water up here. She's very much a city girl.'

Richard tried to smile at his friend's gallows humour.

'Look, if anything should happen to me, as my literary executor, you'll know what's worth publishing and what's not. Don't let them mess about with anything. If I don't finish the book, destroy it.' He was very definite about this.

'Of course. But let's hope it won't come to that. You've got plenty of life in you yet. Unlike these poor buggers.' Richard nodded at the growing pile of fish between them. He got a tug on his line and reeled in another mackerel which he killed as before.

'More than anything I want to finish it. I hate the petty dictators and their apologists with a vengeance and this book could really do a job on them. It sums up just about everything I've been thinking and saying for years. And I don't intend to give it up without a fight.'

'I realise that, Eric, and I know how strongly you feel about all this, but your health comes first. You must look after yourself as well.'

'I know, I know… Well, anyway, the cat's out the bag now. And speaking of which…' George took out a bottle of brandy and two glasses from his fishing bag. He poured a glass for each of them. 'Sonia gave me this. This'll cheer us up. *Slàinte Mhor.*'

'Your good health… And to you… and Sonia.'

I've known for a long time that I had TB. Perhaps I somehow caught it in Spain. The conditions in the trenches were pretty wretched. At any rate Eileen's brother Laurence was a specialist in TB and he diagnosed it after I came back. That's why Eileen and I went to Morocco in 1938 just as war clouds were gathering over Europe. Laurence thought that the dry climate would help me and it did. The TB seemed to clear up after that and, although my health was never good, it wasn't until after the war that it came back. That idiot doctor that Susan called out said it was gastritis but I knew I'd had a haemorrhage of some kind and the cause was almost certainly the return of my TB. Naturally, I didn't want to make a fuss and kept my suspicions to myself. I had a young baby to think about and, in any case, I thought that a summer spent on Jura would make all the difference. And it did – until that bloody awful winter in London practically did me in. The worst in living memory they said – more like dying memory if you ask me. When I did get back to Jura in April I was so ill I was in bed for a week. And although I got better as the weather got warmer, I still tire easily. It's prevented me getting on as far as I'd hoped with this ghastly book but I'm determined to finish the first draft this year. I was going to say 'if it kills me' but that might be tempting fate.

People tell me that my chain smoking can't be helping, but there's no evidence for that. In fact the tobacco companies say it's good for you because it relaxes your muscles and relieves stress. But they would say that wouldn't they? Just about everyone smokes these days and it doesn't seem to make any difference to whether you live or die. I'm certainly not a hedonist of the dedicated Koestler type, but you might as well have some simple pleasures in life, otherwise what's the point? The thing is I know I'm on my way out, and the two most important things in my life are to finish this damn book and to make sure Ricky has the best chance in life I can give him.

Richard is the closest friend I've got, he gave me a break by helping me get my first essays printed in *Adelphi* all those years ago, and I know I can rely on him to carry out my wishes. That's why I had to tell him the truth because if I were to keel over one day before I finish the book I don't want some useless hack finishing it for me. Better to destroy it than let that happen. Av knows how to handle Ricky all right and I feel confident she'd bring him up here the way I'd want him to be raised and would send him to a good school when the time came. I haven't told her my fears yet since I'm determined to live as long as I can to see my son growing up.

There was only one thing that George liked better than sea fishing and that was fresh water fishing. That August he took his nephew Henry to fish some lochans high in the hills on the west coast of Jura. It amused George and the rest of the family to call him Hen but he had seen plenty of action as a young officer in the tank corps and could more than handle himself. The sun was high and the lochan shimmered in the stillness that day as they caught plenty of trout.

'You know we're probably the first to fish these waters for many a year,' George said.

'Well, the fish must be bored and want to get caught the way they're queuing up to bite,' Hen replied.

'Bored or not, they'll make a tasty meal tonight. The girls *will* be pleased.'

When they felt they'd caught enough, they packed their gear and headed back over the hills to the coast. Bare rock glinted everywhere through stunted grass. Even the red deer could hardly survive up here. It was hard going to walk on but what was a little hardship when they had caught so many? As they strode downhill towards a bothy in Glengarrisdale Bay, Ricky came out and ran up to meet them. He opened his father's fishing bag, took out a trout and, to everyone's amusement, shouted 'Fish!' He laughed and danced as it slithered out of his hand. George picked it up, dusted it down and put it back in his bag. The men went into the bothy to change.

Inside the cool, dark room was an earthen floor and makeshift beds with heaps of blankets strewn on top.

Av came from the shore with some driftwood in her arms and shouted, 'Jane! Lucy! Would you collect some more wood for the fire?'

Jane Dakin was a good looking young woman in her twenties and she and her fourteen-year-old sister Lucy were nude sunbathing on the sand behind some rocks after skinny dipping in the freezing west coast waters. They giggled at the idea of collecting firewood in the nude but made a start on it.

George crossed over the rocks and was surprised and embarrassed to see them naked.

'Can I help?' he blurted out.

They laughed and Jane threw him some of her driftwood. 'Only if you get into the spirit of things, Uncle Eric.' She gestured to him to take his clothes off. He smiled at the idea but didn't oblige. The girls put their clothes back on and all three of them started collecting wood from along the shoreline.

When they returned to the bothy, George asked Av, 'Why didn't you get your kit off as well?'

'I did… When you weren't here!' she laughed and pushed him so hard he spilled his pile of wood on to the ground and had to scramble about to pick it up. That night, skin tingling from a long day in the sun, they gathered round a campfire. Sparks flew up into the clear night sky. The trout sizzled on sticks over the blaze and everyone seemed in good spirits. George poked the fire with a stick.

'If only we could live like this all the time, we wouldn't need London or governments or atom bombs.' George was happy.

'Trust you to mention the bomb!' Av joked. They all laughed. It wasn't very often that Av and George enjoyed a laugh together.

'But it wouldn't be much fun when it rains… And the toilets here aren't exactly the Savoy!' said Lucy, holding her nose.

But George was having none of it. 'It's an island paradise. Look at the stars up there,' he pointed and they gazed at them in wonder. 'And anyway, a bit of hardship's good for you... Where else could you get fish like these?' He carefully took the fish from the fire and levered them off the sticks on to their plates. They all tucked into their meal. Trout had never tasted better.

Next morning Av and Jane decided to walk back to Barnhill to make a start on the hay making and helped George, Hen, Lucy and Ricky push off from the shore in their small motor boat. From the bow, Lucy and Ricky waved to them on shore as they put their boots back on and set off. George steered in the stern, Hen was midships, surrounded by blankets, fishing rods, plates and utensils.

The boat puttered steadily along the coast and George pointed out a great northern diver and some guillemots to the others. He steered them into the Gulf of Corryvreckan. Its currents and whirlpools were the most dangerous and notorious anywhere around the British coast and it was classed as unnavigable on Admiralty charts. To the north the Scarba cliffs rose sheer from the sea. The Great Race, as the powerful tidal current was known, buffeted the little boat from side to side. George gripped the tiller more tightly and looked puzzled. He had checked the tide tables and this wasn't supposed to happen. Gradually the rushing eddies became more violent around them and waves started splashing over the side. Ricky seemed to be enjoying this. 'Up-down, splish-splosh,' he said happily. George was becoming more and more alarmed but tried not to show it. Suddenly there was a loud crack and the outboard engine was sucked over the stern.

'Get the oars out, Hen!' George shouted, pointing to his chest. 'I can't help you, of course.'

Hen struggled to get the oars into the rowlocks and rowed his hardest but it hardly moved. All he could do was try to keep it on an even keel. They were at the mercy of small whirlpools as waves surged higher in all directions around them. A seal's head popped up near them.

'Curious thing about seals, very inquisitive creatures,' George said in a matter of fact way.

Hen turned round to Lucy and they looked at each other in disbelief. The currents and eddies whipped them from side to side and Ricky laughed. This was great fun. Slowly they were driven by the current towards a rocky islet. Hen shipped the oars and slipped off his army boots as they drew close, but the swell raised and lowered the boat unsteadily in front of a low cliff. Waiting for the right moment, Hen leapt on to a ledge, the boat's painter in hand. As he did so, the boat capsized and tipped the others under it. Hen stared aghast. There was no one in sight. Underneath the boat George stretched to reach Ricky but the current pulled the boy away from him. Desperately, George dived down to try to find him. Alone with the upturned boat, Hen peered anxiously into the seething torrent. No one. After what seemed like a lifetime, Lucy suddenly surfaced. She was gasping for breath but reached a hand out to him and he dragged her ashore. No one else appeared. Only the racing waters and the clamour of kittiwakes.

Suddenly, George broke the surface with Ricky under his arm. 'I've got Ricky all right,' he spluttered, gripping the side of the boat. Ricky held on tight to him, too shocked to cry. George held the boy out to Hen who hauled him onto the rock. He was the last to be helped out of the water, staggering and coughing. Hen secured the boat to the rock with the painter. They climbed up, collapsed onto flatter ground and looked at each other, amazed at their narrow escape.

George took his lighter out of his pocket and put it on a rock to dry in the sun. 'That was a close one.'

'It certainly was,' Hen agreed, 'We've lost just about everything. But at least we all survived.'

'Well, we must find something to eat. I'll see if I can find any birds' eggs and wood for a fire. I won't be long,' George announced as he trooped off.

'But we ate only an hour ago,' Lucy said, surprised at her uncle's eccentric behaviour.

'Maybe he thinks he's Robinson Crusoe,' Hen laughed.

When George returned he told them, 'Puffins are extraordinary birds, they make their nests in burrows. The place is covered in them. I saw some baby seagulls, but didn't have the heart to... you know...'

They lit a fire and peeled off some of their clothes to dry them. George found a potato in his pocket which they roasted for Ricky to eat. Father and son almost seemed to enjoy this unexpected adventure. Eventually the Corry subsided. After several hours a small boat appeared in the distance coming into the Gulf to the east of Scarba. They all waved their clothes in the air and shouted to attract its attention. It was a creel fishing boat with some passengers on board. As it came close, a man threw a rope ashore which Hen secured to a rock. One by one they clambered upside down along the rope to the boat. George carried Ricky clinging to his front. Hen was the last to go, dragging the empty boat behind him, then tying it to the stern of the other boat. The boat's skipper told them he was Donald Mackay from Toberonochy on the nearby Isle of Luing. 'You're lucky I was taking these good folk out today,' he told George. 'And what were you doing out here at that state of the tide?'

'Well, I did consult the tide tables.' George looked shamefaced.

'Ach well, we've all made mistakes reading them,' Donald reassured him. 'And where were you headed?'

'Back to Barnhill.'

'Of course. You'll be that writer fellow that stays there. Mr Blair, isn't it?'

'That's right.' The local grapevine again.

'Well, I better be getting you all back before you catch your death of cold.'

Donald's small boat was full to bursting as it chugged slowly along the coast. George spotted a little bay up ahead and told him, 'It's all right, if you can drop us ashore here, we'll walk back the rest of the way.'

Hen was fizzing since, unlike George, he and Lucy had no shoes. Donald landed them and their boat on a shingle beach and George thanked him. As they dragged the empty boat up beyond the high water mark, George told them, 'We'll come back for it another day.' Soon he was striding out the three miles to Barnhill with Ricky on his shoulders whilst Hen and Lucy hobbled along behind. When eventually they got back to the house, Av and Jane were making hay in a nearby field. Av shouted to them, 'What took you so long?'

Chapter 10

I REMEMBER ONE of the chats Netta and I had about George back then as if it was yesterday. Glasses of wine in hand, we were staring at a painting of a skeletal, grumpy looking man that looked a bit like him. There wasn't much of a turnout for Bill Coldstream's latest exhibition preview, the tiny gallery was almost empty. My dear friends, the Euston Road painters, were no longer flavour of the month, and these days even Bill's promise of free drink couldn't fill the place. I'd gone with Netta more out of duty than inclination, but, then again, there was the free booze.

'What do you make of George?' I asked her.

'This guy?' She glanced at the painting.

'No, the real one.' I realised she was teasing me.

'Well, you know him much better than I do. But what about Maurice, isn't he the one for you?'

'He's the love of my life. But unfortunately I don't think he'll ever leave his wife and daughter.'

We sauntered on past more paintings, sipping as we went.

'George is a lot older, but that's no bad thing,' Netta said. 'He's successful enough these days, if not quite the genius you're after... But you know what these artist types are like. All they want is a skivvy to iron, cook and clean after them.'

I followed her glance to some bohemian types drinking near the entrance. One of the better looking ones gave her the once over.

'I know. I can still smell the cabbage and unwashed nappies

at his place,' I giggled and she laughed. This wine wasn't that bad. 'Mind you, he's not the worst. He's quite practical and he's also good with his son... But his writing comes before everything... And he's very secretive. Especially about his health.'

'I know, these political types are all cloak and dagger. Robert's the same. He still seems angry about the war, as if it all happened just to get at him.'

'But you're still enjoying married life, I hope?'

'Oh, it has its moments all right,' Netta winked at me. 'So far... It certainly has its compensations. But is George keeping any better these days?'

'He was skinnier than ever the last time I saw him. He seems determined to be a martyr to his book.' In truth, I was becoming more and more concerned about the way he neglected his health.

'If anyone can save him from himself it's you.'

'I couldn't give up everything for George. He wants to stay on Jura and you know I just couldn't face that kind of life. Far too uncivilised for me.'

We stopped in front of one of Bill's portraits of me from years ago when we were going out together. I looked pensive in it.

'Oh, it's just like you, moody as ever,' Netta laughed.

Just then Lucian Freud, another of my old flames, came over to greet us. He looked as gorgeous as ever with his fine features and mop of dark hair.

'Thank you for coming,' he said.

'I bet you say that to all the girls, Lucian!' I nudged Netta and we burst out laughing. Lucian's face went the colour of one of those blushing Renoir girls.

Not long after, I let Maurice sleep with me. I'd played him along as much as I could to keep him interested, but there comes a point when you have to let him have his way or you lose him. Of course, I'd invited him to my flat before but had always stopped him at the last minute. Well, tonight was his lucky night and, after supper and a few drinks, I took him into my bedroom and gave him what he wanted. He wasn't quite as elegant a lover as I'd hoped, but was certainly much more considerate than most of the others I'd had. If George was towards the workaday, 'get it in and get it over with' end of the spectrum, Maurice was nearer the opposite end where the seductive Casanovas of this world dwell. He took his time, tried to relax me with lots of sweet nothings, in French of course, and built steadily to a crashing climax. The French are definitely much more civilised lovers.

'*Enfin*!' he shouted as he climaxed and collapsed on top of me.

'What's worth having…' I suggested as he lay there for what seemed ages. He was squashing me so much I wriggled under him. He took the hint and prised himself off me on to his back.

He looked blissful. 'You certainly made me wait all right.' I moved to get up but he gripped my arm tightly. 'Don't go. Let me enjoy the moment.'

'I've got so much to do…'

He looked disappointed.

'If I got a job in Paris we could be together, couldn't we?' I asked him.

'Of course. Or I could come to London if I could get one here.'

'I'll ask Freddie Ayer if he's got anything he could offer you.'

At that he released my arm. I quickly got up and put on my favourite silk dressing gown. On my way to the bathroom I looked back. He lay daydreaming the way they all do after they get what they want.

* * *

That autumn, Bill Dunn moved into Barnhill from Kinauchdrachd. As George had said, his disability didn't stop him getting about the farm and he had started to knock it into shape. Every day he was up first thing seeing to the poultry and their only cow, then out in the fields all morning, only coming back at dinner time. Ricky tagged along behind him and tried to help in his own sweet little way. Bill found it easier to hirple about on his wooden peg leg rather than the aluminium foot he'd been given in hospital. All he needed, George thought, was a cocked hat and a parrot on his shoulder crying 'pieces of eight', and he could be Long John Silver. And Ricky could be Jim Hawkins, his cabin boy, following him around. The only problem for Cap'n Silver was that after the rain his peg leg often got stuck in the mud when he was out working in the fields. George would see him whirling like a windmill and cursing and swearing as he tried to extricate his wooden leg from some bog or other. But they came up with an unusual solution to this. With Ricky giggling as he tried to help, George fastened a small rubber tyre to Bill's peg leg to spread the weight and stop the peg sinking into the mud. After that he looked more like an alien out of an H.G. Wells science fiction tale than a famous pirate.

Strangely enough, Av's cooking seemed to improve after Bill moved in and she seemed different in some rather elusive way. She became much cheerier and took greater care about her appearance. George noticed that she and Bill seemed to get along really well and he became almost jealous of his sister's blossoming romance. Was he just being overprotective? After all, Av hadn't ever really had a boyfriend, as far as he knew. Well, anyway, he was too busy working on his novel to worry too much about it.

That September the house was packed with friends and neighbours who had come to help with the harvest. George got hold of a large bell tent which he put up at the side of the house where he could sleep out to escape the crowd and in the hope that the warm night air would do him good. It helped, but even the post-harvest party that Av and Bill put on for all the helpers didn't raise his spirits much. That wretched book was getting him down.

Once the hay had been stored in the large barn, Bill dug a series of trenches round the big field using a horse-drawn plough to start with, and manhandled dozens of red clay pipes into position to create drains. The drainage had been long in the planning and the pipes had to be brought to the island by boat and carefully unloaded by hand in case they broke. No sooner had he gone in for his dinner than Ricky got hold of a hammer and went round the field, ding-dong, happily smashing every single pipe. When Bill came out and saw what Ricky had done he was raging and charged back inside to get George to come out to see the damage. But instead of being annoyed with Ricky, George howled with laughter and took the boy inside for something to eat. Bill was so angry he would hardly speak to George for a week.

Having been the cause of the rift between the two men, however, it was Ricky who was to bring them together again. One day he was rummaging about in the garden and came across a different kind of pipe, a white clay one, abandoned by some long lost pipe smoker. He put it in his pocket and, after dinner that day, started rooting about in the fireplace, picking up cigarette ends thrown there by his father and stuffing them in the pipe.

'Can I have your lighter, Daddy?' he asked.

George and Bill looked at each other but didn't say a word. George held out the lighter round the back of his chair and Ricky took it. He tried flicking it the way his father did, but couldn't get it to work so he decided to go outside and try again. As soon as he left, the two men rushed to the window to watch the fun. Eventually Ricky got the pipe to light and began puffing contentedly on it. Next thing he was coughing and spluttering, and became violently sick. George and Bill thought this was hilarious.

'That should cure him,' laughed George.

'Aye, he'll not forget that in a hurry,' Bill chortled. The ice broken, he suggested, 'Do you fancy a beer?'

'It's a bit early, but why not? You only live once.' George sat back at the table while Bill got two bottles of beer and a couple of glasses from the milk room.

'He's quite a lad is Ricky,' Bill said. 'He's not afraid of anything.'

'There's nothing much to fear living here, apart from the adders. But it's good to see him playing outside all day and trying to help you with the farm.'

'He does well. He doesn't get in the way that much and he's keen to learn. He'll maybe make a farmer yet. What age is he now?'

'Nearly three and a half.'

'I must get him a wee something. When's his birthday?'

'The fourteenth of May.'

'What? And he was born in 1944? Why, that's the day an anti-personnel mine blew half my leg off in Sicily!' said Bill, astonished.

'So, the day he came into the world, your foot left it?' George joked.

'You could say that all right. That's extraordinary. I'll drink to that.' Bill clinked his glass with George's. And from that moment on Ricky had a special place in Bill's heart as well as in George's.

* * *

George lay pale and listless in bed. Summer was long gone and he'd thrown himself into writing the book to try to finish the first draft by the end of the year. Days came and went as he typed away in his room, overcome by a sense of despair at the nightmare future he envisaged for the world if people didn't become aware of the reality of what was taking place around them. He'd had this book in his head for over four years now and early on he'd sketched an outline of it in his notebook. It was to become part of a trilogy that included *Animal Farm*, which he'd managed to polish off in a few months. But now his sole aim was to finish this one at all costs.

As I see it, if my fears are realised, the future will be based on the division of the world into three spheres of influence, along the lines of those decided by Roosevelt, Churchill and Stalin at Yalta. The big powers will all possess the atom bomb and will threaten to use it against each other, but won't be able to. And so to keep their arms industries going and their inhabitants in a constant state of alarm, they will engage in a series of smaller wars in different parts of the world, and flying bombs will be dropped randomly on their cities just as Hitler did on London. A kind of permanent war economy. Britain will become a subservient part of the American empire which will be ruled by a one party state, with an inner party elite at the top of a pyramid of power and the mass of proles at the bottom being manipulated and controlled by them. Having seen how totalitarian regimes in Italy, Germany, Spain and Russia maintained their power, I want to show how their methods could be applied in a perverted version of a socialist state in the kind of Britain that my readers are familiar with. One that is recognisable as wartime London with its shortages, its rationing, its blitzed buildings and shattered people. The party's methods of maintaining power will be all-important: mass rallies and film shows at which citizens are whipped up into hatred of perceived enemies such as Jews and Asians. Children spying and informing on their parents and neighbours. Propaganda being pumped out constantly in the media. Thought control and leader worship. The rewriting of history and expunging from the record those who played a part in it. A Ministry of Truth that can create unpersons.

I can see that there is nothing more fundamental in all of this than the methods to be employed to rob people of their sense of right and wrong, of what is true and what is false. Goebbels and Hitler knew this and Stalin learnt from them. There will be organised lying on an industrial scale and the distortion and disappearance of objective truth. Language itself will be distorted, denigrated and used to control minds. Newspeak will be developed to reduce the number of words available and to make it impossible for people to think differently. We can already see this with the spread of Basic English and in the language of the advertising world. Words will be turned into their opposites and lose all meaning: war is peace, freedom is slavery, ignorance is strength. Television sets will be turned into telescreens which will spy endlessly on everyone both inside and outside their homes. Love and sexual activity will be seen as a danger to the party and its control and, as such, prohibited to citizens. There will be agent provocateurs who will entrap rebels against the system. And an all-powerful secret police who will arrest, torture and murder people without anyone knowing.

My hero in the book, Winston Smith, will become aware of all this and join an underground resistance. He will realise his dream of making love to Julia, a bold, desirable young woman. If I cannot have Sonia, at least Winston can have Julia. Winston will see himself as the last man in Europe who sees the way things really are. But, once they are arrested and tortured, he will be betrayed by Julia and will, in turn, betray her. And in the end, like all the rest, he will come to love Big Brother. All life ends in failure. Death is the ultimate end. I can see clear signs of this nightmare already happening around me whilst others are sleeping the deep sleep of complacent England. I feel that if I can take the nature of this nightmare future to extremes through satire, I may be able to jolt people out of their complacency.

One of the reasons I want to warn everyone about the dangers of a police state is that I have personally experienced some of its methods. The police raided my house just before the war and took away banned books written by Henry Miller. I know that letters are opened, phones are tapped and MI5 keeps files on potential subversives like me. I've come to feel, like Winston, that I too am the last man in Europe since it seems that I alone am aware of the way the world is heading and what will happen if people are not wakened from their political slumbers and shown the extreme dangers of what is coming. I've written about some of these things in my essays and newspaper columns, but I know that not many people read essays and today's papers become tomorrow's fish supper wrappers. Surely, if I can finish this book, they will read it and pay attention to its message? The only hope lies in the proles.

All of these thoughts have been going round and round in my head all those years in London, and now they haunt me here on Jura. I've delayed and delayed finishing it and now my health is deteriorating fast. I must complete the first draft this year and edit it early next year to get it out there. It's absolutely imperative.

Av came into his bedroom. 'How're you feeling?'

'I'm done in. It feels like the flu.'

'That dip in the Corry didn't help. You must rest. I'll get you a hot drink.'

She tucked him in and left. He reached for his notebook but was too weak to write. He turned over instead and imagined another scene from his novel.

Winston and Julia lay in bed together in a bedroom above a junk shop. He was thinking how wonderful it was to be able to escape from the watchful eyes of Big Brother and to be here, entirely alone with her. He also registered how amazing it was to be able to make love. He was eating the forbidden fruit. He reached over for her but this time she was having none of it. 'I'm hungry,' she pushed him off and got up to look out the window. He lay there admiring the curves of her young body, relishing the moment. He decided to join her. Arm in arm in their underwear, they gazed outside. In the slum of a backyard a stout woman was hanging out diapers on a line. She was singing an old music hall song.

'You know, the proles are the only hope,' he said.

'There is no hope, they are the dead.'

'You are the dead!' A harsh male voice came from the wall behind them. A clatter of boots in the yard and ladders rattled on the wall below the window.

'The house is surrounded! Remain exactly where you are! Make no movement until you are ordered!' the voice instructed.

Winston and Julia were transfixed. A ladder crashed through the window. Men in black uniforms armed with truncheons filled the room.

***

George woke up with a start. Sweat streamed from his face. His pyjamas were soaked through. 'We are the dead.' he muttered. He opened his eyes and saw the blurred lights of a Christmas tree. Tatty Christmas decorations drooped across the ceiling. He heard the carol *In the Bleak Midwinter* being sung by a group of carol singers at the far end of the long room.

> *In the bleak midwinter, frosty wind made moan,*
> *earth stood hard as iron, water like a stone;*
> *snow had fallen, snow on snow, snow on snow,*
> *in the bleak midwinter, long ago.*

A tear dripped from his eye. Where was he? How did he get here? He thought he remembered. They had dragged him and

Julia away from their secret room above a junk shop and taken him to the Ministry of Truth. Gradually he sensed that some-one else was there. Sonia sat in silence by his bedside. George was delirious. His head jerked from side to side as he spoke in short bursts. 'We're the last ones… The only hope… I'm sorry you couldn't come… But you were always with me.' Slowly he became calmer and more aware. 'Where am I?'

'Hairmyres Hospital near Glasgow,' she replied.

'I thought I was somewhere else. Ah, I remember now. How did you know I was here?'

'Paul Potts told me.'

'Good old Potts,' he mumbled. 'They say I've got TB. I'm not allowed to write anything.'

'I know. When you're better, you must come to London and I can look after you.'

'Let's never be apart again.'

'I'll try to be here for you.' She lifted his hand and squeezed it. He smiled weakly. What a place to be at Christmas, he thought. But at least she was here with him. Or was she? It wasn't like her to come all that way north from London and he only saw her once. Had he dreamt that too?

The days and the weeks went by with him just lying there. If Sonia was there she had now gone back to London and he was alone again with his books. But even reading was a struggle. His typewriter was taken away from him and his right arm was put in plaster to stop him writing. The initial treatment he received was to collapse his lung by sticking a rod down his throat, pulling the muscle aside, exposing the nerve and tweak-ing it with a pair of forceps. The pain was excruciating but his diaphragm jumped and was paralysed for months. A special machine then pumped air into his abdomen through a hollow needle about three inches long. A local anaesthetic was used the first time but after that the doctor just stuck it in. George came to dread this procedure and couldn't relax on the operating table when they wheeled him in. It felt like he was in a torture chamber. Shades of the Spanish Inquisition. But he never complained, or even gasped at the pain. A true stoic, he suffered in silence.

In February he wrote to David Astor saying his specialist had told him it would speed his recovery if a new drug called streptomycin could be obtained. He suggested that, with his American connections, David might be able to arrange to buy it and he could pay him for it. David visited him and spoke about this to the consultant, Bruce Dick, who explained that it would require a special licence to be used, but it could help George. David contacted Aneurin Bevan, George's former editor at *Tribune* who was by then Minister of Health, who gave permission for the drug to be imported. When it arrived, George got one injection each day and it seemed to help at first. But soon he developed a fearsome allergic reaction. All over his body his skin became red and itchy, he couldn't stop scratching it until it bled. His mouth became inflamed and his lips were almost glued together so that he could hardly eat. Ulcers appeared, his eyes were bloodshot, and a lot of his hair fell out. It must have been caused by the high doses of the new drug he was receiving. He felt like a guinea pig and thought of it as a bit like sinking the ship to get rid of the rats. A tube protruded from his mouth and he was in terrible pain. But he didn't cry out.

O'Brien, a fierce looking tormentor dressed in black, slowly walked round his bed. He had come from the future. 'In the future there will be no wives and no friends... There will be no loyalty except loyalty to the party... There will be no love except love of Big Brother.' George was terrified. His whole body shuddered.

George's consultant appeared by his bedside. Bruce Dick wore a smart, grey suit over his giant frame and spoke confidently. 'How are we today Mr Blair?'

'Not bad, but I'm still having nightmares and I'm missing Ricky terribly.'

'Only to be expected. I'm afraid your disease is too infectious for you to see your son. You must be patient,' he smiled at his overused joke and listened to George's chest with his stethoscope.

'I don't want Sonia to see me like this.'

'Don't worry. She won't. I think we'll have to stop your injections. These side effects must be from an allergic reaction to them.' He left as quickly as he arrived.

George struggled to take his typed manuscript from his bedside cabinet. He tried to make changes to it with a ball point pen but dropped it, exhausted. The pen clattered on the floor. He removed the tube and struggled out of bed to retrieve his pen. These kinds of pens were new and difficult to obtain. He didn't want some nurse standing on it. He caught sight of himself in a long mirror. A skeletal shadow of a man. Could this be him? This would be how Winston would look after they had tortured him for weeks on end. A broken wreck who'd lost all self-respect and would do anything to make the pain go away.

It took months for George to regain some weight and for his hair to grow back, but eventually he was able to sit up in bed and to make changes to his manuscript with his ballpoint. It became almost undecipherable except to himself. He was even allowed to type again, smoking a roll-up in the corner of his mouth as ever. He smoked nearly all the time. Lots of people did in hospitals in those days, even the doctors. He shared a double room with another patient who didn't seem bothered about the noise of his typewriter. Perhaps because he was the editor of the *Hotspur* comic which D.C. Thomson produced along with the *Rover*, the *Dandy* and the *Beano*. George took a great interest in the world of comics. They got on well together.

'A strange thing, you know,' George told his neighbour. 'I believe Mr Dick was on the other side from me in the war in Spain. Over there he would have tried to kill me if he could, and I him. But now he's trying to keep me alive.'

'Aye the world's a gey strange place, all right,' his neighbour replied. 'I wonder if either of us'll get out of this place alive.'

At long last summer came. George and Sonia walked through the rolling green grounds of the hospital. It was made up of a scattering of small buildings, built on a hill, all of which gave easy access to the outdoors. A sanatorium really, 500 feet above sea level, near the village of East Kilbride, well away from the noxious tenement slums of Glasgow. However, the village was changing. The area had been chosen as the site of a New Town to house some of the city's slum dwellers, and builders had started to create a market garden town something like Welwyn Garden City. The locals dubbed it Polo Mint City because of all the roundabouts that were being built for cars. Some of the other patients would grumble to George about the changes that were happening around the village. But, remembering the Gorbals slums, he considered it was a small price to pay to enable people to have good quality houses and a healthier place to bring up children. He thought how much better it was for Ricky to grow up in the clean, fresh air of Jura than drab, polluted London with its smokestacks and its smog, its crowded streets and its traffic. George looked a lot better now. His hair had grown back and he'd put on some weight. He felt more like his old self and couldn't wait to get on with finishing his book.

'Please don't go back to Barnhill. Come south where you can recuperate and we can see more of each other,' Sonia said.

George hesitated. He knew this was a crucial decision he had to make: to go south to recover his health and be closer to Sonia or to return to Jura to finish his book. He wanted her so much but he knew she didn't love him. Down there he would also be closer to doctors and medical attention if he had a relapse and it would be easier for his friends to visit him. But he knew what would happen if he did. He would be back where he started, engulfed by all kinds of demands on his time from editors and friends. Ricky wouldn't have the same freedom he had on Jura, his development would go backwards not forwards. But, above all, his novel wouldn't get finished. He had revised some of his first draft lying in his hospital bed, but now the manuscript was an absolute mess and it would take all his concentration to sort out. It was by far the most difficult book he'd ever written. But he must finish it. Only on Jura could he exorcise his demons, put an end to his nightmares and present to the world his vision of the most dire of futures that it was sleepwalking into. If returning to Jura was a big risk in order to achieve that, then it was one he felt he had no option but to take. Besides, he'd been ill before and had always recovered. His health was a price worth paying. He'd been thinking about this decision for months and now it was time to tell Sonia.

'I'm afraid, if I did, I'd get drawn into the same old rut of articles and reviews.'

They sat down on a wooden bench and enjoyed the warmth of the sun. Patients and visitors played croquet on the lawn. He took from his satchel a thick sheaf of papers and leafed through them. The typed pages were covered in pen marks. He told her how Winston and Julia had escaped to the country and how it reminded Winston of a dream he had of a place he called the Golden Country.

A thrush landed on a bush near George and Sonia. It began to sing so beautifully they stopped their conversation and listened. George recounted how Winston lost himself in a bird's beguiling song.

'There's probably no point in me trying to persuade you,' Sonia said. 'But that damn book will be the death of you if you go back to Jura. Come to London with me.'

George was unsure. 'I'd love to, but I can't stop thinking about my book.'

Sonia looked deeply disappointed.

George turned over in bed and remembered where he was. It was so good to see Sonia again. He could remember their conversation, the croquet players, the bench where they sat, the song of the thrush. But had it really happened?

August 1948, Barnhill, Isle of Jura

George looked pale and fragile as he dug the earth with a large fork and weeded his vegetable patch at Barnhill. His lettuces and potatoes were fully grown. Av had put netting round them to keep the rabbits off. Ricky was old enough now to be able to help him by picking up the weeds and putting them in a wheelbarrow. George patted him on the back, pleased to have his son with him after all those months of separation. The boy was taking to country life the way he'd hoped he would. Av came out and grabbed the fork from him.

'You're supposed to take it easy, Eric. You know what the doctor said, you have to look after yourself.'

'I'll try,' he mumbled, unsure what to do now.

'Come on, I've something to show you.' She took him through the house to the main byre. Ricky toddled along behind. Inside she showed them a metal cage in which she'd caught two large rats and two small ones. The rats showed their teeth menacingly at George. Horrified, he jumped back. Ricky was startled too and started crying, so George shielded him from them. That night George lay in bed and could hardly move. He wheezed and coughed up blood into his handkerchief. He struggled to get up. He staggered over to the typewriter on his desk and started clacking away. He wrote the scene where Winston is taken to Room 101 where he will experience his worst nightmare. George smiled as he remembered the meetings that were held in a room with that number when he worked at the BBC – his little in-joke at the Corporation's expense. But his mood quickly changed as he described how O'Brien clamped Winston's face to a cage full of rats. Winston was so terrified by the rats flashing their yellow teeth he betrayed Julia. Everyone could be broken down by torture.

George remained utterly determined to finish his book. The demon that drove him was the realisation that he had to finish it before his health gave up altogether. His obsession with the book had hung over him for far too long, and it was getting him down having to live with that police state, its brutal methods of torture and the knowledge that Winston would submit to Big Brother in the end. It felt at times that he was inflicting torture on himself in the writing of it. He knew that he was damaging his health by driving on with it to the exclusion of everything else. But he'd done it before, he'd overstretched his body and mind, had been seriously ill, but had always recovered. This is what would happen again.

He had gone back to Glasgow in September to be examined by a specialist who'd said that he was in as good nick as when he left them in July. But he hadn't booked anywhere to stay that night and had exhausted himself humping his suitcase around Glasgow trying to find a bed. It felt like that time on Islay only much worse. He'd been ill on his return but forced himself to get back to writing what he now regarded as 'that bloody book'. He had another desperate choice to make. He could rest and hope to recover, then take up writing the book again, but the danger was that he might never be well enough to do so. Or he could carry on writing it to a finish and hope that he would get better afterwards, as he had done before. It was a gamble either way. But he chose to struggle on and finish his book.

He was now a pale shadow of himself. He sat at his desk in

striped pyjamas, gazing dreamily out of his bedroom window. A paraffin heater churned out fumes in a corner. The back wall behind his bed was dripping wet from all the rain they'd had. A thick mist had come down with the dusk. He glimpsed some movement in the mirk and felt afraid. He watched as shadowy figures crept ever closer to the house. He was terrified and muttered to himself, 'The house is surrounded. They've come for it!' He rushed over to his bed and took his Luger from under his pillow. He went into bed and pointed the gun at the door. Nothing happened. He waited for what seemed like hours then put the gun down beside him and lit a roll-up, still watching the door. He drew deeply on it. He reached for his typewriter on his bedside cabinet and managed to lift it and his much annotated manuscript on to his lap. He put in four new sheets of paper with carbons in between and typed madly away, the fag still in his mouth. Richard came into the fug in the bedroom. George looked up in alarm and stopped typing.

'The air in here is awful, Eric. What must it be doing to your lungs?

'It's because of the dampness. It's a grisly job typing out this bloody book. It's sucking the life out of me... But I have to finish it. Fred's given me a deadline of early December.' George started a coughing fit. Richard went over and turned off the heater and opened a window. Gradually George stopped coughing.

'Why didn't you get a typist to do it?'

'I wrote to Fred and Moore, and even Senhouse, but they couldn't get one to come all the way here... And it's such a ghastly mess, I couldn't send it away for typing,' George panted. He looked completely done in.

'Well, you have to ease up and look after yourself more. You'll kill yourself if you don't.'

'I have to get rid of this before they get rid of me.'

'Who do you mean?'

'I saw some figures out there coming towards the house.'

Richard went over to the window and looked out. 'It's just some deer. They must be hungry.'

'Oh, I was sure I saw something else.'

When Richard left, George started typing again. He typed into the night and only gave up when he felt himself dozing off and making a mess of it.

For the next few weeks he sat up in bed typing about five thousand words on a good day, less if he was feeling worse than usual.

At the beginning of December, George tottered down the stairs, manuscript in hand. He was puffing and wheezing. He slowly entered the kitchen where Av and Bill were sitting talking. They looked surprised to see him up.

'Well, I've finished it,' he managed to say.

Av and Bill were delighted. She hurried over to help George to sit down. He was completely exhausted.

'That calls for a celebration!' Bill rummaged in a cupboard and pulled out a bottle of red wine. 'It's the last one.' He poured out a glass for each of them.

'What are you going to call it?' Av asked.

'I think I'll call it *Nineteen Eighty-Four*. Eileen once wrote a poem with that year in the title, so I think I'll call it that.'

'Well, here's to *Nineteen Eighty-Four*!' Bill said.

'To *Nineteen Eighty-Four*!' they repeated.

***

I'll never forget that last time Maurice came to my flat. We had drunk a lot of good French wine and lay snuggled up on my sofa. He started cuddling me but I didn't encourage him. I felt ill at ease because I just didn't know where this was going. If anywhere.

'I never longed for anyone in my life as much as you. Will

we ever be together?' I asked him.

'We are together... But I can't stay here without work.'

'You men and your work... I mean really together. Without you going back to your wife and daughter all the time,' I remember I started to slur.

He was silent for a moment. 'There's a difference between love and being in love. I'm in love with you but I love them.'

I sat up and pulled myself away from him. 'Typical nit-picking philosopher, you just won't commit!' The wine brought out the anger that had been simmering inside me for months.

He looked hurt. 'I once made a commitment many years ago to a friend of Simone's but her parents ended it. She felt crushed between me and them. And she died from a fever.'

I was having none of it. 'We've all suffered loss and feel guilty,' I faced him, my rage boiling over. 'I had to have an abortion because of that bastard Koestler.'

Shocked, he sat up too.

'I'm talking about *our* future. Will you not stay here with me?' I demanded.

'I'm sorry I can't make such a decision right now.' He looked unnerved.

'And yet you can decide to support a regime that engineered the Moscow Show Trials and the murder of the old Bolsheviks?'

'You've crossed the line there!' Now he was angry. 'You just use sex when it suits you!'

'No, you've crossed the line. You're just like all the others. You only do what suits *you*!' And I burst into tears.

He slept on the couch that night. Next morning I slammed doors and clashed plates as I prepared breakfast for us. My anger had become sullen hostility. We ate in silence until I told him, trying to sound as breezy as I could, 'Time to get you on that train, Maurice.'

Chapter 11

CHRISTMAS AT BARNHILL that year was almost as dismal as the previous one when George was in Hairmyres Hospital. Again he had to spend most of it in bed, although this time at least he had his family around him. The goose they had fattened up for their Christmas dinner escaped and was found in a bay about a mile away. Bill took out a gun and shot it. But George couldn't share his son's excitement about Christmas and opening his presents. He was afraid that his tuberculosis could infect Ricky and, much against his will, kept him at a safe distance. The boy couldn't understand why his father wouldn't play with him the way he used to, and it fell to Av and Bill to keep him amused. They were worried that the slightest exertion would send George's temperature soaring. He was in bed over New Year too, but his mind dwelt on the fact that he'd have to leave Barnhill again in January. Since sending off his retyped manuscript to Warburg early in December, he'd made enquiries about various sanatoria where he could go to recover. There was one up north in Kingussie, but it was full. And, in any case, he thought the milder climate of southern England might help him to get through those dreaded early months of the year when his health was usually at its worst. Gwen was still a GP and she found him a place at Cranham in Gloucestershire.

So it was on January 2nd that he took his leave of Barnhill to start his long journey south. He wasn't looking forward to it because even slight disturbances these days seemed to weaken him. It was late afternoon when Bill and Av helped him into the Austin 12 car they'd bought with some of the money from Richard. Little Ricky jumped in the back with his father. The old motorbike stood neglected by the front door. Those biking days seemed long gone since they now also had a lorry that they'd bought. He gave the old place a last, longing look as they headed off down the track. As dusk fell, the rain pelted down and the car's windscreen wipers could hardly keep up with it. The track got muddier the further they went and, with only two miles to go to Ardlussa, the car skidded into a ditch and wouldn't budge. There was nothing for it but that Bill and Av would have to walk back to Barnhill in the dark to fetch the lorry and a rope to try to pull them out. As the car door slammed shut and the pair of them headed off, Ricky was close to tears. He was worried about his ailing father beside him in the back seat and asked, 'Will they be long, Daddy?'

'Oh, no,' George replied. 'Just long enough for me to tell you a story or two and recite some poems. Would you like that?'

'Yes, please.'

'I've also got some boiled sweets. Why don't you have one?' George took a paper bag from his pocket and offered Ricky one. Somehow sucking a boiling seemed to help calm them both down. George was well aware how dangerous the situation was. If he had another haemorrhage he could die before Av and Bill got back, and his poor son would be scared out of his wits. He recited a few simple poems which he thought his son would like and then took up the story of Johnny Morie whose unusual escapades always went down well with the boy. This time Johnny was out fishing for mackerel in the Sound of Jura when he had a real adventure.

'Johnny saw a huge fin in the water near his boat and realised it was a shark,' George went on. 'It swam closer and closer to his little boat.'

Ricky was spellbound. 'What happened to him?'

'When he saw its huge jaws open wide near the surface he desperately hunted for his fishing knife to try to protect himself. The shark had dozens of sharp teeth that looked as if they could chew him into little bits. And it was heading straight for him.'

Ricky looked anxious. Was this the end of Johnny Morie who, in Ricky's eyes, had become like a best friend? The rain drummed down on the car roof and ran down the windows, adding, in the boy's imagination, to his fear of being underwater with a menacing shark coming towards him.

'Then Johnny saw the shark glide past the boat scooping up clouds of tiny plankton ahead of it. And he realised that it was a basking shark. And you know what?'

'What?'

'They're harmless to humans.'

Ricky breathed a sigh of relief and asked, 'And was Johnny alright?'

'Oh, yes,' said George, 'He caught lots of fish that day and took them home for his mother to cook. And they sat down to a lovely supper.'

'Is Av my mother?' Ricky asked.

'Well, not really, son, she's your aunt. I'm afraid your mother died when you were a baby. But Av is just like a mother to you. She loves you just as much as Eileen did. She'll be back soon. Are you getting sleepy?'

'A little bit.' He didn't like to give up.

'Well, snuggle up under the rug, close your eyes and let's listen to the rain.'

The boy did as he was told and in minutes he was fast asleep. George also listened as the rain beat steadily down. I must get better so I can bring up Ricky the way he should be raised, he thought. With the sound of the rain, his mind drifted back to his own childhood. He remembered spending wet days with Jacintha, his first love, watching raindrops running down the windows of the outhouse in her garden where they often played. He remembered standing on his head that first time to get her and her siblings' attention and going on expeditions in the woods with them. Although he had lost touch with her many years ago, he would always cherish the memories of their childhood summers together. The older he got the more they meant to him.

When Av and Bill pulled up in the lorry they were relieved to find George and Ricky fast asleep. Once they'd fixed the tow rope to the car, George awoke and carried Ricky through the drizzle into the front seat of the lorry. Bill revved it up to try to pull the car from the ditch but it was no good. It wouldn't budge. Instead he tried to ease the lorry round the edge of the stranded car and just managed to get it through.

'That was a chance in a million that the ground was firm enough to support the lorry,' George said, 'It was like staking your all on zero.'

'Yes, we were damn lucky,' Bill replied.

It was about ten o'clock that night when they got to the Fletchers' big house at Ardlussa and, after a hot drink, they were soon all tucked up in bed. Early next morning after breakfast they said their goodbyes and Robin Fletcher drove George to Craighouse in his Land Rover. They were in good time and Robin saw George safely onto the ferry. The rain had stopped and the sea was calm as George looked over the side to see if he could spot any basking sharks. No sign of any. As the long coast of Jura retreated into the mist he wondered when next he would see it again. He bade it a silent farewell. At West Tarbert he was met at the pier by Richard who had ar-ranged to take him south to Cranham.

Their familiar journey took them by bus to Tarbert on Loch Fyne then by paddle steamer through the Kyles of Bute to Tighnabruaich, Rothesay, Dunoon and Gourock. This time George remained below decks, unable to take much interest in how things had changed since his last steamer journey. He fell asleep to the steady thumping rhythm of turning paddles. They got off at Gourock and caught a train to Glasgow. It chugged its way along the coast through the industrial bleakness of Greenock and Port Glasgow where shipyard cranes kept watch like dinosaurs. Not for the first time he thought how strange it was that people could turn these beautiful hills running down to the sea into a scene of urban squalor. People need to work. You couldn't make a living out of lovely scenery. Their train arrived at Central Station on time and Richard helped George walk the short distance to platform two where the trains left for England. They had a first class compartment all to themselves and settled down for the long trip south. The city looked as black as ever, its factories run down, the faces of workers pinched and drawn, as they sped past. No sooner had they left the outskirts of the city when George remarked, 'The weather seems to be just the same in England.'

Richard looked at him in disbelief, 'We've another hundred miles to go before we're in England, Eric.'

'Oh, have we? Geography was never my strong point, you know.' He didn't seem in the least ashamed of his ignorance.

'Well, we're still in the Scottish Lowlands and over to the west is Ayrshire. You know, Robert Burns country? And further south is Ecclefechan where Carlyle was born, and, of course, Walter Scott made the Borders famous in his novels.'

'Ecclefechan, now there's a word to conjure with. Carlyle was an important figure in his time, though he's hardly read nowadays. And, of course, you can't escape Burns – well ahead of his time in so many ways.' George loved nothing better than discussing other writers and so the conversation rambled on for quite some time about the relative merits of Scottish and English writers. Then, as they reached Carlisle station, out of the blue George asked, 'Do you think it's possible for the trains of one railway company to run on the tracks of another?'

Richard looked astonished by his friend's seeming lack of common sense, or his failure to observe the bleeding obvious, or both. 'I suppose it must be possible, since they use the same tracks and the same stations.'

'Yes, I suppose you're right. Funny how these thoughts come into your head.' George looked tired and soon dropped off, leaving Richard to muse on his strange, yet endearing, friend who often came out with such curious notions.

Darkness fell early at the beginning of the year and George slept on whilst Richard enjoyed having the time to read some more of *David Copperfield*. It was late when they got to Birmingham, and, when they disembarked, they checked into separate rooms at the station hotel. Next morning they caught a train to Gloucester where it had been arranged that an ambulance would meet them and take them on the last leg of their journey some five miles to Cranham Sanatorium. By the time they arrived, George was completely exhausted.

It was built on a hill about 900 feet above sea level and designed so that patients with lung conditions could have their beds wheeled out from their room onto an adjoining balcony where it was thought the fresh air would do them good. George had his own private chalet and spent an hour or two outdoors each day in all weathers, mostly in the cold. On his bedside cabinet beside his pile of books he placed a framed photograph of himself with Ricky seated in a pushchair that Vernon Richards had taken at Canonbury. He found the routine at Cranham very different from that at Hairmyres. Having his own chalet meant that it was much quieter here and everything seemed to be done in a more leisurely fashion. The staff brought in breakfast, lunch and supper like waiters, whereas at Hairmyres they would be wheeled in on trolleys that rattled up and down the ward. There was much less noise from radios too, because all the patients had headphones which were tuned to the BBC Home Service, whereas at Hairmyres they seemed to blast out

Light Programme music all day long. Here he could even listen to birdsong when he was wheeled outside onto the glass-roofed verandah, one of the benefits of paying twelve guineas a week to be a patient there. He would try to identify the birds by the sounds they made and look up the ones he wasn't sure of in a bird book. At first the main treatment was simply to raise the height of the foot of his bed to encourage sputum to come up. But it seldom did.

A few weeks after he arrived, George was visited by his publisher Fred Warburg and his rather pushy wife Pamela. His chalet seemed bitterly cold to them and Pamela wasted no time in telling George so. 'Don't you feel cold in here, George?'

'It's a bit cold sometimes, but they're going to let me have an electric blanket,' George replied.

'Well, why haven't they given it to you yet?'

'I expect it'll be here tomorrow or perhaps the day after.'

'Why not today? Ask them for it. Why don't you? After all, you're paying for it.'

'I don't want to make too much of a fuss. In case they see me as a nuisance.'

'Well, what I'd like to know is what the doctor thinks about your condition.'

George said nothing.

'Don't tell me he hasn't told you what he thinks,' she went on.

'As a matter of fact, I haven't seen him yet.' Pamela looked ready to erupt. 'But a woman doctor comes and visits me every morning.'

'Well, what does she think?'

'She asks me how I feel and that sort of thing.'

'Is that all? Doesn't she listen to your chest with that thing?'

'A stethoscope,' at last Fred got a word in.

'No, I'm afraid she doesn't. I expect they're understaffed here. She probably hasn't got enough time.'

'But you've been here for ages, George. It's monstrous. Absolutely shocking.' Pamela's temper showed. 'Now, you must ask to see the doctor in charge today or at the latest tomorrow.'

'I expect he'll come and see me fairly soon. The place is really very comfortable and they look after me quite well. I expect the doctors know what they're doing.'

'George, I want you to see Dr Morland,' she didn't let up. 'He's a top specialist in this field. He'll come and give you a thorough examination and he may be able to take you into University College Hospital. And of course, your friends could come and see you there. Will you let me ask him to come and see you?'

'I'll think about it.'

It was to be another three months before George agreed to let Dr Morland come. In the meantime, although he wasn't well enough to do any serious writing, he was able to write business and personal letters by hand and to correct the proofs of *Nineteen Eighty-Four* which he returned promptly to Roger Senhouse at Warburg's. He spent day after day reading and kept a list of the books he'd read each month. He'd had enough of political tracts for now and so it was mostly novels he read, everything from D. H. Lawrence to Edgar Allan Poe, *Jude the Obscure* to *New Grub Street*. He got through about three books a week since he was allowed to do little else. As time passed he read more and more of Joseph Conrad and Evelyn Waugh's work and decided to make notes on them in his notebook with the intention of writing extended essays about them. As his mood became blacker he even began reading Dante's *Divine Comedy*. He wanted to see what might lie in store for him, whether it be Heaven or Hell – or somewhere in-between. It felt like a touch of heaven when Celia Kirwan wrote to him and visited Cranham in late March. She had not long returned from working in Paris and had got a new job.

After the usual formalities of enquiring after his health, she asked, 'Can I ask you something in the strictest confidence?'

George was intrigued. This always meant something interesting was about to be said. 'Of course.'

'I've started working for the Information Research Department which Bevin has set up to try to counter the Soviet propaganda machine. Stalin is trying to starve West Berlin into submission with a blockade and would like to take over as much of Europe as he can. We're looking for authors who'd be willing to write books and pamphlets from a democratic standpoint and wonder if you would be willing to help us?'

She looked as beautiful as ever. A sight for sore eyes as far as George was concerned. He wanted to feel useful. And if he was, perhaps she would visit him again. 'Well, I'm afraid I'm too ill to write anything myself and, in any case, I don't do my best work on commission. However, I can think of some writers who would make a good job of it. For example, Franz Borkenau on Russia, Ruth Fischer on Germany, Darlington on the science of eugenics.'

'I'm sorry you're not well enough to write for us yourself, George. Perhaps once you're better? But I'll pass on these names. Now, this is even more sensitive. Are there any writers you can think of whom we shouldn't approach?'

'You mean Stalinists, fellow travellers and the like?'

'Yes, I suppose so.'

'Well, there's no shortage of them around. It might be easier to say who isn't. But, as it happens, I have a list of some of the usual suspects at Barnhill. Richard and I used to have fun playing a bit of a guessing game about who was and who wasn't.'

'That could be very helpful.'

'I'll see what I can do. I'll write to Richard to ask him to send me my notebook. You know, there's no shortage of Soviet agents in intellectual, government and even secret service circles. And they can do a lot of harm. I believe one of them advised

Cape not to publish *Animal Farm*. Anyway, I'll have a look at what I've got. But I'd need to have it back fairly quickly.'

'That would be marvellous, George. And, of course, anything you can provide us with would be returned right away and would be in the strictest confidence.'

Quite soon afterwards, George wrote to Richard who didn't take long to send him his notebook from Jura. George had a good look at it and then sent Celia a list of thirty-five names with comments attached of people he felt could not be trusted to write counter-propaganda for the British Government. Some were well-known Stalin supporters like the Labour MP Konni Zilliacus with whom he'd crossed swords in the letters pages of *Tribune*, others were more speculative. But it was highly unlikely that the likes of Charlie Chaplin or Paul Robeson would ever have been asked to write this kind of thing in any case. George had coined the phrase, the 'Cold War', to describe the new world political situation, and he had personal experience of the way the Stalinists had attacked, killed and tortured others on the left in Spain. He still thought fondly of Bob Smillie, the young Scottish ILP volunteer he knew, who had died at their hands in prison. He thought they were just as bad as the fascists but he still regarded himself as a social democrat and a critical supporter of the Labour Government. So, he believed it was his patriotic duty to act in this way. However, he realised that not everyone would see it like that.

On Easter Sunday his treasured peace and quiet was shattered by the arrival of lots of visitors to see the patients in his, the most expensive, block of chalets. What a hubbub of upper-class English voices they were: extremely loud, over self-confident, overfed, expressing ill-will towards just about everyone, and indulging in braying laughter about nothing. George had been out of earshot of voices like theirs for almost two years and had grown used to the generally more discreet tones of working class and lower middle class Scots. To his ears these toffs seemed the enemies of everything that was intelligent or sensitive or beautiful in the world, and the epitome of everything that was wrong with England. No wonder everyone hates us so, he wrote in his notebook.

His main concern, however, as the months went by, was missing Ricky so much and he became afraid of him growing away from him. He would soon be old enough to go to school and then he would hardly see him at all. Although still worried that his disease could be infectious, he wrote to Av and asked her to bring him down from Jura to visit him that summer. When there seemed little improvement in his condition, streptomycin was tried again but his allergic reaction was so severe that it was stopped immediately. Typically, he continued to bear with grim stoicism the painful weekly collapsing of his lung. Although he was now very weak, he was allowed visitors, so long as they didn't tire him out too much. And now that he was within easy travelling distance of London, a lot more of his friends came to see him than when he was in Hairmyres. Fred was as good as his word and pushed ahead with bringing out *Nineteen Eighty-Four* as soon as possible. In June, it came out in Britain and the United States to great acclaim and massive sales. Not only that, but soon afterwards it became the American Book of the Month Club choice with a huge print run.

One hazy evening that summer David Astor visited him. 'George, you've painted a terrifying vision of the future. No wonder it's caught the public imagination.' George couldn't see David and, when he raised himself up in his bed, he had gone.

Instead, he had been replaced by Malcolm Muggeridge and Cyril Connolly. Or so it seemed. 'My dear boy, this time you've excelled yourself. I'm afraid we're all doomed,' Malcolm chortled.

'Pay no attention to him, Eric, always the cynic,' Cyril chipped in. 'The critics just love it. Gollancz must be kicking himself for letting you go. Now, is there anything we can get you? Of course, with your latest marvellous success, money's no object.'

But before George could reply, they too had gone. He started to wonder if he was hallucinating as a result of all the medication he was on. Then Richard appeared. 'How are you, Eric, old chap?'

'Mustn't grumble. They're looking after me quite well, I suppose. I'm not allowed my typewriter, or even a pen and paper, but I can still read,' George pointed to his pile of books.

'I just got back from Barnhill. Av and Ricky and Bill send their love. The lad's coming on leaps and bounds. Now, you must let me know if there's anything else you want sent on to you and I'll arrange it.'

'Thank you, I'll let you know. How's the book doing in America?'

'Thanks to that Book Club edition, it's already a bestseller in the States. Your money worries are well and truly over.'

'That's good to hear, Richard. But, you know, the money's no good to me now. It's fairy gold, fairy gold…'

But Richard was no longer there. Instead, by his bedside sat Paul Potts. 'You know, you couldn't have smashed their statues better if you tried. Everyone's talkin about it. Look, I've brought you some scones and raspberry jam. I know how much you like them. What about your tea, is it strong enough?' Paul asked.

'You know me,' George raised half a smile, 'it's never strong enough for my liking. But I'm slowly getting them used to my ways.'

'Good,' Paul said, 'You deserve only the best. You know, your book has really got them worried. You've exposed the dictators and the cruelty of their methods, and no mistake.'

'It's certainly a good idea all right but I ballsed it up rather, probably because I was so ill when I was writing it.' George reached out for the scones and jam but Paul had gone and there was nothing there. Now if Paul was real, he thought, he'd have taken a scone or two with him when he left me some.

Ricky, looking even bigger for five years old, came over to his bedside. 'Where does it hurt, Daddy?'

'Nowhere really,' he replied sadly. 'My, aren't you getting big?'

'I'm staying with Mrs Wolf at Whiteways and I play at the camp every day.'

'And is she nice?'

'Oh yes. She's old, but she's very nice.'

'That's good, son. These anarchists are nice people. I'm glad you like the camp.'

'And I caught a fish!' he grinned.

'In a river?'

'Yes, in a big river. And at home I've been fishing in the sea too.'

'Good for you. Well done, son!' George smiled proudly. He reached out to pat his head, but Ricky too had gone. Were they all real or had he imagined them?

Chapter 12

November 1980, Blakes Hotel, London

I HEARD NOT long after Maurice and I broke up that George was in hospital in Cranham and decided to go and see him. I hadn't had much contact with him after he left Hairmyres and went back to Jura to finish his book. He did write me a love letter or two but I was still hopeful that things would work out with Maurice and didn't reply. Anyway, he told me that it was his birthday on the 25th of June and asked me if I could visit him then. It only took me a few hours by train and taxi from London, much shorter than the long journey to Glasgow. Cranham looked rather run down to me. Like George, it had seen better days. But I was shocked when I saw how frail he looked lying flat on his back in bed. He seemed to have lost that old sparkle in his eyes that was one of his most appealing features. It was as if that damn book had drained all the life out of him, leaving only a husk of a man instead of the intriguing character I had known. At that point I could only feel concern for his well-being, not love. I wondered how, or even if, I could help him. I sat by his bedside and handed him some grapes, 'Not much of a birthday present, I know.'

His eyes lit up a little, 'You're all the birthday present I need. I'm so glad you could come.'

'I'm glad too. How've you been keeping?'

'Some days are better than others, I suppose. But this is definitely one of the good days now that you're here.' He gave me a lingering look that seemed full of regret and said in a faltering voice, 'I wish I hadn't gone back to Jura… I should have come here where you could be with me… But I had to…'

'I know. It's all right. I understand,' I tried to make it easier for him.

'They say I've a good chance of being around for some years if I stay still and don't do any work… I still love you, you know.'

He didn't hang about in letting me know that his feelings for me were just as strong. 'I know you do. But I don't know if I can ever love you,' I replied. I know I was being rather blunt but I've always believed it's better to be honest with others. Especially with someone who tells you they love you.

He looked disappointed but gamely persevered. 'I could become what they call a good chronic, and, if we were married, you could manage my affairs and learn how to make dumplings.'

'I'm not sure that I'm really cut out for making dumplings,' I smiled, trying to make light of the situation.

'You could have as much freedom as you want when it comes to… you know. It's being emotionally faithful that matters.'

'I know.' Since it looked like George was no longer capable of any kind of sex life, he could hardly expect me to give up mine.

'You would help me to get better,' he went on. 'And if it didn't work out, you'd be a rich widow.'

Even I was taken aback by his matter of fact approach. 'It sounds more like a business proposition than a marriage proposal, George… I'll have to think about it.'

Well, it wasn't at all the kind of conversation I'd expected. I'd just gone along to keep him company for an hour or so on his birthday for old times' sake and here was I on the receiving end of a marriage proposal again. I decided to talk to Fred Warburg since he'd recently visited George and had been in touch with his friend Doctor Morland about his prospects. I knew, of course, that Fred had a vested interest in keeping George alive as long as possible since the success of *Animal Farm* and *Nineteen Eighty-Four* had put his publishing house on the map in a big way. One afternoon, a week or so later, his secretary ushered me into his spacious office. It was stuffed with books and ornaments and paraphernalia he must have picked up all over the place. His desk was piled high with books, papers and what must have been manuscripts. It was a wonder he could ever find any of them to read. The hopes and dreams of scores of would-be authors lost in a jumbled mess. I'd soon have sorted that out if I'd been working for him. Fred was a rather ugly looking man by my standards, but he was well turned out and his long cigarette holder gave him something of the appearance of a suave businessman.

'Good afternoon, Sonia. Would you like some tea or coffee, or perhaps something a little stronger?' He motioned to his cocktail cabinet. 'How about a G and T?'

He'd obviously heard I was partial to a little snifter whatever time of day it was. 'Why yes, that would be quite refreshing,' I replied.

He called his secretary on the intercom who quickly came in and made us two G and Ts whilst we engaged in small talk.

'Cheers, my dear,' he said.

'Cheers.'

'How's our patient then?' he asked.

I waited until his secretary had left and closed the door. 'Not so good, really. That's what I wanted to talk to you about. George has asked me to marry him.' I always believe in coming straight to the point.

Fred's eyes lit up but he didn't seem that surprised. 'Well then,' he said, rubbing his chin and not wanting to show his hand too soon until he knew what I was thinking. 'And what did you say?' he asked.

'I said I'd think about it. But I would like to know what you think before I give him my answer.'

Fred realised he would have to come off the fence. 'Well, as with all such things there are pros and cons to consider. He's clearly a very ill man and the doctors don't think he'll ever fully recover. He'll likely be bedridden for the rest of his life, so there are all the implications of that to consider.'

'Is that what they said to you?'

'Well, you know what doctors are like, they never want to be too specific in case you quote it back at them or think about suing them. But that's the gist of it. You'd be tied down to looking after him and, of course, there's bringing up his son to consider. George would also need to take into account your needs, if you know what I mean?'

'I know what you mean.' I took another gulp of my drink. He was being rather blunt but I prefer that. 'And what about the pros?'

'Well, of course, you two have a lot in common. You've a shared interest in all things literary, and I'm sure with your experience at *Horizon* you'd be a great help to him in dealing with the many demands of his literary affairs. He wouldn't have asked you if he didn't think you could handle all that with his best interests at heart. George and I have agreed to bring out a uniform edition of his work, so, of course, you'd have to read all his books.'

How did he know I hadn't? He made it sound like a business proposition in the same way George had, but it was good to know that Fred thought the same way. 'I've read a lot of his work and I worked with him when we published some of his essays in *Horizon*. Are you expecting the new book to do well in the States?'

'It already has, and with his royalties from the American Book of the Month Club, he won't have to worry about paying hospital bills, however long they keep him in.'

I nodded at this reassuring news. 'If I said yes, I wonder if it might help him to get better?'

'Yes, that's the most important thing. It would cheer him up no end and give him a real boost knowing that he had a life with you to look forward to.'

I'd heard enough to know that Fred would be a useful ally if I decided to accept George's proposal. I finished my drink and shook hands with him. It felt like we were sealing a business deal.

'Let me know what you decide,' he said as he saw me to the door. 'Whatever it is, I'm sure you'll do the right thing. And if there's anything else, don't hesitate to give me a call.'

'I will. You've given me a lot to think about.'

When I got home I phoned Netta and asked her to come round to my place for a couple of drinks the following night. Well, as usual, when the pair of us got together, 'a couple of drinks' meant a bottle or two of quality wine. And in no time at all we were getting quite merry.

'Well, put me out of my misery,' she said. 'What's your big news on the George front?'

'Well, he proposed to me again.'

'*He* didn't waste much time.'

'And on his birthday, too.'

'How touching.'

'What do you think I should do?'

She thought for a moment then said, 'I don't know. Do you love him?'

I hesitated. 'Well, you know as well as I do that Maurice is the real love of my life… But it's obvious he won't leave his wife and daughter for me… I don't love George in the same way, but he needs me so much. Perhaps I could give him something to live for?'

'You're right. You've no real future with Maurice. And you'll soon be out of a job when *Horizon* closes.' Netta could be just as frank as I could, but I knew she was trying to help me make a decision. 'And, well, you've always wanted to be some kind of guardian angel to a famous author…'

I butted in. 'He says he'll get better if I marry him, so I've really got no choice.'

'There's always a choice. But maybe you still feel guilty that you've taken a life… And perhaps now's your chance to give one back. You're George's lifeline and it may be that you're his only hope.'

'Yes, I suppose that's it.' Netta was a true friend. She knew almost everything about me and I could always rely on her to help me do what was best for me. 'Maybe I'll come to love him in time.'

Now that the serious business of the night was over, we could enjoy ourselves and it wasn't long before we polished off the last of the wine. It felt that a weight had been taken off my mind and I knew that, one way or another, my future was secure. George was bound to get better with my help. I would cheer him up no end and could really help him with his literary commitments – of which there was no shortage. I went back to Cranham about a week later and sat down beside him. This time he lay propped up in bed and looked a bit brighter. I could see how anxious he was and decided to cut to the chase. 'I've thought a lot about it.' I took a deep breath. 'And I've decided to marry you.'

He looked as if he was going to jump out of bed and hug me. 'You can't imagine how happy you've made me!' He spoke like a man whose dream had come true.

'I can't promise to love you but I will look after you.'

'That's all I ask.' He didn't seem to care. He had got the answer he wanted.

I visited him every week after that and he seemed much more cheerful and hopeful of a full recovery. His friends also noticed the difference when they visited him, especially David

Astor. The one thing that troubled all of us was that his doctor hardly seemed to bother about him and he could go for days without even a visit. Like Pamela, David also suggested that George should move to University College Hospital, London, so that he could be under Morland and receive specialist treatment. Well, I thought, that would suit me down to the ground. I could walk there from my flat and visit George every day. He agreed and we both got excited about the idea and started making plans for our wedding. We decided to delay a decision about the date until he had settled in at his new hospital. Once again he was taken by ambulance and, indeed, he seemed rather impressed that it was one of the new luxury ones and was equipped for just about every eventuality. He told me later that he got particularly excited when it rang its bell to cut through the queues of traffic in Euston Road. He could be quite boyish that way.

His private room, Room 65, as I recall, was on the top floor of UCH and quite cramped compared to Cranham. There was no outdoor balcony for him to be wheeled out onto but, of course, if there had been, the city's fumes would have done him no good whatsoever. At least here he could get the best of medical attention and Morland came to see him every day to check on his progress. George and I settled into a daily routine in which to all intents and purposes I became his personal assistant, typing his letters and seeing to all his business needs, of which, as a highly successful author, there were many. I still worked for Cyril in the mornings but my job at *Horizon* was winding down and its last issue was scheduled for the end of the year. Cyril had long since lost interest in it.

'Ten years is a good innings for any literary journal,' I remember him saying. 'We showed the world that English and, indeed, European, culture was something worth fighting for, and we should be proud of that fact.' I often thought that the magazine was his way of avoiding war service and enabling him to continue to enjoy the extravagant lifestyle he was used to. He had his faults all right, but I did agree with him that we showed our culture at its best in the magazine.

One of the letters I remember typing at George's dictation was to Francis Henson of the United Automobile Workers Union in the United States. He practically whispered the words to me as he sat in his chair and I typed away for all I was worth. He was at pains to make clear that *Nineteen Eighty-Four* was not aimed at attacking socialism, rather the perversions to which a centralised economy is prone as seen under fascism and communism. It was set in Britain to show that we were not immune from totalitarianism but that it could happen anywhere if not fought against. He said he was in fact a supporter of the British Labour Party.

That was as far as he got that afternoon. 'Sorry, I'm a bit tired. I really don't know how I'd manage without you.' He looked exhausted so I stopped typing at once and helped him get back into bed. His pyjamas hung off him, his long frame was terribly weak and he felt like a skeleton through them.

'Not to worry, I'll be back tomorrow and we can finish it then.' I put the cover over his old Remington and went over and kissed him on the cheek – in case he was still infectious. I left him to rest up and was soon out and about in that bright other world of busy Bloomsbury.

Sir Richard Rees was another regular visitor. He'd stayed at Barnhill with George the previous year and, indeed, had put up some of the capital to set up George, Av and her one-legged Scotsman Bill Dunn to try to make a go of the farm. I don't think it did very well because David told me that the land was pretty stony and Atlantic storms could blow up quickly and destroy just about anything you tried to grow. However, you couldn't stop George trying out all kinds of hair-brained schemes once he got them into his head. And he would forever be asking how things were doing back on the farm. One particular day, though, their conversation was rather different.

'Do you think it's possible that one cannot die if one still has a book in mind one wants to write?' George asked. Well, you could have knocked me over with a feather duster.

'I'm not really sure. It would be nice to think so… Though maybe writing one or two really great books is enough.' I had to hand it to Richard, he was tactful to a fault.

'Maybe so,' George seemed somewhat consoled. 'Morland told me "Yes, you can have a book in your mind and still die," but I don't think that's so. I've got a trilogy of novels in mind and I've even made some notes for a long short story. I'd also like to write something more substantial about Conrad and Waugh. I've been reading some more of their novels recently.' As if that wasn't enough, George proceeded to go on about another of his favourite topics. 'You know, Morland also treated old D.H. Lawrence for tuberculosis. He died because his philosophy of life became completely untenable. He would have no plausible attitude towards events today.'

Well, that was the last straw as far as I was concerned. 'Oh, George, do stop talking like this. Let's talk about something more cheerful. What do you think of my engagement ring, Richard?' I pushed the large diamond and ruby ring on my finger under his nose.

'It's lovely,' was about all Richard could offer.

'Isn't it? George gave me a blank cheque and I chose it myself. Now, George, tell us about that little poodle you used to have. What was it called?'

'Marx.'

I knew he was weary of telling this much told tale but I had to get him off the subject of death. 'And what did you use its name for again?'

'I could tell the politics of visitors by whether they thought it was named after Marks and Spencer or Karl Marx, or Groucho Marx.'

That little tale of his never failed to raise a chuckle. Then I remembered, 'Oh, I almost forgot, I have to go to a cocktail party later and won't be back this evening.'

'But…'

I knew George wouldn't be happy about this, but I had to have a bit of a life beyond his cramped little room even if he couldn't. Sometimes I just had to ignore his feeble protests and get out there amongst others again.

The big day soon came along. George still wasn't well enough to get out of bed so we had to be married in his hospital room. David pulled a few strings again, this time with the Archbishop of Canterbury no less, who gave a special dispensation for the hospital chaplain, the Rev William Braine, to conduct the service there. Although George wasn't a practising Christian or believer, he was a traditionalist and thought it would only be right and proper to be married by the Church of England. He was full of contradictions of that kind. Naturally, Netta was my bridesmaid, and very lovely she looked too. She was accompanied by her handsome little husband, Robert Kee, who had been a fighter pilot during the war and was now a journalist. He 'gave me away' as the saying goes. David was George's best man and he was as urbane and charming as ever. How on earth would George have managed without him? He and Malcolm had scoured gents' outfitters all over London to find a velvet smoking jacket for George and now there he was, sat up in bed, looking as debonair as you like in a very smart cerise one. He was still as thin as a rake, and looked just as frail, but was very, very happy. We all gathered round his bed as the vicar went through the marriage vows with us and we exchanged rings.

'And will you Sonia Brownell, love, honour and obey Eric Arthur Blair till death do you part?'

I wasn't too sure about the 'obey' bit, but I said 'I will' in any case.

'Then by the grace of God and the power vested in me I now pronounce you man and wife. You may kiss the bride.'

I leant over the bed and we kissed each other on the cheek. George was elated. He had that real sparkle in his eyes that I hadn't seen for a long time. And everyone seemed very happy for us.

'My sincere congratulations, Mr Blair,' said the vicar as he formally shook George's hand.

David broke open the champagne and gave everyone a little, even George. Netta almost emptied hers in one gulp. She seemed very emotional and had probably been eyeing the bubbly throughout. It helped take the edge off what could easily have become quite a sad occasion. We all engaged nervously in small talk. But soon it was time for us to go.

Robert came over to the bed and gave George a warm handshake. 'Many congratulations, George. Look after yourself now.'

Then it was Netta's turn, 'Take care, George, we'll come and see you soon.' She touched his wasted arm and looked pityingly at me.

David was the last, 'I'll see you tomorrow, George. Don't worry, I'll make sure she behaves herself.' He was clearly moved by the occasion. As indeed we all were. And soon it was over. They all filed out. We were alone.

'I don't want to leave you,' I said.

'Somehow I don't think the Ritz would let me in like this,' he smiled ruefully. 'You run along now and celebrate for both of us… You must enjoy yourself, it's your wedding day. And don't worry about me, you've made me a very happy man. I'll be fine… See you tomorrow.'

I managed to hold back the tears and kissed him again on the cheek. 'I'll try to. Yes, see you tomorrow.'

Out in the corridor I almost broke down. It was just so sad to see him like this and to leave him lying there alone on his wedding day. He had looked forward to this for so long. But what else could I do? A small reception for close friends at the Ritz is what we had agreed and it was too late to change it now. I walked along the corridor to where the others were waiting for me and tried to put on as cheerful a face as I could when I approached them. We had a nice time at the Ritz, the champagne was flowing, and our meal was superb. A small, intimate gathering of friends it was, with all of us hoping for the best.

I went back each day after that and George's face always lit up when I came into the room. His health seemed to improve in the months that followed, but I could see that he was worried about how long he would last. His thoughts seemed to keep returning to his childhood growing up in Oxfordshire, to the fields and woods where he played and the rivers and pools where he loved to fish. This was his Golden Country. And he wanted so much to return there if he couldn't go back to Jura. It seemed at times that this was the one thought that kept him alive. Anyway, I don't really know why his medical condition got worse, but he seemed to go downhill with the onset of winter. As the nights drew in, his mood became darker. I tried to cheer him up, but it wasn't easy. He was a man who looked reality straight in the eye and didn't usually like what he saw.

Christmas was a pretty glum affair despite the colourful decorations above his bed and the little Christmas tree in the corner. George lay on his back on Christmas Day but Malcolm Muggeridge and Tony Powell dropped in later on and George regaled them with tales of his exploits in the Home Guard and in Spain. However, there was very little Christmassy about the occasion. I noticed how dismayed they looked on their way out. The New Year celebrations almost passed us by, apart from when George toasted someone called Robert and some friendly people he'd met in Glasgow one New Year whom he thought would be enjoying themselves that day. The only real sign of hope was that, in January, Morland thought it would be a good idea for George to go to a sanatorium in Switzerland. So, with Lucian Freud's help, I arranged a special flight to take him there. Money wasn't a problem by then since the royalties from *Nineteen Eighty-Four* kept pouring in. Lucian became a regular visitor after that.

'Just think, this time next week we'll be in Switzerland and you'll be able to breathe all that fresh mountain air,' I told him. 'And once you're a bit better, you'll be able to fish in the rivers and lakes. It'll be our honeymoon.'

'I'd like that. But maybe Morland just doesn't want me to die here,' George replied.

'You mustn't think like that. When we get back, we'll find a nice place in the country. And you'll be able to write again while I deal with all your correspondence and entertain our friends.'

George smiled sadly at the thought. 'That sounds nice. And we can have lovely meals together… I have everything I want now… Except my health.'

'Don't worry, I'll look after you and make sure we've lots of delicious things to eat and drink.'

'I feel better just thinking about it.'

Well, after that George wrote to Av and asked her and Ricky to come and see him before we left and to bring his fishing rods with her. They came not long before we were to fly out and his rods were carefully placed in a corner of the room. The little fellow looked bigger and brighter than ever and was overjoyed to see his father again. Av looked less happy when she saw how much more wasted her brother looked.

'I went to the zoo with Tony and Violet,' Ricky said, all excited.

'Did you now, and what did you see?'

'I saw lions and tigers. And they were in big cages.'

George's eyes sparkled, 'Just as well. And did they look fierce?'

'Oh yes. But I wasn't afraid.'

'Well good for you. That's my boy,' George ruffled his hair. Father and son looked as pleased as punch.

Av didn't seem at all pleased that we had got married without telling her, but came round a bit when she saw how happy it had made her poor brother. Ricky started telling him about all the fish he had caught back on Jura, when there was a knock at the door and this little old man put his head round.

'May I come in?' he enquired.

Although George was lying flat on his back he recognised who it was and said, pointing to a chair, 'Of course, Mr Gow. Please sit down.'

'I was visiting a chap from Trinity and heard you were here, so I thought I'd take a look in to see how you are,' Gow said. He was a quiet-spoken, severe little man, almost bald, but with big bushy eyebrows and side whiskers.

'Mr Gow is a Fellow of Trinity College, Cambridge. He taught me Greek at Eton,' George explained. 'This is my wife, Sonia, my sister Avril and my son, Richard.' It was all very formal.

'Pleased to meet you,' he said, showing little interest in us. 'And how are you then, Blair?'

'Oh, not so bad. I've been better, though.'

'And are they treating you well here?'

'Oh, they're very good. It's almost like a hotel, really. The room service is rather good, I've even got my own phone,' George said, pointing to it beside the books on his bedside cabinet. 'But I'm looking forward to going to Switzerland next week. If I can manage the journey the mountain air should do me some good.'

'And when do you leave?'

'Next Wednesday. I hope to do some fishing over there. If I'm well enough,' George gestured towards his fishing rods in the corner.

'I see. Yes, I seem to remember at school you had some secret pool where you fished.'

'I'm going to school,' Ricky piped up. 'And I catch fish.'

'Is that so?' Gow said.

'Yes. And at Christmas my Uncle Bill shot a goose and there was bloody blood on the floor. It was a bugger.'

George looked embarrassed at Ricky's new favourite word being used in front of Gow. 'Av, could you take Richard out for a little while, so Mr Gow and I can have a chat?'

'Of course,' she said. 'Come on Ricky, let's go exploring. We'll come back soon.' She didn't look too pleased, but Ricky seemed happy enough as they left.

'Sorry about that. Young lads nowadays…' I couldn't understand why George was apologising for his son. Who was this self-important little man?

'I remember you were a bit of a handful yourself as a boy,' Gow said. 'And you've certainly gone your own way as a writer.'

'Have you read my latest book, then?'

'Yes, I have. That's quite a thesis you've set out there. That the state can control everything and destroy anyone who rebels against it.'

'Well, I'm not saying it will happen, just that it *could* happen if people aren't careful and don't do something about it.'

'I must say I found it all rather gloomy, indeed pessimistic. There must be some hope for humanity, don't you think?'

George gave Gow a strange look at the mention of the word 'humanity'. I could see that this discussion was tiring him out, and decided to butt in, 'George has warned people what the future could bring, now it's up to them to stop it happening.'

'Well, we all do what we can, I'm sure,' Gow replied. His dismissive tone seemed to me typical of his supercilious donnish type. 'But I see you're getting tired, Blair. I better leave you in peace. Take care now.' And with that he upped and left.

'What a strange little man. All those questions. It felt like he was checking up on you.'

'Granny Gow was his nickname at school, he had his favourites – if you know what I mean. And I wasn't one of them. Especially after I gave the game away in a little ditty I wrote. I went to see him after I came back from Burma and later we exchanged a few letters. But we were never close. Strange that he should come and see me now after all these years.' He looked slightly worried.

Av brought Ricky back in after she saw Gow leaving, 'What was that all about?' she asked.

'A good question,' George replied. 'Perhaps it'll all become clear one day. Anyway, son, tell me more about that goose that Uncle Bill shot.'

Ricky picked up his story where he left off and George looked really proud that he could have a proper conversation with him. Especially after those early years he told me about when he used to worry how slow he was in starting to speak. Av and I sat back and enjoyed seeing how well the pair of them got on and how much they loved telling each other stories about the outdoors. They spoke about adders and caterpillars and how basking sharks weren't like other sharks. That's when it struck me how close they were and how important his son was to George.

Unfortunately, it was soon time for us all to go and George bade them a fond farewell. 'I'll see you both when we get back from Switzerland. I'll be a new man by then. Look after yourselves, now.'

'You too, Eric,' said Av, squeezing his hand and giving him a bit of a hug. 'Don't worry, we'll be fine.' Ricky had enjoyed his time with his father and went away quite the thing.

Next day I asked George, 'Have you thought any more about why Granny Gow came to see you?'

'I have, but I must say it's still a bit of a puzzle. It's unlikely he heard by chance that I was here when he was visiting someone else. Who could that have been? And his talk that there must be some hope for humanity set alarm bells ringing in my head. In my experience, those who go on about humanity are often amongst the least caring people you could possibly meet.'

'Well, anyway, enough speculation, what else do we need to do before we go?'

'We must get the final changes to my will completed.'

'Don't worry, it's all in hand. It should be returned in a day or two for you to sign.'

Well, his new will was signed later that week and Gwen O'Shaughnessy countersigned it as a witness. He left just about everything to me apart from the proceeds of an insurance policy which were to go to Ricky to pay for his education whenever I thought best. Poor Av was to get nothing – apart from the pleasure of bringing up Ricky. The nay-sayers and gossipmongers talk about me being a gold digger and say I only married him for his money. But that wasn't at all the case. I think he felt that I was the best person to ensure his literary legacy would be looked after, and so he wanted to make sure I was well provided for. That's also why he made me his joint literary executor with Richard, whom his previous will had specified was the man for the job. By that time his mind was very much concentrated on coming to terms with death, no matter what I said. It was round about then that he told me about a dream he had.

'You know the other night I dreamt I was wandering about the empty streets of a city full of skyscrapers. They looked like central London only different. It was sunny and I felt quite happy, even though I was lost. It seemed to me that the towering buildings represented death and I know that it's closer.'

'Why do you think that?' I asked.

'I can't really explain it. But I've had these kinds of dreams before and they become more frequent when my health gets worse and I despair of recovering. Since I'm not afraid of death, why do they keep recurring? Why, when I feel so happy now? I don't want to die. I want to live! I want to live to be with you and to see Ricky growing up to be a young man.'

I didn't know what to say. I had no answers to his questions. It seemed to me he'd had another nightmare. But I couldn't tell him that, even though he must have known that's what it was. He said another strange thing that puzzled me.

'Have you ever thought about what the world would be like without you?'

'No, I can't say I have. I suppose the way it is just now when you're in hospital.'

'That's the common sense view, of course. But I mean when you're permanently gone. It's strange to think of everyone in the world going on living just as before. And you're no longer there to witness it or to be able to influence it in any way.'

'Well, the way your books are being bought these days, I'd say, you're going to go on influencing it for a long time to come.'

'I certainly hope so. It's one of the reasons I was so desperate to finish it. It brought together all my thoughts and fears for our future. There's no such thing as immortality, whatever priests say… but perhaps we writers live on a little through our books. Anyway, I hope people really do see what's happening to the world and take action to prevent it.'

'I'm sure they will, George. I'm sure they will.' I felt that he needed to understand how much he had achieved. If nothing else, it might help him to content himself with the thought that he had done as much as anyone could to make the world a better place. I knew how important that was to him.

Chapter 13

I DIDN'T SEE much of George after that godawful winter when he had to burn his boy's wooden toys to keep the three of them warm in their flat. He returned to Barnhill to finish his book but I never went back there. How could I when that dragon of a sister of his was still there? But when I heard he was in hospital at Cranham I visited him a few times and, of course, I saw him more frequently when he transferred to UCH. He always seemed pleased to see me and we used to reminisce about how he taught me to fish and how I nearly published *Animal Farm* from my Whitman Press. I still reckon I could have sold a barrowload round the Soho pubs. However, I noticed a huge difference in him by then. He always looked older than his years, but now the deep lines on his face had become chasms and he looked like a man whose life was hanging by a thread. I reckon he almost killed himself finishing that blasted book. But, you know, he never was one to look after his health. He smoked like a chimney, and he seemed completely oblivious to danger. He certainly got himself into some scrapes over the years. Between going off to Spain to fight not long after he got married and almost blowing himself up in the Home Guard. And then practically drowning himself and his family in that treacherous whirlpool.

He was totally obsessed about the totalitarian future he could see was coming. He wanted to warn us all about the dangers of it happening and just seemed to lose his bearings altogether. Of course, it was a tour de force for sure. We could all recognise what had become of London in a future age when flying bombs were again dropping on it all the time and television sets had become spying machines for the state to keep track of every detail of our private lives. I reckon that the seedy prole area he described in the book was based on Islington where he and I enjoyed more than a few adventures together. He told me he thought it could have been a better book if he hadn't been so ill when he was writing it. But I'm sure his illness made his vision of the future all the more harrowing because he'd experienced the horrors of losing his hair and becoming a skeleton as a result of the side effects of some of the drugs they gave him. And he must have felt like a prisoner when he had to spend so much time in bed because of his illness. No matter, the book was a huge success. And everyone is now much more aware of the dangers of Big Brother watching us than they would have been if he hadn't sacrificed his health to finish it.

I remember that last time I visited him at the hospital not long before he was to leave for Switzerland. It was during the evening visiting hour, but he was all alone in his private little room. Before going in I looked through the small window on the door and saw that he was lying in bed sleeping soundly. He looked much thinner and his cheeks were shrunken, but I was reassured by how peaceful he looked. Almost happy. The pile of books on top of his bedside cabinet was as high as always and there were two fishing rods in a corner. I wondered what he thought he was going to catch there. Maybe he was going to teach Sonia to fish the way he had me? I had brought him a bag of his favourite Ceylon tea, but I didn't have the heart to waken him. I knew he needed as much sleep as he could get. So I left it on the doorstep for him, feeling sure that a nurse would give it to him when he woke up.

Chapter 14

I FELL ASLEEP early last night and woke up again around two o'clock. Now I can't get back to sleep, my brain's too alert. The only sound is my breathing and occasional coughing. The rest of the hospital seems to be fast asleep. I'm being well looked after here and the doctors and nurses have been much more attentive than at Cranham. Yet I feel I'm getting worse. And that last time Tony and Malcolm visited me you would think they'd seen a ghost. Well, boys, I'm still here. I might be thinner and weaker, not unlike Winston, but there's life in the old dog yet.

There's no doubt that marrying Sonia has given me hope. And where there's life... She's cheered me up no end and she's very practical and enjoys organising things like our flight to Switzerland. Whatever she says, I still suspect Morland doesn't want another corpse on his hands and that's why he wants me to go. He could probably see the headlines now: 'First Lawrence then Orwell. Who's next?' I don't really mind that Sonia's bringing along her former lover Lucian Freud since I can't fulfil her needs in the state I'm in. Although I'm only forty-six, I've not had a bad innings really. And if I'm bowled out, I'm sure Sonia and Richard will look after my work the way it should be taken care of. My last two books caught on with the public and I've managed to achieve what I set out to do – to warn the world about the dangers of totalitarian rule. It's up to them now as to whether they're smart and committed enough to stop it happening. I'm sure there will be other would-be dictators in the future but it'll be up to the people to stop them too. I still believe in the common decency of ordinary people, they're the best guarantee of our freedom in the future.

I feel I've done my bit, and now I'd like to live long enough to indulge my interest in other writers like Conrad and Waugh, and to write another novel or two like the short one I've already started. I can just see me fishing in those turquoise Swiss rivers once I'm better. And, once I return, I'd like nothing better than to show Ricky how to catch trout and tench in the Upper Thames where I grew up. I can see us now, casting into some deep, dark pool and the fish lazily swimming about choosing their moment to pounce on that fly. And us on the bank waiting patiently for them to bite… Dace and tench swimming languidly, trout and…

In the early hours that morning George's room was dark and completely silent. The corridor light shone a beam into the room and his fishing rods still stood propped up in a corner. On his bedside cabinet a bag of tea sat next to his pile of books along with framed photographs of Eileen and Ricky, and one of Sonia. George lay face up and perfectly still in his bed. Blood seeped from his lips on to his thin chest forming a large, dark pool.

Chapter 15

I SAW GEORGE that afternoon as usual and he seemed tired but in good spirits. He was looking forward to going to Switzerland the following week and talked of catching some trout in Swiss rivers. I knew that was something of a fantasy in his condition but didn't wish to discourage him. That night I went out for a meal with Netta and Lucian and we finished up in a late night bar in Soho. I remember I was tired and anxious. The strain of it all had got to me and we'd drunk quite a lot into the early hours.

'I'm not sure how well George will cope with the flight next week,' I said.

'Don't worry, we'll be there in no time,' said Lucian.

I remember the barman had started to clear the tables and came over to me. 'Mrs Blair? There's a call for you.'

At first I didn't know who he meant. Hardly anyone called me Mrs Blair. Anyway I went over to the bar and took the call. No sooner had I picked up the phone and heard a voice I didn't recognise than I felt dizzy and dropped it. I lurched back to our table. 'He's dead... All alone...,' I stammered. 'I thought I could save him... He seemed to be getting better...' I could hardly take it in.

Netta started to cry. 'Don't blame yourself, you did what you could for him. It wasn't your fault,' she tried to console me. Lucian looked stunned.

'I really do love him,' I sobbed. 'But I was too late. What have I done?' I was heartbroken. How cruel that it was only then that I realised how much I truly loved him. They tried to comfort me but I was inconsolable.

The funeral service and burial were arranged by David and Malcolm but it was all a bit of a blur as far as I was concerned. Over the years since that terrible night I've tried to carry out George's wishes. I've done my best to protect his reputation and publish whatever would enhance it. I suppose the high point for me was when I collaborated with Ian Angus in bringing out the four volumes of George's *Collected Essays, Journalism and Letters*. They did a great deal to show that there was a lot more to his work than just his two most famous novels. In those last weeks I persuaded George that it wouldn't be in his interest to have any biographies written about him, and I did my level best to make sure that none were. Malcolm made a start on one but said that there were too many things about George that couldn't be written about. Well, that was fine by me. I burnt most of George's personal letters to me and mine to him before offering his and my papers to University College London.

However, when George became so famous that it became impossible to stem the tide, I had hopes that Bernard Crick would focus on George's books and his politics and reluctantly gave him my blessing. But, once I read the manuscript, I tried to prevent it from coming out because there was just too much personal stuff in it that George would have hated.

I failed, and now I feel very guilty that I let George down. However, I helped other writers like Jean Rhys in any way I could, and I used what income I got from George's royalties for quite a few worthwhile literary causes. I've never been good with money so I didn't understand for a long time why the income I received from his book sales was so little. It was only fairly recently that I found out that most of it was being kept by George Orwell Productions, the company that George had set up near the end, and by that crook of an accountant,

Jack Harrison. Well, I sued them for a lot of money and separately for the ownership of George's copyrights. My solicitors were confident that I would win both my cases but, when it turned out that I had a brain tumour, they advised me to settle rather than face a gruelling cross-examination in the witness box. So that's what I aim to do. And whilst it will cost me what little money I have, I should get George's copyright back to give to his son Ricky. I shall die a pauper, but Ricky will inherit the fruits of all his father's labours. That pleases me no end. I once went to see the little fellow at Barnhill and found that he was perfectly happy growing up there with Av and Bill. But I was shocked how bleak and remote a place it was and it confirmed my belief that I could never have lived there. I never went back.

One thing that's bothered me all these years, however, was that strange visit by Granny Gow to see George when he was practically on his death bed. Until now, that is. You see, Thatcher recently announced in the House of Commons that Anthony Blunt was the fourth man in the Cambridge Soviet Spy Ring with Burgess, Maclean and Philby. That's what got me thinking and talking to some of my friends and contacts. I still have some, you see. They told me that Blunt and Gow were both dons and very close friends at Cambridge. And that they shared a common interest in Impressionist Art and young men of a certain bent. I also heard that David and Malcolm, and even Freddie Ayer, had worked for the intelligence services during the war, and perhaps even afterwards. Some of George's best friends were spies. And he seemed to like all that cloak and dagger stuff. But the Cambridge Spy Ring were double agents who were passing on all kinds of secrets to their Soviet spymasters. Now, it's common knowledge that George was paranoid that Stalin's agents were out to get him ever since Spain, and especially after *Animal Farm* and *Nineteen Eighty-Four* came out. But let's face it, who did the Soviets more serious damage than George? If Stalin had a hit-list, which he almost certainly did, George must have been Public Enemy Number One on it after he'd disposed of Trotsky. And one of the strangest things was that the day George died was the 21st of January, the same day that Lenin died in 1923. A coincidence? Perhaps not. Some historians say that Stalin had Lenin killed so he could take over.

That's when I remembered what George had said about those people who go on all the time about 'humanity'. It seems that Burgess worked in the Information Research Department alongside Celia Kirwan. He could easily have heard about George's list and passed this news on to his spymaster. And he and Maclean must have been getting very jumpy around that time because they fled to Russia not long afterwards. They may have been concerned that their links to Blunt, and even Gow, could come out. Could it be that Granny Gow was on a scouting mission to see what could be done to put an end to George before we left for Switzerland? Did he report back what he learned that day to his controller who decided they had to act before he went? The Communists had members in most of the unions in those days and they could easily have given them instructions not to check on George during the night and not to try to save him if he haemorrhaged. Or even worse, a nurse or janitor could have come into his room and simply put a pillow over his head or done something to make him bleed. George once told me that he used to sleep with a pistol under his pillow and at the time I thought he was paranoid. But maybe he wasn't paranoid enough?

I know this might sound like a scene out of *The Godfather*, but you have to understand that George was a clear and present danger to the most powerful dictator in the world at that time. A tyrant who had managed to insinuate his agents into the top echelons of the British Secret Service. I realise you might think I'm imagining all this, and maybe, like Winston

Smith eventually did, I'm adding 2 + 2 and getting 5. But one day George's dire warnings about the possibility of a permanent war economy, a surveillance society and its thought police could all come true. And, as he himself said, perhaps the truth about Granny Gow and why he came to see him just before he died, may also come out. At any rate, this cancer is killing me. I don't have long to live, so I've got nothing to lose. They say that the approach of death sharpens the mind and the senses. Well, George was very sharp in both respects until the night he died, and I've done my best to be true to him in everything I've said and done since then. I know ours was far from being an ideal marriage and it wasn't really about love, at least on my part at first, but I do still miss him terribly and I feel really guilty that I've let him down in spite of my best efforts. Most of all I regret what might have been, if only he'd lived longer. As his childhood sweetheart Jacintha Buddicom used to say in her letters to him, Farewell and Hail, dear George.

Chapter 16

AV LOOKED SADLY out of the front window at Barnhill. She had heard of Eric's death on the BBC eight o'clock news on the wireless and had gone to the funeral service in London and to the committal in that little graveyard in Oxfordshire. The service had been a gloomy affair which was conducted by a vicar as Eric had wished. David had used his influence as a landowning parishioner with the vicar of the village of Sutton Courtenay to have him buried in Church of England soil. She remembered seeing some giant cooling towers in the distance and thought it somehow appropriate that her brother was laid to rest in sight of them. Bill had looked after little Ricky until she got back to Barnhill. He was a good soul and now that she had learnt that 'that woman' had got all of Eric's money, perhaps she would marry Bill to give Ricky some sense of security and of being part of a family. Her own family was decimated. First her father, then her mother, then Marjorie and now Eric. She and Ricky were the last of the Blairs and she was determined that he would be brought up in a good, loving home and have the best possible chance in life. That she would do, as Eric had wished.

Chapter 17

RICKY WAS PLAYING happily on the grass outside Barnhill with the wooden lorry his father had made for him. He never seemed to tire of it. He liked machinery that moved. A rabbit was nosing about nearby. Inquisitive, it stopped and looked at the boy. He saw it and smiled at it. He pointed his hands towards it and imagined he was shooting it the way his father used to do. When he was a bit older perhaps he would be allowed to shoot rabbits and go fishing on his own. He would stand on the rocks at the bay and cast his line out into the water and slowly reel it in. He would feel a tug on the line and then another. That's when he'd get excited. But he would follow his father's advice and concentrate on steadily reeling it in, loosening the line a little, then reeling it in some more. Then he'd see two silver fish jumping to the surface, unable to resist the steady pull of his line. He would land them and be full of joy. That would be his future.

Timeline of George Orwell's Last Years

1943

November   George Orwell/Eric Blair resigns his post at the BBC and becomes Literary Editor of *Tribune*. He writes an 'As I Please' weekly column for it.

1944

February   *Animal Farm* is completed but no publisher will accept it due to the wartime British alliance with Stalinist Russia.

May   His affair with his secretary Sally McEwen upsets Eileen Blair. He ends it.

June   He and Eileen adopt a three week old child whom they name Richard Horatio Blair – born 14 May 1944.
Their home in Mortimer Crescent is bombed and they stay in the flat of Inez Holden.

September   They move to a top floor flat in Canonbury Square, Islington.
Animal Farm is accepted for publication by Fred Warburg.
He visits Barnhill for the first time.

1945

February   He becomes a war correspondent for *The Observer* in Paris and Cologne. He probably meets Hemingway in Paris.

29 March   Eileen dies in Newcastle from a heart attack caused by the anaesthetic administered for a hysterectomy.

June–July   He covers the first post-war UK election campaign – a landslide Labour victory.

July   He employs Susan Watson as a housekeeper and throws himself into journalism.

August	*Animal Farm* is published by Secker & Warburg and is very successful which greatly improves his financial situation.
Autumn	He proposes to Sonia Brownell.
Winter	He proposes to Celia Kirwan with whom he spends Christmas in a Welsh farmhouse as guests of Arthur Koestler and Celia's twin sister Mamaine. Sonia and Celia both turn him down.

1946

February	His *Critical Essays* are published by Secker & Warburg and are well received. He suffers a tubercular haemorrhage in his flat.
March	He proposes to Anne Popham who turns him down.
Spring	He writes his essay 'Some Thoughts on the Common Toad' about the joys of spring.
3 May	His elder sister Marjorie dies as he is about to leave London to live in Barnhill, a remote farmhouse on the Isle of Jura.
23 May	He arrives at Barnhill and is joined by his sister Avril a week later. He rests from writing by gardening, peat cutting, fishing etc. His diaries record the weather, gardening and wildlife.
July	He brings his son and Susan Watson to Barnhill. Avril does not get on with his friend Paul Potts or Susan. Potts leaves.
August	He starts to write *The Last Man in Europe*. Susan and her boyfriend David Holbrook, a Communist Party member, leave.
September	Fifty pages of *The Last Man in Europe* are complete.
October	He returns to London to stay over the winter, the coldest one in many years, which, along with too much journalism, seriously worsens his health.

December   He goes north to plant fruit trees and roses at
            Barnhill and spends two nights in Glasgow at New
            Year.

1947
January   The BBC broadcasts his adaptation of *Animal Farm*.
April   His final 'As I Please' column appears in *Tribune*.
            He returns to Jura but is ill in bed for a week.
August   He almost drowns with his son, nephew and niece
            in the Corryvreckan whirlpool.
December   He finishes the first draft of *The Last Man in
            Europe*. Before Christmas he enters Hairmyres
            Hospital, East Kilbride, near Glasgow, with tuber-
            culosis of the left lung.

1948
January   He receives painful treatment and a new drug
            streptomycin which causes hair and weight loss and
            bleeding blisters, but gradually his health improves.
July   He returns to Jura and, despite declining health,
            redrafts the book.
November   He can't get a typist so he types the book himself.
December   He finishes the book, which he renames *Nineteen
            Eighty-Four*. But he has fatally damaged his health.

1949
January   He enters a sanatorium in Cranham, Gloucester-
            shire. Some of his friends and his publisher visit him
            there.
March   He corrects proofs of *Nineteen Eighty-Four* in
            hospital.
            He hands a list of pro-communist writers and others
            to Celia Kirwan who works for a Foreign Office
            unit, the Information Research Department, set up

to publish anti-communist propaganda.

8 June	Secker & Warburg publishes *Nineteen Eighty-Four*.
13 June	Harcourt Brace in New York publishes *Nineteen Eighty-Four*. It is an immediate, outstanding success.
25 June	He proposes to Sonia Brownell on his birthday.
September	He is admitted to University College Hospital, London.
13 October	He marries Sonia Brownell in hospital.

1950

January	He plans to go to Switzerland with Sonia on his discharge from hospital.
18 January	He makes his will. His wife Sonia and Richard Rees are named his literary executors and she is left his entire estate and the royalties from his books.
21 January	He dies suddenly, aged forty-six, of pulmonary tuberculosis at University College Hospital. Following his instructions, he is buried according to the rites of the Church of England at All Saints, Sutton Courtenay, Oxfordshire.

Writing *Barnhill*

I FIRST WALKED in to Barnhill on the Isle of Jura in September 2006 but didn't go inside the gate. I knew that George Orwell had written *Nineteen Eighty-Four* in that remote farmhouse but was puzzled by the contrast between his dark, dystopian novel and that beautiful location by the coast. I could see a little of Jura behind Scarba from Cullipool village on the Isle of Luing where I came to live in 2007 and I began to research Orwell's life and work. I came up with the idea of writing a

The author at Barnhill beside what is thought to be the remains of George Orwell's motorbike.

View of Barnhill from the Sound of Jura.

feature film screenplay and novel about his last years on Jura and elsewhere. After successfully applying in 2011 to DigiCult's Incubator scheme funded by Creative Scotland, I worked with Paul Welsh, a Scottish film producer, to develop and write the film script. In 2014 I was awarded a Creative Scotland artist's bursary to undertake research and professional development to write my first novel, about Orwell's last years, drawing on my work on the screenplay with Paul.

I continued to read lots of biographies and memoirs about him and the other main characters, his letters, diaries, essays and novels, and carried out research in the Orwell Archive at University College London. In October 2014 I visited Orwell's former flat in Canonbury Square. It was smaller than I had imagined it and Orwell's workroom was much narrower, but I had a much better picture of where he, Eileen and Ricky lived in London at the end of the war. I also discovered that Donald Mackay, the creel fisherman who rescued Orwell, his son, nephew and niece in the Gulf of Corryvreckan, came from the

Rear view of Barnhill.

village of Toberonochy on the Isle of Luing.

I attended novel writing courses at the Moniack Mhor Creative Writing Centre in the Highlands, at Ty'n y coed in North Wales and an Emergents novel editing course at Portree on Skye. I wrote the novel throughout this time and finished it in early summer 2017. In June 2018 I visited Barnhill with Richard and Eleanor Blair and a large group of other members of the Orwell Society. It was a dream come true finally to be inside the house I had imagined and written about for many years, to be in Orwell's kitchen, to see his free-standing bath and to stand in the upstairs bedroom where he wrote most of *Nineteen Eighty-Four*. Amazingly, some parts of what might have been his motorbike were carried out from the barn. There was still a strong sense of Orwell about the place. Please note that Barnhill is a private residence – visitors to Jura should respect the privacy of its occupants and should only visit it by arrangement with the owners.

After I had finished my novel and it was to be published, it

The Paps of Jura

was quite a shock to learn that an Australian author Dennis Glover had also written a novel about Orwell's final years – great minds… – although perhaps not that surprising considering the significance and appeal of *Nineteen Eighty-Four* and Orwell's dramatic struggle to finish it on Jura. Whilst covering similar themes in Orwell's life, our approaches to the story and styles of writing are different and equally valid. My novel focuses on the last six years of Orwell's life and is told from Sonia Brownell's point of view as well as his. It is a continous dramatic narrative that portrays several other key characters in his life as well as him.

As the timeline indicates, *Barnhill* is based as far as possible on the actual events of the final years of Orwell's life. However, some incidents have been altered and recreated, and others invented for dramatic effect, and these and the dialogues have been imagined as they might have been. Whether and where Orwell met Hemingway in Paris is uncertain. He didn't have a sidecar for his motorbike. The women in the Compton Arms in Islington and the couple in Port Ellen jail are fictional characters. There is no record of how Orwell spent two days in Glasgow at the New Year of 1946–1947, so I have written what I imagine he might have done and some of the people he could have met. Similarly, there is no evidence of Sonia meeting with George after he went to Jura and no record of her visiting him at Hairmyres Hospital. She did visit him at Cranham and accepted his marriage proposal. Of course, Sonia did not write about her life with Orwell as she was dying in November 1980, but her point of view is essential to the story and I have tried to convey it as fully as possible.

Some say that Orwell was paranoid because he carried a gun in his last years, but evidence was uncovered in Russian archives by one of Orwell's biographers, Gordon Bowker, that David Crook, a young Communist Party supporter who spied on George, Eileen and the Independent Labour Party contingent fighting with the POUM on the Republican side in Spain, was trained by Ramon Mercador who murdered Leon Trotsky with an ice axe in 1940. It is quite possible that Stalin's NKVD (KGB) would do anything they could to stop him finishing *Nineteen Eighty-Four* after the popular success of *Animal Farm* and would want to see him die in hospital. Some of MI5's files on Orwell have recently been published and his house was raided by police in 1939 and banned books by Henry Miller were taken away. Paranoid? If not, he had good reason to be.

The role of Andrew Gow, Orwell's tutor in Greek at Eton, is also an interesting one. The art critic Brian Sewell, who hid Anthony Blunt in his flat after Blunt was exposed as the fourth Soviet agent in the Cambridge Spy Ring in 1979, was convinced that Andrew Gow was also a Soviet spy. When Sewell asked Blunt directly if this was the case he did not deny it. Sonia's speculation at the end of the book is based on that evidence.

Open relationships were quite common in free thinking artistic circles in the twentieth century. It was considered by many

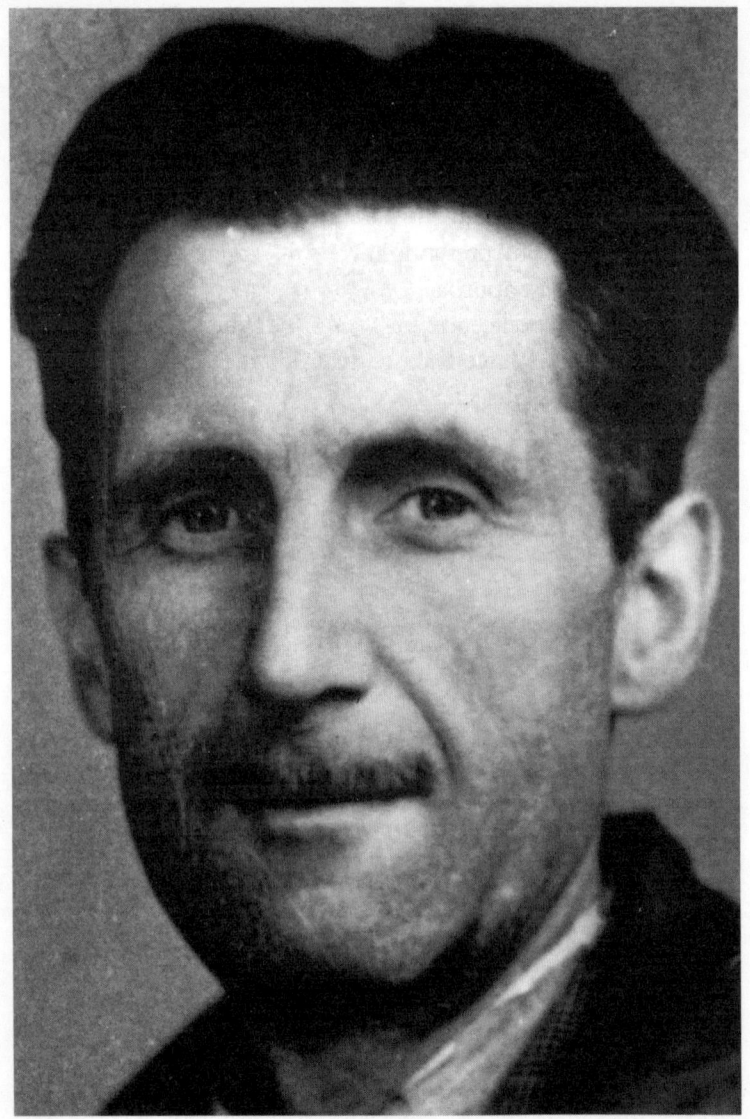

George Orwell

(Photo: Wikimedia Commons)

that monogamy was unnatural and the Bloomsbury Group was well known for such relationships, as were Simone de Beauvoir and Jean-Paul Sartre in France. Eric and Eileen Blair made an agreement of this kind until his affair with Sally McEwen went too far for Eileen and she insisted he end it. Orwell's attitudes and behaviour towards women were fairly typical of men at the time. Judging him by present day moral standards and attitudes may not be the best approach.

Although poetic licence has been used where appropriate in writing *Barnhill*, I have tried to remain true to the significant events of Orwell's later life.

Acknowledgements

The assistance of Creative Scotland for the award of an artist's bursary to undertake research and professional development to write this novel is gratefully acknowledged.

Many thanks are due to Paul Welsh for his personal contribution to the development and writing of the story and original screenplay commissioned by DigiCult Ltd, as part of the Creative Scotland funded Incubator scheme, which *Barnhill* is partly based upon. DigiCult Ltd continues to develop our original script about Orwell's last years.

Many personal thanks are also due to:

Anne Scott, writer and lecturer, for her very helpful advice and comments on the manuscript;

Peter Urpeth, writer and musician, for his support throughout the writing of this novel;

Leela Soma, writer and teacher, for her support and helpful comments on the manuscript;

Larry Flanagan, General Secretary of the Educational Institute of Scotland, for his helpful advice and comments on the manuscript;

Birgit Whitmore, my partner and artist, for her boundless patience and unfailing support in the writing of this novel;

My son Gordon, my daughter Susan and my grandson Callum Bissell for their belief in me and encouragement over the years;

Gavin MacDougall, Alice Latchford and Maia Gentle for their very helpful advice, suggestions and support in the final editing of the manuscript;

The Orwell Society for its unrivalled knowledge of and enthusiasm for George Orwell and his work;

Richard Blair, son of George Orwell, and his wife Eleanor, for their friendship and encouragement.

Web Links

The Orwell Society
www.orwellsocietyblog.wordpress.com
www.facebook.com/TheOrwellSociety
www.twitter.com/Orwell_Society

The Orwell Foundation
www.orwellfoundation.com
www.facebook.com/OrwellFoundation
www.twitter.com/TheOrwellPrize

The Orwell Archive
www.ucl.ac.uk/library/special-collections/a-z/orwell

Orwell Today
www.orwelltoday.com

Norman Bissell
www.normanbissell.com
www.facebook.com/norman.bissell.writer
www.twitter.com/nbissell

Isle of Jura
www.isleofjura.scot

Further Reading

Nineteen Eighty-Four, George Orwell, Penguin
Animal Farm, George Orwell, Penguin
Down and Out in Paris and London, George Orwell, Penguin
The Road to Wigan Pier, George Orwell, Penguin
Homage to Catalonia, George Orwell, Penguin
Essays, George Orwell, Penguin
The Orwell Diaries, Penguin
George Orwell: A Life in Letters, Penguin
Seeing Things as They Are: Selected Journalism and Other Writings, George Orwell, Penguin
George Orwell, Gordon Bowker, Abacus
Orwell: The Life, D.J. Taylor, Vintage
George Orwell: A Life, Bernard Crick, Harvill Secker
The Girl from the Fiction Department: A Portrait of Sonia Orwell, Hilary Spurling, Penguin
The Orwell Tapes, Stephen Wadhams, Locarno Press
Orwell Remembered, Audrey Coppard and Bernard Crick, Ariel Books
George Orwell: English Rebel, Robert Colls, Oxford University Press
George Orwell: A Personal Memoir, T.R. Fyvel, Hutchinson
The Crystal Spirit: A Study of George Orwell, George Woodcock, Fourth Estate
The Road to 1984, William Steinhoff, Weidenfeld and Nicolson
The Larger Evils: 'Nineteen Eighty-four' – the Truth Behind the Satire, W.J. West, Canongate
George Orwell on Screen, David Ryan, McFarland & Company

Luath Press Limited

committed to publishing well written books worth reading

LUATH PRESS takes its name from Robert Burns, whose little collie Luath (*Gael.*, swift or nimble) tripped up Jean Armour at a wedding and gave him the chance to speak to the woman who was to be his wife and the abiding love of his life. Burns called one of the 'Twa Dogs' Luath after Cuchullin's hunting dog in Ossian's *Fingal*. Luath Press was established in 1981 in the heart of Burns country, and is now based a few steps up the road from Burns' first lodgings on Edinburgh's Royal Mile. Luath offers you distinctive writing with a hint of unexpected pleasures.

Most bookshops in the UK, the US, Canada, Australia, New Zealand and parts of Europe, either carry our books in stock or can order them for you. To order direct from us, please send a £sterling cheque, postal order, international money order or your credit card details (number, address of cardholder and expiry date) to us at the address below. Please add post and packing as follows: UK – £1.00 per delivery address; overseas surface mail – £2.50 per delivery address; overseas airmail – £3.50 for the first book to each delivery address, plus £1.00 for each additional book by airmail to the same address. If your order is a gift, we will happily enclose your card or message at no extra charge.

Luath Press Limited
543/2 Castlehill
The Royal Mile
Edinburgh EH1 2ND
Scotland
Telephone: +44 (0)131 225 4326 (24 hours)
email: sales@luath. co.uk
Website: www. luath.co.uk